FALLEN ANGELS

Fallen Angels
The Reign of Hell
Austin Golemon

Acknowledgements

An enormous thanks to all of my family, who had to hear me talk endlessly about this book to get their opinions on it, as well as help me edit it more times than I care to remember. A second thanks goes to my sister, my first fan, and the person who convinced me to publish. A third goes out to my friends, who encouraged me and inspired me to finish this and still remain sane. And last, but not least, to anyone who cared enough (or was bored enough) to read this. You are all awesome.

First Printing: 2014

ISBN 978-1-312-49475-6

Golemon Publishing
8309 N Switzer Rd
Brimfield, IL 61517

Visit us on Facebook: www.Facebook.com/TheReignofHell

Ordering Information:

Special discounts are available on quantity purchases by corporations, associations, educators, and others. For details, contact the publisher at the above listed address.

U.S. trade bookstores and wholesalers: Please contact Austin Golemon: Email: TheReignofHell@gmail.com

For Tyler. Without him, this book wouldn't exist.

Contents

Prologue: Into the Night

Jasmine breathed out slowly, adjusting her night eyes on her face. They looked like sunglasses, wrapping around her eyes, preventing anyone from seeing their color. She glanced sideways, the silhouette of her partner barely visible in the fading light to anyone else. To Jasmine he was easily visible, her night eyes even picking out the small details of his face.

He smiled at her, noticing her glance. She was always amazed he knew whenever she was looking at him, night eyes or not. She shifted her position, careful not to make any noise. The two of them were crouched on a small ledge, their bodies contorted to keep ahold of the wall.

They waited patiently as the darkness of night fell, covering their forms with a blanket of shadow. When the night was at its blackest, they dropped, falling silently to the ground below.

Jasmine led the way, her slim form visible only to her partner. They snuck across the ground like wraiths toward the Keep that towered above the cracked earth, its jagged spires stabbing towards the sky. When they reached the base she stooped, letting her partner find the best area to scale the wall.

He searched for several seconds, and then stopped, crouching. Jasmine froze, sensing something was wrong. She followed his gaze with her eyes, and held back a gasp. Visible only to their night eyes, a dark form slowly glided across the sky, its wings barely visible even to her.

They watched until it vanished, Jasmine holding her breath in controlled fear. As soon as it did, her partner gestured to her and squatted, his powerful legs flexing in anticipation. Backing up, she ran forward, jumping as he grabbed her foot and hoisted her upward. She soared upward in a small arc, landing on a ledge several stories above him. Unclamping the rope at her waist, she secured it to the parapet and threw it down to him.

He climbed it easily, wrapping the rope as he went and handing it to her at the top. They briefly stopped as she secured the rope again, and then continued on silently.

They simultaneously removed their gauntlets, replacing them with gloves containing carefully crafted spikes, and climbed. They scaled the wall for several more stories and stopped, circling around a window in order to remain unseen.

Jasmine paused, her muscles tight as she briefly looked down. She immediately looked up again, automatically reverting to training exercises to keep her mind calm. She focused on her partner as he carefully latched himself to the stone above the window and attached himself to a rope at his belt. Passing the rope down to her, she latched herself on as well, breathing large, slow breaths to prepare herself.

She tensed as he held up a hand with three fingers, counting down. As the last finger dropped, so did he, smashing through the window below, the sound of splintering wood and glass loud in the night.

She immediately followed into a brightly lit room, the torches on the walls throwing their forms into sharp relief. They were both garbed in tight, black armor, with various weapons and tools hanging from their belts and back.

They both unsheathed their swords as the man in the room whirled, half dressed, his well-muscled chest gleaming in the torchlight. He sized them up quickly as they rushed him, rolling between them and coming up with a sword, its crystalline blade gleaming as he raised it, preparing himself.

He shouted once, probably for guards, but Jasmine didn't listen as she circled around him, trying to get behind him. He wasn't stupid, however, and his flashing sword quickly drove her back. It did give her partner enough time to spin a spell to hold the door, though.

Pounding on the door followed shortly after, and she attacked him again, trying to overwhelm him quickly. He retaliated just as fast, and she would have died if her partner hadn't slashed at him from behind. He rolled to the side, careful not to cut himself, and they advanced on him. He held his ground warily, his golden eyes burning in the light.

As they drew near, he abruptly slashed at her, catching her by surprise at his quickness. Despite her reflexes, a line of searing pain told her he had managed to cut her arm. She fell back, and her partner engaged him in a whirlwind of blows, their blades flashing in the light.

Reaching to her belt, she removed a single throwing knife. Rolling it on her palm, she gripped her sword tightly in her left hand. She rushed him from behind, tossing the blade over his head as she attacked him. He ignored it, knowing it wouldn't hit him, and blocked her strike, knocking her back with strength belying his form.

She rolled and returned to her feet, ready for attack, but it didn't matter. He lay on the floor motionless, her knife lying beside him. He had forgotten her partner, who had caught the knife and threw it, hitting him hilt-first in the back of his head, knocking him out.

Ignoring the banging on the door, she dressed her wound as her partner lifted his slumped form. Nodding to each other, they exited through the window they had entered in.

By the time the guards broke through the door, they were long gone.

Sparks

Kenneth Sanderz walked slowly up the road to the bus stop, his fair hair tousled slightly by the wind. First days of school were always the worst in his mind. This Monday would be a nightmare, as his life had been a nightmare ever since he had moved from his small home in Indiana to Montana a week previously. He knew almost no one in the city. His thoughts flashed back to the conversation he had with his father when they had announced they were moving to Montana.

"What if I don't want to move?" he had yelled at his father, "What if I like it here and want to stay? Why do I get no say in what we're doing before we move halfway across the country?" His father had tried to reason with him, his voice calm and reassuring. "But Ken, I can get a better job there. The country is nice; it has some beautiful mountains and waterfalls in the area we can explore, and it has a fantastic city you can go to high school in." Kenneth listened to none of it as he ran off to his room, fuming as he slammed the door behind him. He still hadn't made up with his father; they hadn't talked at all, except short formal exchanges in day-to-day life.

Kenneth's swirling thoughts were interrupted when he saw the bus coming down the road. Sighing, he stepped onto the bus and resigned himself to a day of everyone staring, whispering, and the frantic input of names to remember. He nodded respectfully to the bus driver and listened carefully to the rules of the bus. It paid to be cautious. Making his way to the back of the bus, he sat down in an empty seat and tried to remain as casual as possible. In his experience, confidence in oneself kept the local bullies away.

Not that he had needed. As he looked around the bus, few of the inhabitants looked the bully type. Many were bordering towards scrawny and avoided eye contact. Only one even looked at him, so he sat across from him. The dirty-blonde haired student merely nodded, his earphone wires swinging as the bus rumbled down the road. Sliding his bright blue eyes back to his phone, he began ignoring Kenneth. *Great*, he thought, *I have the loser bus.* Not that he intended to be a loser himself, but in high school, your first impression was everything. Looking around the bus again, he came to the realization that not many people must ride this bus. They were already making their way to Crater High, and the bus was barely half filled.

Kenneth exited the bus carefully, keeping his eye out for any teachers to ask what he was supposed to do. Unfortunately, there were none. He entered the school hesitantly, looking at its white, stone walls and tan colored tiles decorating the floor. Spying the school office, he made his way towards the secretary.

"Hello? I'm Kenneth Sanderz, the student from Indiana Community High School. I was wondering if you had a copy of my schedule for the day. I didn't have one sent in the mail since we moved recently."

The secretary looked at him and smiled. "That's Mrs. Howell's job. Go in the back and find the room on the left with her name on it." Kenneth smiled back and made his way down the sparsely decorated hallway she had indicated. Walking quickly now, he made his way to the door with the correct nameplate on it and knocked.

"Come in!" a voice from inside called. Opening the door, Kenneth made his way inside and started as he saw Mrs. Howell. He had been expecting a small cranky old woman, but was instead greeted by a young and striking woman with stark, black hair and warm, brown eyes. Shaking hands with him, she said, "Sit down, sit down! I've been expecting you. You are Kenneth Sanderz?"

"Yes," replied Kenneth, "but it is pronounced *Sanderez.*" He sat at one of the many chairs around her desk, looking around her room with no small amount of interest. It was fairly unadorned, but here and there were pictures of a man he assumed was her husband, a dog, and two children.

"My apologies Kenneth, I will do my best to remember. Do you need a copy of your schedule?" She said, and when Kenneth nodded, she continued, "Good, I have it prepared for you." She handed him a sheet of paper with his name in bold letters across the top. "Is there anything else I can do for you?" Kenneth shook his head and left, thanking her. Looking at his schedule, Kenneth frowned. The eight block periods were set up into A days and B days, with his first class as *Spanish I-First Semester.* No problem. He had taken Intro into Spanish his 8th grade year.

Looking at the map of the school on the back of the schedule, he located his room with relative ease. He slowly made his way through the halls of the school towards his room, watching the commotion around him. Students filled the halls, locating their lockers, organizing their notebooks, and greeting old friends. Everything was so unfamiliar, and he felt a spike of anger as he thought of his friends in Indiana. Reaching the door to the classroom, he opened it and was greeted by the teacher inside.

"Hello! You must be Kenneth. My name is Mrs. Wolls. It is nice to meet you," said the elderly woman. She was short, barely reaching Kenneth's shoulder, and had a sweet grandmotherly smile. "Your seat is over here," indicated Mrs. Wolls, and Kenneth sat in the seat, staring around the room.

It was filled with posters written in Spanish, showing pictures of beaches and rainforests in beautiful splendor. One depicted a map of Spain and all of its terrain.

Kenneth was the only one in the room except the teacher. Soon, a flood of students was coming through the door, and many of them gossiping quite loudly about 'the new kid'. Kenneth shrugged his bulky shoulders uncomfortably as he heard one of the girls mention his eyes. He had strange eyes, never quite one color, changing with the weather and the colors around him. He ran his fingers through his blonde hair, slightly unsettled.

The bell and Mrs. Wolls saved him. She swept up from where she was sitting and slapped her hand on her mahogany desk with a loud crack. Staring the room to silence, she began speaking.

"Good morning freshmen. My name is Mrs. Wolls, and as you should know if you are in the right classroom, I teach Spanish I. Most of you are sitting in the correct spots, but as we do roll call, I will point to where you need to be and expect you to move there with efficiency." She acted immediately upon her words, leaping about in a frenzy of movement and speech, organizing the students to her satisfaction. Eventually, when everyone was accounted for and in their assigned seats, she got out a large stack of books and told everyone to grab a copy.

The room erupted into a flurry of movement as the students rushed to get a good copy. Some of the books were fairly new, but most of them had fallen into the hands of the ingenious graffiti artists of the modern day. Kenneth snatched his copy quickly and got out of the way as some of the kids started a small fight for the one of the better copies. Looking up, Kenneth saw the teacher leave the room, muttering something about extra copies. The fight intensified with the absence of the teacher. Kenneth tried to stay out of it. He was built enough to handle himself, but this was the first day and he didn't want to get caught with the wrong crowd.

Kenneth thought back to his conversation with his dad again. *Right, this is such a great school we fight for good textbooks—*

Wonderful. He stiffened in anticipation as one of the bigger kids swaggered towards him with a scowl on his face. "You have a better book than mine," he growled. He was tall and fat, with ripped jeans and a Nike shirt with a football in the background. Looking at the larger student's book, Kenneth had to agree. Kenneth's book was of better quality—an advantage of sitting in the front rows. As a result, the other kid's book was close to falling apart.

When the other kid didn't continue with his sentence, settling on looking menacing instead, Kenneth prompted, "And?"

The other kid scowled, looking angrily at Kenneth. "Do you know who I am?" the kid growled, his face starting to turn red. Kenneth looked around, noting the unsurprised faces as he realized he was about to become a display of a resident bully's power. Swearing silently, he turned to face his assailant.

"No," he said shortly, "but I'm hazarding a guess if I asked someone, they probably wouldn't answer with the name Lucy." Out of the corner of his eye, he saw someone stifle a giggle. Focusing on his now blustering oppressor, he assumed the guise of a surprised and slightly taken aback person, carefully hiding the fear that was threatening to show on his face. "Oh, I'm sorry; did I get the name right?"

"My name is Richard!" the bully raged, spit flying from his mouth. Students behind him snickered as Kenneth said, "Oh, my apologies Dick. I can call you that right?" Richard, completely infuriated now, lashed out at Kenneth with blistering speed. Kenneth, expecting this, leaned backward, letting the fist pass neatly in front of him, then stepped forward and caught his upper arm while the bully staggered forward.

"Whoopsie, there! We don't want to fall now do we?" Kenneth said mockingly. Instead of stabilizing him, Kenneth gave him a small nudge that sent him reeling backward into a desk behind him.

Richard righted himself, and was about to take another swing at Kenneth when one of the other students whispered fiercely. "Teacher!"

Richard calmed himself immediately. Mrs. Wolls stepped in, and looking at the circle of people around Kenneth and Richard, said in her motherly voice, "Oh dear, we aren't fighting are we?"

Kenneth shook his head. "Nope!" he said cheerfully, "Dick and I were just getting acquainted, seeing as I'm the new student and all. I think we're going to be good friends."

A ripple of laughter went around the room as the teacher said, "Good! I'm glad you and your new friend Dick there are getting to know each other. It is good to have friends in a new environment." Turning around she walked to her desk and set down a stack of papers and a few extra copies. Turning back, she exchanged the copies for the older books.

Immediately everyone sat down in his or her newly assigned seats, although Richard flipped him off behind her back, mouthing *I'll get you later*. Kenneth shrugged. He doubted it. Realizing the teacher was finished and had started talking, he looked forward.

"…And as you can see, there are many different forms of one verb, which is why you will probably only learn one verb tense. That verb was *ser,* meaning 'to be'. I will give you a list of words you would do well to memorize in your free time, as these are going to be the terms I use in day-to-day teaching. Learning those words will make understanding the later words easier. Since this is the first day, therefore a half day, you have the rest of the fifteen minutes to talk. *Adios y buenos dias.*" Mrs. Wolls sat down and began working on her computer.

Immediately the room burst into chatter, and Kenneth's attention was drawn to a student sitting directly to his right. She was of the shorter persuasion, with medium length dark hair, and emerald green eyes. "That was hilarious! Did you see the look on his face when you asked him if his nickname was Dick? Priceless!" she gushed. "My name is Kali by the way. Kali Ross. What is your name?"

Kenneth raised an eyebrow, his nervousness overcome by amusement over her outburst. "My name is Kenneth." She only nodded, talking nonstop until someone else interrupted her. The rest of the morning went as a blur, with him becoming instantly popular as the story of him standing up to Richard circulated around the school. The inflow of names was nearly overwhelming, and he was sure it would take him many weeks to learn just the freshmen's names. Kali stuck with him and turned out to be a valuable friend since she knew everyone's names and their reputations from the constant gossip she loved.

Lunch hour eventually came, with Kali leading him to the commons so they could get in line first. The commons was huge, holding nearly four hundred people, most of them forming an enormous line.

Kenneth moved to get in line, but Kali shook her head and pulled a lunch card from her pocket. "You get VIP service today, Kenneth. You have to get your lunch card first," she said motioning towards the kitchen. Kenneth rolled his eyes and headed towards the direction she was pointing.

Making his way to the back of the kitchen amidst the smells of lunch, he approached a cook and asked nervously, "Um, am I supposed to get a lunch card?" Turning, she appraised Kenneth and said, "Of course! How else are you to pay? What's your name, son?" the cook asked, slapping her ladle against her enormous thigh. Kenneth told her his name, and she nodded, her multiple chins dancing. "Of course, you're the new kid from Indiana! I have your card here in the change box." She bustled over and hit a button that made the change box pop out. "While you're here you might as well get your lunch, and I'll swipe your card."

Kenneth walked over, grabbed a lunch tray and she dumped some of the colorless mush onto it, adding in an apple almost as an after thought. Swiping his card, she said, "You have about two hundred dollars on the card now, so you know!" Kenneth nodded his thanks and went out to the commons to sit down.

The commons was filled with round tables of five; the high ceiling and enormous windows making the room seem much larger than it seemed. Spying Kali over by a window, he wove through the multitudes of sitting students and sat by her.

She immediately grabbed his lunch card from his tray. Waving away his protests, she flipped it over and said, "No fair! You have an updated picture! Mine is still from when I was in fourth grade, and I look hideous!"

"Get over your picture Kal; it's not any worse than the rest of ours." The speaker sat down, a skinny, older looking boy with dark eyes, golden loops in his pierced ears, and wild, bright green hair spiked so it looked like the wind was blowing on it. He rolled his eyes at Kenneth and said, "My name is Flammeth, many curses to my idiot parents who thought they were being so original."

Kenneth stifled a laugh and held out his hand. "My name is Kenneth," he said.

Flammeth grinned, white teeth flashing against his tanned skin. "I know," he said, "your morning exploits have been all over the school and back again. And I see you have already met my girlfriend, Kali."

Kenneth turned and raised an eyebrow at Kali, and she giggled. "She's been a lifesaver," he said honestly.

Flammeth nodded, and greeted the newest person that was sitting down. "Hey there, fatso," he said easily, looking at the monstrous pile of food on his tray. The newcomer grunted, and

Kenneth immediately noted the bulging biceps that miserably failed to hide in his T-shirt. He had silver—not grey, but bright silver—hair that was tied in a ponytail in the back, and had intense black eyes.

He nodded to Kenneth and sat down, ignoring the jibe from Flammeth and eating his lunch in silence. As far as Kenneth could tell, all of his enormous bulk was muscle. Kenneth found himself wondering if he had been held back a year. There was something to him that made him look older than a normal high school student.

When he stayed silent, Kenneth looked at Flammeth, who shrugged. "This is Gabriel, he doesn't talk too much. He is our personal bullyguard at the moment because if he sits on you, you don't get up again." Gabriel nodded again, mouth filled with food.

Kenneth smiled, saying, "It's nice to meet you."

Gabriel studied him with an impassive face for several long seconds, then looked at Kali. "Does he play the piano?" His voice was all quiet intensity. Kenneth looked at him in confusion.

Kali shrugged. "I assume so."

Kenneth shook his head. "I don't know how to play the piano. I've never really thought about learning." He had no idea why it mattered.

Gabriel smiled, the edges of his eyes crinkling, picking up his fork. "Then let me borrow your fork." He said in his quiet voice. Taking Kenneth's fork from his outstretched hand, he bent the metal as easily as a paperclip, threading the fork tines together and bending the handle into a bracelet. Giving the newly formed bracelet to Kenneth, he went back to eating lunch.

Kenneth inspected the deftly created bracelet, acutely aware of how much finger strength it took bend the small pieces of metal into a bracelet. The threads were tightly woven, and when he put it on, it fit almost perfectly. Looking up, he saw Gabriel still smiling at him, and he thanked him. Gabriel merely nodded again. *He is the perfect gentle giant,* Kenneth thought.

Flammeth motioned and held up a hand. On his wrist was a double fork bent into a bracelet, exactly like the one Kenneth was now wearing. Looking over, he noticed Kali was wearing one as well. Realizing he had been officially let into their little group, he smiled to himself about what had happened: he had friends.

Kenneth finished his lunch, and stood, intending to put his tray away, when a girl close by their table fell out of her seat with a crash, thrashing about on the floor. Her friends screamed in shock and fear as she struggled, her blue streaked hair fanning out behind her as she fought empty air. Kenneth reacted immediately, flipping out his cell phone and calling 9-1-1. As the call forwarded, he was dimly aware of other people screaming in fear as well, and adults rushing forward to hold the thrashing girl still.

Stammering out the school's address into the phone, he hung up and was immediately assailed by Flammeth, who shouted, "Good thinking! Now get everyone to calm down!" Kenneth nodded and tried to calm people down as they were carrying the girl to the stretcher. She now hung limp, her face pale and covered in sweat, shivering uncontrollably and moaning.

It was practically impossible to calm things down; girls were crying, boys shouting, and sirens from the ambulance were going off. Looking over, he saw Gabriel walking towards him. As he walked, people around him immediately calmed, and as he got closer, he could almost feel the waves of tranquility pulsing out of him, eliminating the little bottled panic he had. Gabriel continued to walk among the students until everyone was calm, then came and stood by Kenneth and the others at the window.

As Gabriel neared, Kenneth spoke, "How did you do that?" he said incredulously. "I could practically feel the calm flowing off of you!" Gabriel looked at him strangely, and Flammeth and Kali stared at him in shock. Eventually, Flammeth spoke. "What?" Kenneth looked to Kali, whom had an eyebrow raised.

"Well... you know...how he just walked around and everyone near him got calm or something," said Kenneth.

Flammeth slowly shook his head. "I have no idea what you're talking about. You're not on drugs are you? Makes you see things, or so I've heard."

Kenneth shook his head. "Never mind," he said, feeling like an idiot. Looking around, he noticed nobody else had seemed to feel the same calm that had come over him. *I must have imagined it.* Kenneth thought. *After all, who can create calm?* Shaking his head, he went to see if he could help.

"The new kid has a savyl. He felt me today, without any training. Either he's been trained before, or he's powerful." The listener on the other side of the phone nodded thoughtfully.

"Pick two emergency scouts. Watch him constantly until he is alone. Then approach him to see what he knows. And be careful, that incident in the lunch room was not normal."

Nora sat, relishing the solitude. She was slight of build, with long, straight black hair, full lips and intense scarlet eyes. They sparkled in the darkness, unnatural to all who looked upon them except her.

Despite the room being pitch black, she could see fine, her eyes picking up the infinitesimal waves of light that bounced around the room. It was a barren room, empty except for a single bed and dresser. There was, of course, more to it than the eye could see.

Time trickled by, in a way. Although time passed, the room was separated from the fabric of time, existing in all times and the current time as well. But time did pass in the room.

Nora shook her head, her hair swirling as if in slow motion, and sighed. Soon her solitude would end, and once again she would have to dwell in the outside world. Turning, she picked up her cell phone a second before it rang and answered it.

"Hello Patsy," she said, knowing it would annoy him. She heard the controlled release of breath from the other end, and waited until he was just about to talk. "I assume you have another job, since that is the only reason you ever call," she observed, and was rewarded by again hearing a vexed sound from the other end of the phone. She let herself smile.

Kenneth lay on his bed, staring at the ceiling in a sullen silence. He had fought again with his dad, yelling and slamming things in the house, until he had finally stormed up to his room. His thoughts swirled. Why couldn't his dad understand? Why did they have to disagree on practically everything? Why couldn't he realize…

His cell phone interrupted Kenneth's thoughts. Picking up the beeping device, he quickly read the text message sent by Flammeth: 'Hey man, I just realized the movie *Eagle* just came out. Want to go see it with us? It shows at 9.' Kenneth looked at the clock by his bed. Eight thirty. There was plenty of time to walk there. His dad would never miss him.

Typing out a text message answering 'I'll be there', Kenneth went over to the window and eased it open quietly. Slipping outside, he hung on the windowsill, and then dropped to the ground. It was a short fall; he was on the second floor. Brushing off sticks and grass, Kenneth set off towards the local cinema.

It was a relatively short walk, but even so, Kenneth found himself a little jumpy. Kenneth could hear only the crunch of his feet on gravel and the distant traffic. The buildings on this side of town seemed dark and gloomy, the streetlights throwing forbidding shadows across walls and grass.

He jumped as he heard the sound of voices down an alleyway. Peering around the corner of the alley, he saw nothing but graffiti covering the brick walls. He walked slowly into the open, and then down the rocky road, but still no one was to be seen.

Mentally berating himself for getting distracted, Kenneth spun on one foot and began walking back towards the alley's start. But when he faced the way he came, his path was blocked by five angry-looking teenagers, one of them Richard. They were walking forward with a drunken swagger, the smell of stale alcohol reaching Kenneth before they had taken two steps.

Kenneth swore violently under his breath and turned quickly, looking for anything that could be used as a weapon. He found nothing in the alley but mud and grime. Turning back to his assailants, he noted one of them was carrying a bat. Backing up slowly, Kenneth found himself creating and ditching scenes of escape at high speed.

They were closing in now, Richard in the front with a sneer curling his lip, slapping the bat in sharp tattoo on his hand, his rag-tag cohorts circling behind him and cracking their knuckles. He spoke in the careful tones of a drunk, "Not so smart-mouthed now, huh? What, cat got your tongue?" His friends laughed menacingly and Kenneth found himself speaking.

"That's such a cliché, Dick. Cat got your tongue?" Kenneth mimicked. "Really?"

Richard snarled and moved forward clumsily, and time *slowed*, all of his movements seeming to take forever. Kenneth saw the bat rise up and swing towards him, and every second was an eternity. Kenneth could feel his adrenaline pumping through his veins, seemingly setting his mind on fire.

Time sped up again, the world moving in a frenzy of movement. Kenneth moved without thinking, spinning with the force of the bat, grabbing it and flipping Richard. He staggered as someone hit him in the back, and the world exploded. Light flashed and fire roared, deafening him. Colors swirled, and Kenneth found himself lying on the ground, spots flashing before his eyes, his head spinning.

Sound was confusing at first, and as he sat up, he saw only blurs of motion, like something moving almost too fast for the human eye to see. Eventually his head cleared, and he could make sense of the yelling.

"You complete and utter fool! What do you think you were doing, attacking a mortal like that?" It was Kali, barely recognizable in the half-light, bending over something that was smoking, and let off a horrible smell. Kenneth gasped as he got a closer look at what she was looking at. It was Richard, his arm torn off at the shoulder, revealing the muscle and bone underneath. He was barely recognizable, with half his face looking as if it had been burned off, flesh and hair melting together, and most of his skin torn off, leaving gaps that showed the skull beneath. As soon as he saw him, he became aware of a horrible smell in the air. It was the smell of burned flesh and hair, heavy and revolting.

Richard was barely breathing, short gasps erupting periodically from his mouth, and he was sobbing uncontrollably with his only eye, his tears leaving a trail in the soot covering him head to foot.

Kali looked up, and shouted to somebody nearby, "Ellie! Get over here now, he's barely alive!" A young girl, probably thirteen years old, hurried out of the shadows. Bending over, she placed her hands on Richard's mutilated form. Kenneth gasped in astonishment. Richard was glowing, a bright white light that pulsated softly around him. His wounds were healing, the cuts and burns shrinking and closing before his eyes. His missing arm and eye were suddenly *there*, as if they had never been gone. His breathing stabilized, and soon he was normal again, sleeping.

Kenneth was gaping at her now, not believing what he'd seen. "W-what...what did you do?" he stuttered. Ellie sat back, and even in the growing darkness Kenneth could tell she had gone immensely pale, and her hands were shaking.

She turned to Kali, brushing her brown hair out of her eyes. "That took more effort than anything I've ever done." She had a soft voice, and it shook with exhaustion.

Kali tossed her head in anger. "That's because you've never had to heal someone who has had such extensive injuries." She spun to face Kenneth, who cringed as she yelled, "You had no call to do that! What were you thinking, blowing his arm off like that?"

Kenneth could only shake his head, "I don't know what you're talking about!" he sputtered. This was a different Kali than the girl he had met earlier.

Kali growled at him, stepping forward, still shouting, "What do you mean you don't know what I'm talking about! You nearly killed him!" Kenneth took a step back, hopelessly confused and horrified, and Ellie stepped forward, looking slightly exasperated.

"Perhaps he doesn't know what he did, who we are, or how he did it Kali. We need to take him back with us to find out more before you get angry enough to knock him out like the others," Ellie said reasonably, her purple eyes gleaming in the darkness. *Wait,* Kenneth thought *purple eyes?* But they were there, a glittering oddity. Kenneth looked about, his mind registering what she had said, just now noticing the unconscious people that were spread-eagled everywhere.

"You knocked them all out?" he said weakly. "How? That fast, and they weigh probably forty more pounds than you..." His voice trailed off slowly as he saw the look of danger growing on Kali's face.

Kali spun, grabbing on to his arm and pulling him forward, Ellie following his staggering form behind him. "Come on," she said, "You need to talk to Yigil."

False Memories

They walked for a good hour, with Kenneth being shushed to silence every time he attempted to speak. He had tried checking his phone for the time, but when he reached into his pocket, it was missing. Looking back, he remembered it slipping out of his pocket into a muddy puddle when he had fallen.

He was filled with curiosity and revulsion as they wandered seemingly randomly about the city. His mind was whirling; images of the burned and blackened body of Richard kept invading his thoughts. Eventually, they arrived at their destination.

They were at the town's cathedral, its spires reaching towards the heavens, gargoyles and statues adorning its outer walls. Instead of entering through the front doors, Kali led him around to the back, where she walked up to a statue of Jesus and said, "A wanderer of the Lord seeks shelter." And in saying so, she pricked her finger on one of the thorns surrounding the statue's head, and smeared a small bead of blood over his heart. "True blood beckons," she whispered.

To Kenneth's astonishment, the bricks in the wall of the cathedral behind the statue shimmered and formed into a door.

Walking up, Kali grabbed the door's handle, and pushed the door open saying, "Come on! Don't just stand there with your mouth open!" Closing his mouth with a click of his teeth, Kenneth walked through the door, going down the stairs into a large room.

The room had obviously been used recently; there was food on the round table in the middle of the room. There were couches lining the wall, and comfy looking lounge chairs surrounding a large, flat-screen TV. There was a small kitchen off to the side, with a mini-bar closing it off to the rest of the room. Doors lined the walls, and Kenneth could only guess at what lay behind them.

The entrance door shut with a bang, and Kenneth jumped at the unexpected noise. Turning to face the stairs, Kenneth got a better look at the two girls. They were dressed in some sort of uniform, completely black jumpsuits studded with what appeared to be armor. Ellie was looking pale still, her strange purple eyes looking bleak.

Ellie immediately grabbed an apple from the table and collapsed on one of the lounge chairs, clearly as exhausted as she looked. Kali merely sighed, grabbing hold of Kenneth's arm again and half dragging him toward one of the doors lining the walls.

Kenneth struggled to get out of her grip, but it was like iron, so he resigned himself to asking, "Where are we going?" Kali didn't answer, pulling him through the door and down a spiral staircase. Leading him down past a door marked TRAINING AREA - NOT IN SESSION, she took him to the bottom and led him through another set of doors into a library.

The library was much larger than the public library in the town; rows and rows of bookshelves filled Kenneth's vision, each book thick, at least five hundred pages apiece. Following Kali to the back, he found himself in a small study area occupied by a tall woman.

She was sitting in a chair, the desk covered with books and a computer. She had brilliantly white hair streaked with black that fell loose on her shoulders. She was a good head taller than Kenneth, and when she turned to face him, he saw she was blind. A white cloth surrounded her head, keeping her hair back and covering her eyes, and Kenneth could see two dents where her eyes should have been.

"Why have you brought the boy here?" Her voice was as sharp and cold as ice, each syllable clicking into place with forceful precision when she spoke. Despite her blindness, she seemed to be able to interact with her surroundings easily, swinging her chair around and standing, arms folded. "Was he not supposed to be secured first? Do my orders mean nothing to you, girl?"

Kali bristled, obviously trying to keep calm. "Our position changed. He blew a boy's arm off, and as far as I can tell, doesn't know how. He needs training. We barely saved the boy, and Ellie is exhausted." Kenneth opened his mouth to speak, but closed it as he got a heated glare from Kali.

The woman spoke again, this time with a softer tone, "I see. Then you did the right thing. He is clearly dangerous, so you couldn't have left him to wander after Ellie healed him and the boy."

Kali interrupted, "He didn't need to be healed. Only the other kid needed healing, and that's what sapped her strength so much."

The woman nodded slowly. "You boy!" she unexpectedly snapped, and Kenneth jumped. "Are you Christian? Jewish? What religion are you?"

Kenneth, caught off his guard, managed to stammer, "Catholic."

"Excellent." The woman whirled around and grabbed a book off the table, opening it up to near the beginning. Flipping through pages, she looked up and said, "Are you familiar with the workings of the church?"

"Somewhat," Kenneth replied, wondering where this was going. Once again noticing that she appeared to be able to see without eyes made gooseflesh rise on his arms and neck.

"Then read this passage," she said, holding out the book. It was the Bible, and was opened to the sixth chapter of Genesis. Looking at the highlighted section that she was pointing at, he read aloud, *"At that time the Nephilim appeared on earth, after the sons of heaven had relations with the daughters of man, who bore them sons. They were the heroes of old, the men of renown."*

Kenneth looked up at the woman who said quietly, "This is your parentage Kenneth."

Kenneth shook his head, confused. "I don't understand. What do you mean this is my parentage? It's just a passage from the Bible."

The lady tisked, "You're half angel. The Bible tells of the first Nephilim, for that is what you are called, that were made in the first hundred years of humanity's creation."

"You know the stories. In the beginning, for that was a beginning and an end, God created the heavens and the earth. First he created the heavens, and all the angels and archangels, thrones and dominions, then he created the earth and all its inhabitants. The earth was on a different dimensional plane, and so heaven was invisible. Eventually the first angels fell and were banished from heaven. In this time, Adam and Eve were expelled from the garden because of their infraction against their only law. Later, the angels saw the humans and 'married' them, in a way, giving birth to the Nephilim."

The lady seemed to be staring at him, the sunken cavities of where her eyes should be thoroughly creeping him out. Kenneth shook his head, "I don't understand," he said, "How can you tell I'm Nephilim?" The woman sighed.

"You will understand with time. Tomorrow you will know more. For now, you should get some rest." She turned, picking up the Bible, and went back to the computer, tapping away at the keyboard. To his irritation, Kali grabbed his arm again, and led him back up the stairs.

"Would you please tell me what is going on?" he complained to her as they climbed back up a staircase. His head hurt, and everything seemed befuddling. The events of the day had completely outpaced him. Kali sighed, sounding much like the other woman, and said, "You'll understand eventually. Yigil will teach you all you need to know."

"Who's Yigil?

"You were just talking to her."

"Oh. Why is her name so weird?" Kenneth asked.

Kali looked at him, startled, then laughed at the question in spite of herself. "Her name is Hebrew. It means 'you shall be redeemed."

Kenneth's brow furrowed. Who named their child in Hebrew? They walked on, and Kenneth blinked as they stepped into the brighter light of the upper room and gasped, jumping backwards as he looked across the room *at himself*. He was sitting on a chair by the table, eating one the many apples in the bowl, and as far as he could tell, it was an exact replica. "Wha—how—I'm…"

The duplicate turned and laughed. He shimmered, growing taller and thinner, with spiked hair and golden loops in his ears. Flammeth, for indeed it was Flammeth, tilted back the chair and roared his mirth, all the while a stammering and confused Kenneth stood there awkwardly.

Kali sighed and muttered under her breath as she walked over to the couch area. Kenneth half noticed, through his astonishment, Kali easily picking up the sleeping form of Ellie and carrying her through another door.

Flammeth watched her go, a small smile on his face, then walked over to Kenneth and clapped him on the shoulder, his smile apologetic. "I shouldn't have done that to you, but I couldn't resist."

he said, wiping tears from his eyes. "You still have no idea what's going on do you?" Kenneth shook his head, more than a little frustrated. "Ah, I'll explain. Yigil always tries, but she's not very good with people." Flammeth led Kenneth to the sitting area, and sat down, legs crossed.

"In the beginning," Flammeth began, "there was only God. Then, God created Earth right? So after he created Earth, He made animals and plants, including humans. Still with me? All right. That's about everything everyone knows. However, angels were also made a little before the creation of humans. When the angels saw the humans, they were all like, 'Whoa! They look pretty awesome!' So they married some of them. We are the offspring of angels and humans."

Kenneth frowned. "This is real?"

Flammeth chuckled, looking him in the eye. "After everything that's happened, are you sure you can ask me that question?" Kenneth nodded, acceding his point. Flammeth nodded and sat back. "Nephilim exist," he stated, "And you're one of them. So are Kali, Ellie, and I."

Kenneth's mouth dropped open. "So... My mom was an angel?" He said disbelievingly. Flammeth shook his head.

"Angels who mate with females produce Nephilim, who are half angel-half human, but angels who mate with male humans don't ever have children," Flammeth explained.

Kenneth shook his head. "I've always lived with my dad though, " he said, confused, "He said my mom had died at childbirth…"

Flammeth shrugged. "That's not uncommon. We'll find out what's going on eventually."

Kenneth nodded, still feeling shell-shocked and stunned. "You still didn't explain how you looked like me, though!" he accused, and Flammeth laughed again.

"Okay, so maybe I didn't," he chuckled. "Nephilim sometimes inherit powers from their heavenly side. I can change my shape and appearance at will. Ellie can heal other people's injuries and sicknesses, and Kali's savyl is movement."

"Even if they don't have any extra power, all Nephilim are naturally stronger, faster, and more intelligent than normal mortals. We also live longer than humans, and seem to age slower. Nephilim scientists have actually studied the differences in our DNA, and why we can do what we can."

Kenneth nodded again, thinking back to what happened earlier. "What exactly do you mean by 'her savyl is movement'?" he said slowly.

Flammeth sighed. "It's hard to explain. She has a grace of movement. She can move faster and more efficiently, jump higher, leap farther, and react faster than any of us here. In a fight against any one of us, except probably Gabriel, she would win every time."

"Gabriel's a Nephilim too? What are his powers?" Kenneth exclaimed.

Flammeth nodded, the smile coming back on his face. "He's our captain, and the one who said to watch you tonight. Good thing he did, too. But yeah, it's savyl, not powers, and he's rare. He's called a disavylus, meaning he has two different savylus. The first is strength. His second is the ability to manipulate the emotions of others."

"So," Kenneth began hesitantly, "Earlier when I felt calm rolling off him, I wasn't imagining it?"

Flammeth nodded. "We suspected you might be Nephilim because of the way you approached Richard, but we weren't sure. Remember when Gabriel asked if you "played the piano"? He was actually asking if you were Nephilim, but Kali only suspected at the time. Since we suspected, he gave you your fork bracelet to notify any other Nephilim you might meet. But when you noticed his calm, we immediately became aware that you were Nephilim, and he contacted Yigil shortly afterward. We thought you might already be trained because you immediately noticed the manipulations of emotions. So we decided to ask you meet us outside in order to find out more about you. What happened out there? All I got was the call to meet you guys here."

Kenneth paused, then explained what happened after he had gotten the text message from Flammeth. Flammeth listened in silence, an intent look of concentration on his face, until he reached the point where Richard and his gang were about to attack him.

"They attacked you?" he burst in. Kenneth nodded and opened his mouth to continue, but Flammeth interrupted him again. "Did something… strange happen? Anything to point to whether you have a savyl? Or do you already know what it is?"

Kenneth shook his head. "I have no idea what my savyl is. When they attacked me, something exploded, and Richard was severely hurt." He shuddered at the memory of burned and blackened bones and flesh. "Ellie healed him and Kali… She knocked everyone else out."

Flammeth's face was grim. "That sounds like Kali. You won't be able to go home anytime soon, though. Nor will you be able to go to school." Kenneth made a noise of protest, but Flammeth cut him off. "You don't understand. The humans will notice this, and you will likely be accused of attacking Richard while his gang helped 'defend him'. You will be wanted as a criminal. It's best you lay low here until we can figure something out."

"But my dad!" Kenneth exclaimed.

Flammeth made soothing motions. "We will probably be able to let you see him tomorrow, and if he is the right guy, explain to him the situation. For now, it is ten thirty, and I'm tired. We should both go to bed. Come on, I'll show you where you can sleep tonight."

Nora stood, wind whipping at her glossy black hair and eyes looking like pools of shining blood, surveying the room. She was dressed in studded leather armor, enchanted so it blended into her background. In her hand was a picture of a young man in armor, handsome and fair-haired, with eyes a burnished red-orange.

She turned to the two guards that escorted her into the room. "You may leave me now," she said. The guards protested, but fled after another look at her eyes. Alone now, Nora closed her eyes and looked with her savyl.

The room took a bluish cast, with all the normal colors inverted, and she turned slowly. It was a large room, with black stone and dark walnut furniture. It was obviously the man's bedroom, as a large gilded bed was in the corner of the room. It had several windows, and a fine carpet covered the floor.

Holding up the picture of the man, she lifted it to her line of sight. Immediately an image appeared of the man in the room, and started to move. He was going about his normal activities, so it seemed, moving in a way that suggested him tidying up the room, then removing his armor and clothes in a methodical manner.

He abruptly jerked, head up, eyes searching. Soon he was ducking and rolling, grabbing a sword and slashing at invisible objects only he could see. Eventually, his head moved in an awkward position and he collapsed. A couple seconds passed, then he rose off the ground and floated out the window.

Nora opened her eyes and walked to the window. After careful examination, she found a scuffmark on the black stone. Taking off her boot, she flipped it upside down. On it were metal spikes used for gripping slippery objects. Holding up the boot, she slapped it across the stone. The boot made a mark almost identical to the one beside it.

Nodding thoughtfully, Nora walked to the door and opened it. Outside were two embarrassed and frightened guards who followed her as she continued along the hallway. After a couple minutes of navigating, they reached a large double door entrance like they had left only moments before.

Entering without knocking, Nora walked in and sat down on the nearest couch.

"Do you always intend to be rude to me?" said the man behind the desk in the room. His voice was deep, smooth, luring. He stood and turned, walking into the light, revealing well-defined muscles, long dark hair, and a dark cast to his silver eyes.

Nora smiled, a feral baring of teeth. "Why, what ever do you mean, Patsy?" she said, watching his jaw muscles work. "You know that I am most civil to the Lord Patrik."

"And you know that I am called Iephus," the man said. "To call me otherwise mocks my past."

"Oh, I never would mock!" said Nora sardonically, raising her eyes imploringly.

Iephus growled, anger showing in the readiness in his body. He relaxed, suddenly, though Nora knew it was only on the surface. "You came to me to talk. Have you found him?"

"Of course not. You have only given me an hour. I have, however, discovered how he was taken."

Iephus nodded as if he had expected nothing less. "Then you came to discuss the price of finding him." Nora smiled and nodded, settling back to debate her terms.

Kenneth awakened gradually, as if he was slowly surfacing in water. Sound and feeling came first, everything sounding far away. Then memory came, the events of the previous day bursting inside his head. In an instant he was awake, shuddering, feeling sick as he once again saw Richard, face and arm burned off, flesh gaping and showing bone and muscle normally hidden beneath.

Forcing himself out of bed and Richard out of his mind, Kenneth dressed in the same clothes as the previous day. He would have to find clothes to wear since he had no extra clothes in the hideout below the church.

Sitting on the bed, Kenneth looked around the room. He hadn't paid much attention to the room when he had first walked in. He had been too tired, and had barely taken the time to strip out of his clothes and collapse on the bed before falling asleep.

The room was sparsely furnished, with the bed in one corner and a dresser in the other corner, with a mirror mounted on top. A clock was mounted on the wall directly across from the closet, which was relatively small, and was covered by a curtain. The clock read nine thirty, and as Kenneth walked out the room, he could almost hear his dad berating him for sleeping in again.

But the hallways were silent, the quiet pressing in on Kenneth like a blanket, with every step he took echoing slightly, and a quiet ringing in his ears the only other sound.

Retracing his steps, Kenneth managed to find his way to the room nearest to the top of the underground fortress, and found Gabriel sitting at the kitchen table with an enormous stack of pancakes and waffles. He was already eating, but a second place was set on the table, so Kenneth sat down. Gabriel merely nodded to him and kept chewing, motioning him to take what he wanted. Filling his plate, Kenneth drenched his pancakes with syrup and ate, acutely aware of Gabriel watching his every move. After a several minutes of eating, Gabriel sat back, wiped his mouth with his napkin, and began to speak.

"I understand that events are happening to you very quickly. Hopefully I can answer any questions that Flammeth has not already answered for you, and show you around our little home here underneath the cathedral. Possibly later today, when things in the town have calmed down, we can contact your father and explain to him the situation. For now, while you eat, do you have anything you want to ask me?"

Kenneth swallowed a mouthful of pancakes and thought to the conversation that he had the night before with Flammeth. "Flammeth said you were the Captain?" he asked, swirling his forkful of food in the syrup on his plate.

Gabriel nodded, folding his arms. "I'm in charge in this base aside from Yigil, who is my advisor and overseer. She helps with many things, but I end up deciding who does what and how things run around here. When it comes time for battle, I lead in tactical decisions and strategy. I also am the one who is 'sick' and misses school when we have a new member in the town to show the inductees around."

"You have battles?" Kenneth interrupted, his voice cracking a little.

"Where angels exist, so must demons," Gabriel said, "and worse, fallen angels. You'll understand the difference later, and I don't have time to explain now. But yes, every now and then we have a rogue demon that enters the town, and we have to fight him off before we have any problems." Gabriel stood up and grabbed his empty plate and headed into the kitchen to wash it off. Kenneth followed him and listened as Gabriel continued. "You will learn more about the battle front later, and, depending on how good of a fighter you are, you may even fight there for awhile. But for now, let us explore your new home."

Gabriel closed the door on the now clean dishes and addressed the room. "This is the food and entertainment area. We eat and play games here. It is the central part of the safe house, with staircases leading to every other room. You have already been to the library, but next to it is the training room." Gabriel walked to the staircase and led Kenneth through the door marked TRAINING AREA-NOT IN SESSION, and flipped it so it now read IN SESSION. Turning, he took the room in with a sweep of his arm.

The ceilings were high, around thirty feet, with several beams and bars up high in the rafters. Rows upon rows of weapons were hung upon the walls, from swords to quarterstaffs, and shields to armor, and all were neatly kept and labeled. Several gymnastic mats were laid on the floor, and in one corner was an array of lifting equipment.

"This is the room we train in. We learn everything from hand to hand fighting to learning how to use all those weapons on the walls," explained Gabriel. Walking across the room, he grabbed a wooden sword, padded with cloth, and walked to Kenneth. Grabbing the outstretched blade, Kenneth felt its weight.

"It's heavy!" Kenneth said, surprised.

Gabriel chuckled. "It's about twice as heavy as a normal blade. We practice with heavier blades when learning the basics to increase muscle strength and speed. When you get more advanced we will use blunted blades." Returning to the wall, Gabriel grabbed another blade, similar to the first, but about twice its size. "Let's see how good you are with the sword," he said, swinging the blade casually in one hand.

"What? No practicing first?" Kenneth squeaked, looking at the muscles flexing in Gabriel's arms.

"I want to see how much natural talent you have in the blade," replied Gabriel, slowing the blade and bringing it up in front of him. "We will start...now."

Gabriel swung the blade, and to Kenneth's astonishment, so did he, parrying the stroke neatly and moving his blade to counter. The world condensed, becoming simpler, everything sharper, with every movement noticed. It was all action and reaction, no thought, as

Kenneth swung and sliced, not noticing the concentration on Gabriel's face, or the speed that he was starting to use.

Suddenly the realization that he was holding his own against Gabriel crashed into him and he fumbled, unsure what to do, and Gabriel's blade slammed into his, knocking it out of his hand, and flicked up to his throat.

Gabriel stared at him, face betraying nothing, before carefully placing both swords back on the wall. Kenneth followed him as he continued down the staircase, leading him to the library.

"Didn't you say you weren't going to show me the library because I had already seen it?" Kenneth asked, but Gabriel only replied with a curt "Be quiet" before leading him into the library. He walked to Yigil's desk, where, apparently unmoved, Yigil was working on the computer.

She turned as they approached, and inhaled sharply, face tilting towards Gabriel, sunken eyes seeming to bore right through him. She stood, navigated her way through the desk and books that surrounded her, and entered a door behind the desk. Gabriel gestured sharply for him to enter, and Kenneth hesitantly followed.

It was not a large room, but it was carefully organized to maximize the space in the center. The walls were covered with shelves and cupboards, and were lit with candles. As soon as he walked in, Gabriel shut the door behind him, and lit the rest of the candles. Yigil grabbed a chair and set it in the middle of the room, all the while muttering to herself, words inaudible.

Kenneth moved, and Yigil's head snapped up, causing him to freeze. "Come here, boy," she snapped, "Sit in this chair." Kenneth sat, wiping his palms on his pants and waiting as she went to one of the cupboards and rustled around. Gabriel grabbed a chair of his own and pulled it to the side and sat, waiting.

Finally Yigil found what she was looking for. Turning, she held what seemed to be a bowl of water in her hand. Setting it on a table, she turned her face, sunken eyes meeting his, and said, "Why have you come here, boy?"

"I-I don't know what you mean," stammered Kenneth, unsure by what she was asking.

Yigil hissed. "You make a poor liar, boy. Now tell me, why have you come here to spy on us? What cult are you from? Ospiron? Girideal? Tell me," She growled, her voice low and menacing.

"I'm not a spy!" exclaimed Kenneth, bewildered. "How could you think I was a spy? Who would I spy for?"

Gabriel spoke up, voice grim, "There are several reasons." He said, ignoring his second question. Kenneth looked at him in astonishment. "The first was that you immediately became friends with the only Nephilim group in the High School. The second was a little less subtle. You can already use you savyl. You attacked the boy Richard on the way to meet Flammeth."

"He attacked me!" Kenneth said, incredulous, "And I don't even know what my savyl is!"

Gabriel shook his head. "Later, during breakfast, you didn't say a prayer before you ate, even though you claim you are Catholic.

You also immediately accepted the idea that you are Nephilim. Not many people believe that they are part angel right away. Furthermore, you claim to have lived with your father, but we found where you said you had lived, and the place has been abandoned for five years. And finally, for a person who never picked up a sword in his life, you fought in a windsinger's battle at a blademaster's level, despite your 'fumble'."

Kenneth was speechless. He looked from Yigil to Gabriel and shook his head slowly. "I'm not a spy..." he said weakly.

Gabriel looked at Yigil. She slowly stood, fumbling with something on her pouch. "There is a way to find out if you are a spy or not," she whispered, "Take off your shirt."

"What?" said Kenneth, startled.

"I said to take off your shirt. Is this too much to ask of you?" she said, and Kenneth shook his head and took off his shirt, feeling extremely self-conscious. Yigil walked up to him and passed her hand over his head, showering him with a golden dust. It settled in his hair, on his face, and seemed to stick to his skin, glowing. Abruptly it *pulsed*, and vanished. Immediately, all over his arms, chest, and back, a tattoo shimmered. It spiraled and swirled, ending in jagged edges and wrapping around his arms.

Kenneth stared at himself in amazement, looking in the mirror. He looked dangerous now, with the tattoo even on his face, and when he turned, he saw two black angel wings on his back. Gabriel's face reflected his own astonishment, and when he turned, he saw Yigil smiling coldly.

"Not a spy…" she whispered, "Then where did this come from?"

The Sign of the Fallen

Nora crept, her armor taking on the colors of the dark background behind her as she snuck her way across the courtyard. Shadows played off the walls, and the sound of marching sentries echoed in the night. The smell of earth and grass gently fragranced the air, and the quiet rustling of Nora moving abruptly stopped. She breathed slowly, silently, listening intently for anyone near her.

Satisfied she would not be seen, she put on gloves with small metal spikes on the ends, used for climbing. Scaling the wall next to her carefully, she slowly made her way to the top, nearly three hundred feet high.

The stone was slippery, but she had done this many times. Carefully, she lifted herself on the edge of the highest window, metal spikes grinding on her calloused hands, and stood on it. Wind blew, and she suppressed a shiver; she was high enough her breath was showing and icicles had formed at the top of the window.

Thick metal bars covered the window, and as she scooted closer, she saw that they were completely silverlight. *Someone wanted to make sure that no one could get in or out with their savyl,* Nora thought. Silverlight resisted all magical energy that touched it, but it was extremely expensive and hard to craft. Reaching into her pouch at her waist, she took out a small flask filled with a dark liquid. Unstopping the flask, she drank.

The world darkened, color draining, everything going gray scale. Only the bars retained color, changing into a bright, shining white. Reaching out with her hand, she grabbed the bars.

They held firm, but that didn't matter. Focusing, Nora kept her hold on the bars and passed through the stone beneath them, using the silverlight for support. Letting herself meld back into the real world again, she stood up in the chamber.

It was small, built to hold a very dangerous prisoner. There was no door, only a hatch on one of the walls to insert food. There was a rough cloth in one corner, probably for the prisoner's bed, and a bucket that she guessed was their bathroom. Looking around carefully, she saw nothing out of ordinary, but she closed her eyes and looked again.

The room took on that bluish cast, with all colors inverted; white colored stone changed to black, and the wood of the hatch flashed to a bright blue. The bars in the window glowed a bright white, and when Nora looked carefully, so did something by the blanket. Kneeling, she lifted the blankets edge and gasped silently.

Glowing on the floor in dark red edged with white, was scrawled the Sign of the Fallen.

Kenneth was at a loss for words. He didn't know what to think with everything that was going on. He merely looked at Yigil, confused and slightly hurt, and every now and then glancing at the strange tattoo shimmering on his body. Several times he tried to speak, but no words would come out.

Finally Yigil sat back. Turning her head towards Gabriel, she spoke, "I am going to attempt a spell. Protect me." Gabriel nodded, and held out his hands, a massive sword appearing between them, its blade slightly frosted. Kenneth looked nervously from him to Yigil, but nothing happened that he could see.

Eventually Yigil stood, and a bluish light appeared around her and the chair that Kenneth was sitting in, and Kenneth found he couldn't move from chest down aside from breathing. Yigil faced him and spoke, "I have now cast a spell on you that will prevent you from speaking lies. If you do not speak, you will not live. Tell me, have you been with the Fallen? Have you fought for them?"

Kenneth opened his mouth to deny it, but no words would come out. He tried and tried again, but whatever he did, no sound was heard. Yigil looked from him to Gabriel, expression grim.

"But I don't remember anything like that! How can I be a spy if I don't know anything about them? I swear! I am not a spy!" Kenneth burst in, and to his relief he could speak. Yigil's expression changed to surprise, and Gabriel interrupted.

"Does the spell work even if you haven't asked a specific question?" he interjected. Yigil nodded slowly, and Gabriel harrumphed, but looked thoughtful. "Release the spell for now," he said, and the bluish light dissipated. Walking up to Kenneth, he looked at him for a long time, then finally spoke. "Do you know a spell that can read minds?" he asked Yigil.

"In a way," she answered, "It doesn't read thoughts, it reads memories."

Gabriel nodded thoughtfully. "Can you read his memories to see if he ever served the Fallen, or somehow managed to avoid the spell's effects?"

"Yes, but his consent is required," answered Yigil, grimacing. She was seemingly watching Kenneth, even though she had her blindfold over her empty eye sockets.

"I give it," Kenneth said nervously surprising them both. He wiped his sweaty palms on his pants, watching Yigil tensely. She nodded and walked up to him, placing an ice-cold palm on his head, and the world went dark.

When he reawakened, Yigil was talking to Gabriel, her words garbled and not making sense. "I've never seen anything like it! He has no memories aside from those starting two days ago. All the rest are gone, vanished! Very few angels have that power. The memories will come back eventually—no mortal can suspend them completely—as he sees things that will trigger them. If he is carefully handled, he should stay as he is now, well mannered and talented."

"And if he is not?" came Gabriel's voice, sounding as though it were through water.

"If he isn't, he will return to the Fallen. He is powerful and high ranking in their society. On his chest is the Sign of the Fallen. Only the Semiazas get those, and you are only a leader if you are extraordinarily dangerous and intelligent. As you know, they are usually co-leaders, so that if one was killed, the other could still run the Fallen's Nephilim and choose the new co-leader. They will either be searching for him, or he will be presumed dead, and they will be looking to replace him. And if they are looking for him..." Yigil's voice trailed off.

"Could Sekai or Nora have..." came Gabriel's voice.

"Quiet! He's waking!" hissed Yigil, and Kenneth opened his eyes. Not much time seemed to have passed, but both Yigil and Gabriel seemed to have moved. The air smelled of slightly burned hair, and when he touched his head, the area where Yigil had touched him was slightly singed. The smell reminded him of Richard again, and he immediately felt sickened.

Yigil approached him. "We have decided that you most probably served in the Fallen's regiment." Kenneth sucked in his breath, feeling like he had been hit in the stomach. "However," Yigil said, "Your memories of that time are gone, leaving half formed subconscious thoughts, instincts, and reflexes of the past."

Kenneth looked at her strangely, and she nodded. "We won't hold you captive, but realize that Gabriel will keep a close watch on you. We won't tell the others, and if they find out, we will swear them to silence. Your memories will probably come back, and as they do, please tell us. Hopefully you will see us as helpers. I also apologize. I over-reacted slightly earlier, and was not very nice. I am not normally good with people, but that was unacceptable." She nodded once to him and walked out of the room.

Kenneth, astonished, looked at Gabriel. He nodded, "Everything she said is true. We will continue your tour of the facilities another time. We have decided on a story for your father as well, because he does not actually exist. We also retrieved and checked your phone for any contacts, but the only ones present are Kali, Flammeth, and myself. I also apologize, but don't regret my action. It was warranted. So instead, I wish to introduce to you the rest of the Nephilim in the area." Gabriel stood, motioning to Kenneth to follow, and led him out of the room.

"Are there many Nephilim in the town?" Kenneth asked hesitantly.

Gabriel shrugged. "There is a fair number, around eight in this town, which is normal for a Nephilim population. Nephilim aren't necessarily common, and very few towns are completely Nephilim. Even those are hidden away, kept out of sight from most mortals."

Gabriel walked up the stairs, talking while leading Kenneth. "The Nephilim who live in this area are specialized for the training of new soldiers for the Ranks of the Light, so most of the people here are either retired soldiers or spies." Gabriel turned off a passage on the staircase, leading Kenneth down a corridor full of doors. He stopped near a door at the end of the turn, and said, "I would put your hands over your ears." Kenneth looked at him oddly, but did as he said. Gabriel opened the door, carefully stopped up his ears with his fingers, and walked in.

Kenneth followed, and as soon as he walked through the door, he was hit by a wave of sound. Metal hitting metal in a loud ringing reverberated around the room, making his ears hurt. Pushing his hand harder to block out more sound, he searched for the source of the sound.

It didn't take long. Towering over an anvil in one corner of the room was a man even larger than Gabriel, his bald head nearly brushing the ceiling. He turned around, noticing they were in the room, and set down the large piece of metal he had been working on, silence covering the room like a blanket.

Gabriel walked up to him. "Aaron Gormley, I would like you to meet our newest Nephilim, Kenneth Sanderz." Aaron turned, and regarded Kenneth. He was a massive man, all built at the same proportion, with arms like tree-trunks, and legs like an elephant. He held out a hand twice the size of Kenneth's, and Kenneth gingerly shook it, expecting his hand to be crushed at any second.

"Well at least he isn't as jumpy as the last one!" he boomed, and Kenneth looked at Gabriel as Aaron laughed. Gabriel simply smiled, and Aaron said, "Last time he introduced me to someone they flinched every time I moved. You would think that I look scary or something!" Aaron laughed his loud laugh and smacked his trim stomach. Kenneth smiled weakly, and Aaron walked back to his anvil, stoking the fires next to his workstation.

Gabriel led Kenneth out of the room as the peals of the hammer restarted, and once they left the room, silence once again ensued.

"Aaron makes all the weapons and armor for us here, and has extraordinary craftsmanship, especially for unique sets of armor. His savyl gives him a type of magnetism to all types of metal, which allows him to shape it easily. He doesn't enjoy fighting, despite his looks." Gabriel shrugged, "Just don't annoy him." Kenneth shuddered, envisioning the giant angry.

They walked for a while, heading back towards the stairs and down to the training room. Gabriel directed him inside, and spoke quietly, gesturing to a ledge near the ceiling of the room. Kenneth could make out a desk and a bed, and a humanoid shape sitting on the edge, watching them in silence.

"Up in that corner of the room is Gimelli Savoy. His savyl allows him to speak to birds. He is the head of our spy organization here, and uses the birds to gather information about the Fallen. His spies are everywhere, and come to him when they find anything. But the reason I am speaking so that he won't hear is because he was captured by the Fallen five years ago. They tortured him in order to find out how he was finding out all the information about them. He didn't tell them anything, and was eventually rescued in a raid three months later. But something broke inside of him in those months, and he is a little insane."

Kenneth looked at him, and Gabriel motioned him out into the corridor. They walked in silence for a little while, and eventually Gabriel said, "Those are all the Nephilim here except two. The first is Aaron's son Aelex, who has a savyl that allows him to switch between his normal vision and infrared vision. He is on patrol right now, and the other one…"

Gabriel was interrupted when he opened the door leading to the top room, and Flammeth nearly slammed into them. He was laughing, watched by Kali and Ellie, and staggering around like he was drunk. Gabriel looked at him as if he was crazy, shook his head, and left the room, shutting the door behind him. Flammeth gave one last chuckle and fell over, holding his head, as everyone else laughed.

Kenneth helped him up. "What were you doing?" he asked, trying, but failing, to hold down bubbles of laughter as Flammeth staggered over to a chair and sat down.

Flammeth grimaced. "They," he said, pointing at Kali and Ellie, who were still laughing, "told me that there was no way that I could spin in circle for a full minute and walk down the stairs. And they were so right." Kali and Ellie high-fived each other, and sat down as well.

Flammeth sighed and shook his head, shooting another glare at the two girls. His glare faded quickly into a smile. "I give in, that was funny!" he gasped, and started laughing. Standing, he walked shakily over to Kali and sat beside her, putting his arm around her shoulders. He absently stroked her hair for a second, then focused on

Kenneth, "So how did your day go? Did Gabriel run you through the hoops?" Kenneth shrugged uncomfortably and nodded.

"He showed me around and introduced me to everyone that was here," he said. "The only thing we haven't talked about is my power." The others nodded like this was natural, and Flammeth hopped up from where he was sitting and walked toward the kitchen.

"We can figure out what your savyl is after I eat my second lunch. If you haven't eaten yet you should eat too. A Nephilim burns a lot of calories." Flammeth began taking food out from the refrigerator, salads and yogurt and fruit, and placing them on the table. He looked at them with partial disgust, and muttered, "What Gabriel makes us eat around here..." and sat down.

Kenneth walked over to the table with the others and sat down with them as the said the prayer for the meal, listening carefully so he would remember it in the future. They began eating with gusto, despite what Flammeth had said. After a little bit, the consumption of food slowed, and Kali spoke up.

"I can go to Yigil and talk to her about finding out your savyl. By the time you guys are finished, she will be nearly set up." Flammeth and the others nodded, food still in their mouths, and she left down the stairs.

Flammeth watched after her with a bemused expression on his face, then said to Kenneth, "She still doesn't like you for some reason."

Kenneth jerked, startled. "How can you tell?" he asked curiously.

"I've been with her a long time," he answered thoughtfully. "I can tell. I just can't tell why." He looked up at the ceiling, and gradually slid his eyes to where Ellie was eating. "If someone would tell me, I would be ever so grateful…"

She looked steadily back at him, her purple eyes glittering. "Boys," she snorted and turned back to her food. Flammeth shrugged and turned back to Kenneth.

"It was worth a try," he said with a rueful smile.

Kenneth chuckled and asked Ellie, "Why do you have purple eyes? Is it a Nephilim thing, or is it just you?"

Ellie chewed slowly, and looked at Flammeth, who answered for her, "A Nephilim's eyes are directly related to their savyl. The color of the eyes shows whether or not the Nephilim's powers are mental or physical, the more earthy colors being the physical, and the lighter colors mental. If their savyl is spiritual, like Ellie over here, they are exceedingly strange. Healing doesn't fall into either of these categories; therefore, after many years of research, someone discovered spiritual powers. It's not actually healing. Instead it's an extreme form of compassion. She feels such compassion for the injured that she can sacrifice some of her own health to speed the healing of others. Compassion is spiritual, and therefore an abnormal color."

Kenneth nodded slowly. "So Aelex—the blacksmith's son—what's his eye color?"

"Aelex's eyes are bright blue. And his father's are brown," replied Flammeth. Kenneth opened his mouth to ask another question, but was cut off by the door opening. He turned to look and noticed a short young woman about his age that he did not recognize. She walked with a deadly grace, and had eyes so dark that they looked black. Her hair was shoulder-length and a glossy black that looked wet. She was garbed in a uniform similar to that of Kali's from the previous night, but it seemed to suck in shadow and hide her from sight, making her difficult to see even in the bright light of the kitchen.

Everyone in the kitchen fell silent when they saw her, and when she looked over she gasped, her almond shaped eyes flying to Kenneth's face. She took a step back, broke eye contact, and practically ran down the stairs. Kenneth, surprised, asked Flammeth, "Who was that?" Flammeth didn't answer, and when he turned and looked at him, he saw that Ellie had gone pale and Flammeth had a scowl on his face. "What?" he asked.

Flammeth grunted. "That was the other Nephilim who 'lives' here. Her name is Saskia Ying, and she comes and goes at random times, and rarely stays more than a few days." He looked at Ellie who was still pale, but slowly regaining color. "We are all at least a little afraid of her," he admitted.

Kenneth remembered the strange shadows that seemed to cling to her, and her black eyes. "What is her savyl?" he asked, watching Flammeth curiously.

Flammeth exhaled slowly. "Similar Ellie over here, she also has a spiritual savyl. Like all spiritual savylus, it is based on a certain emotion. But she is very, very different than Ellie, who has a nice emotion, like compassion. Her savyl is fear. She can learn what your fears are by looking at you, and can bring them to life using her savyl. The stronger you are feeling fear towards that fear at the time, the easier she can bring it to life. So, say, if you are terrified of spiders and there is one in the room, and you make her angry, she might cover you with spiders the size of your hand. Now, she probably won't make them poisonous, but you still wouldn't be happy." Ellie shuddered and left the room at high speed, looking sick. Flammeth watched her go with sympathy in his eyes.

"She did that to Ellie?" Kenneth asked in a low voice. Flammeth nodded and Kenneth winced in sympathy. Flammeth and Kenneth were silent for several seconds, and Flammeth cleared his throat.

"Lets go down and find out how Kali and Yigil are doing." Flammeth stood, pushing back his chair and leading Kenneth down the stairs to the training room. They were silent on the way down, and they still said nothing as they opened the door.

Kenneth walked in first and immediately jumped in the air, a scream locked in his throat. He scrambled backwards, pointing and stammering to Flammeth, "T-t-t-tiger! T-t-there's a huge tiger!"

Flammeth looked in said with a smirk, "Oh, her? That's Gabriel's little pet. Big kitty, ain't she?" Kenneth looked at him in disbelief, and Flammeth chuckled. "Don't worry, she doesn't normally attempt to kill new-comers." Flammeth walked in, leaving Kenneth shaking from adrenaline. Not entirely reassured, he followed Flammeth.

Across the massive training room sat an enormous tiger, standing taller at the shoulder than the massive blacksmith he had met earlier that day. It was striped white and blue, with muscles rippling beneath the long fur. It turned its head to gaze at Kenneth with its bright blue eyes and yawned, its long, crystalline fangs glittering in the light.

"Magnificent, isn't she?" came Gabriel's voice from behind them. He walked up beside them, looking at the tiger with his hands behind his back. "I got her as a gift many years ago, and she's been my loyal friend since she was a cub. She's quite intelligent, so she will understand what you say. Is that not so, Fang?" She growled, a deep throaty sound that shook her fur.

"Fang. He had to name her Fang," muttered Flammeth beside him. "What's the matter with something original? Why not name her Abby? Better than Fang! Or if that's not scary enough, we could call her Ice-tiger-mauler-and-tearer! A little wordy, perhaps, but very frightening." Kenneth looked at him with bemusement, and Flammeth glanced back at him with a wink.

"Abby is nice." ventured Kenneth but stopped when Yigil entered with Kali at her side. Gabriel nodded to them both, and walked to a bench by the wall and sat down.

Yigil approached them and spoke, "I was called to test your savyl. We spoke a little bit earlier about it, but I feel that we should find out specifically what it is."

Kenneth nodded, then realizing that she was blind, he said, "Okay."

Yigil gestured with her hand, and an area to the side of her cleared itself of training equipment. "In order to test you safely, we have developed a spell that will show the results of your savyl, but not let it effect anything. This isn't necessary for some savylus, but since you have had a past history of danger, it is better safe than sorry." Kenneth squirmed uncomfortably, realizing that she wasn't referring to his encounter with Richard.

Yigil raised her hand again and spread her fingers. Orange light flashed and converged to a spinning point in front of her. It hovered for a moment before spreading into a large circle. Kenneth watched in fascination as it broke into runes that spiraled outward sinking into the floor, glowing. She turned and motioned for Kenneth to enter the circle. Kenneth walked hesitantly into the circle, expecting to feel different, but he felt nothing as he passed through the circle of runes.

He looked at Yigil expectantly, who was intent on her spell, lips forming the frames of words, and hands flicking every now and then. Gabriel stood and walked to the circle, drawing Kenneth's attention away from Yigil.

"In order for you to access your savyl, you must concentrate. If your savyl is physical, you won't have to, but we doubt that it is. Most likely you have a mental savyl, and therefore have to access it with your mind. When I control the emotions of others, I have to use my mind to discern what emotions that they are feeling at the time and how I want to change them. This took practice, but I feel you are able to use your savyl for many reasons." His eyes flicked to where Kali and Flammeth where standing, and Kenneth realized that Gabriel was trying to keep them from knowing where he came from.

"I want you to try to do something with your savyl right now. We know you can already—you did *something* last night, and that means you can replicate it." Gabriel folded his arms and looked at him expectantly. Kenneth shrugged uncomfortably, and closed his eyes. *What am I doing?* He thought to himself. *I don't even know what I am supposed to be doing!*

"I don't think this is working," Kenneth said after several long seconds, acutely aware that everyone was staring at him, waiting for something to happen. Gabriel looked at him for a moment and nodded decisively.

"Let's try a different way," he said, and for a second Kenneth felt relief. Gabriel walked over to the wall and took down a sword, and walked into the circle. He swung the sword with a soft *wum-wum*, and took a ready stance against Kenneth.

Kenneth swallowed, anxious, and said, "What are we doing now?" His adrenaline slowly started pumping, and the hairs on the back of his neck rose. Gabriel didn't answer, and without warning rushed forward, swinging the sword in a deadly arc towards Kenneth's head.

Kenneth shouted in alarm and threw up an arm, light flashing from it with a loud hiss. It exploded silently, fire spraying to the edges of the circle. He froze, the tip of the sword between his now golden eyes, with Gabriel looking at him with a smile.

"What happened?" he asked Gabriel as he stepped away from him and sheathed his sword.

Yigil answered, "You first used your savyl subconsciously, so he attacked you to force you to react with your savyl. It would seem that your savyl is the element of fire." And in saying so, she turned and left, leaving the dancing orange runes to fade slowly into the concrete floor.

Glass shards glittered as light reflected off of where they lay covering the carpet next to the shattered window. The robber took no notice of this as he leapt through the window, his boots crunching against them. He carried a sack with him, similar to a backpack, and if all went well, it would soon be filled with valuables.

He went through the rooms quickly, looking for small, expensive items, occasionally breaking something large that looked expensive. Picking up some cash on a desk, he grabbed the paperweight and flung it at the flat-screen, laughing as it smashed into it with a crunching noise.

The thief walked to the stairs that led to the upper floor and froze as a scent wafted in his direction. It was the sickly smell of blood, and as the robber looked, he could see that the walls of the upper floor were spattered with a dark red. The smell made him retch, and he covered his mouth to mask the scent.

He walked up the stairs slowly, retrieving his pistol from his pocket and holding it in front of him with both hands. He turned the corner slowly, and was met by a child.

She was a young girl, not older than six. She sat with her back turned away from him, playing with a red pillow. He approached her silently, and swallowed a scream.

What was left of a young woman decorated the walls. She was staked to the wall with wood ripped off of a mangled chair, her skin peeled back from her head. Her eyes were open, staring, and she ended abruptly at the lower half of her body, her blood dripping slowly to the floor. The rest of her splatter-painted the room.

He took a step back, sickened, and the child turned with a chilling grace and stood with pudgy legs, staring at him, and he screamed, aloud this time, as he saw the child completely.

Her eyes were completely black, even around the whites, and blood slowly drooled out of the corner of her mouth as she smiled and laughed a girlish baby laugh and clapped her hands, dropping the pillow—*it was a heart*. He raised his pistol and struggled to stop shaking and fire, to do *anything*.

The man's screams did not last long.

Swords and Fallen Angels

Everyone watched Yigil leave in silence, standing awkwardly for several long seconds. Eventually Kenneth broke the silence, "What does she mean by the 'element of fire'?

Flammeth answered, "There is one other type of magic that you don't know about. Elemental magic changes a person's eye color to that of the color of their magic. It is considered the most powerful type, and is usually similar to a physical magic, causing strain on the body instead of the mind. Elemental magic is usually something like water or air, officially known as *aquamanipulation* or *aeromanipulation*. Since you have fire, you can control everything about fire, and even create fire."

Kenneth stared at him with astonishment, looking to Gabriel for confirmation. Gabriel nodded and cleared his throat. "We might as well do our sparring session now, seeing as we're all here," he said, setting his sword point-first on the floor and leaning on it. Kali nodded happily and ran to grab a thin blade from the wall. Flammeth and Ellie also grabbed weapons, and Gabriel handed his sword to Kenneth and grabbed the blade that he had sparred with earlier.

Gabriel stood to the side, and pointed to Flammeth. "You first," he grunted. He turned to Kenneth, "The room is permanently warded to prevent the swords from leaving anything but a bad bruise. Occasionally we may get a bloody nose, but that rarely happens," he explained. Kenneth nodded as Flammeth approached Kali. She stood perfectly balanced, the tip of her sword pointed slightly up as she faced him. They stared at each other for a moment, motionless, and then Flammeth moved.

He rushed forward, sword raised and whistling through the air toward her head, but she wasn't there. She had dodged, rolling to one side and already moving in on a counterstrike. Flammeth seemed to have anticipated this, however, and managed to block the near-deadly stroke.

Gabriel spoke to Kenneth while they fought, blades flashing and faces locked in concentration. "There are three main stances that Nephilim fight in: The mountain stance, the windsinger's stance, and giant stance. Each is useful in its own way, and used for different types of fighting. Mountain stance is used for total defense, waiting for your enemy to make a mistake so you can quickly defeat them. This is usually taught to foot soldiers, and requires the use of a shield. The second, windsinger's stance is used when facing an enemy larger and stronger than you, and incorporates the force of the enemy's strength and momentum to help give your own swings more power. The last, giant's stance, is used when you are larger and more powerful than your opponent, but slower. It is all about overwhelming your opponent as fast as you can."

Kenneth nodded, watching them fight. It was obvious that they had fought each before, and were fairly evenly matched because of it. Flammeth was slowing though, and Kali showed no signs of stopping. Soon she had him disarmed and her blade at his throat. He nodded in deference to her and walked over to where Kenneth, Gabriel, and Ellie where standing.

"She went easy on me today," he said to Kenneth as he leaned against the wall, panting.

"What do you mean?" Kenneth asked.

"You'll find out," was all he got, and Gabriel walked to Kali and took his battle stance. Kali took a deep breath and charged him. Kenneth quickly understood what he meant as he watched her fight Gabriel. She was everywhere, swinging and ducking and rolling, her hair flying and face locked in a fierce concentration.

Gabriel blocked and parried, turning and dancing about as he stopped stroke after stroke. His blade was a blur, carefully keeping her away from him as he wove a barrier of moving steel around himself. They fought for several minutes, blade matching blade until there was a smacking sound, and Gabriel stopped, holding his side and coughing.

Kali stopped immediately, still in a ready-stance, and Gabriel smiled and dropped his sword. She carefully flicked his sword away with her own and walked over to help him.

Kenneth turned to Flammeth. "Why did she not help him until after he dropped his sword?"

Flammeth laughed. "Last time he beat her because he pretended to get injured. She dropped her guard and went to help him, and he 'killed' her. She doesn't take chances after something like that happens." Kenneth nodded.

Gabriel motioned at Kenneth. "It's your turn. Do your best, and remember our short sparring session from earlier." Kenneth looked at him in disbelief and slowly walked out to meet Kali, who wasn't even short of breath.

He held his sword up in the ready position that he saw Kali in, and waited, his nervousness dampening his palms, making his grip on the blunted sword slickened. He breathed slowly through his nose in an attempt to calm himself as Kali prepared herself, a slightly contemptuous look on her face.

He held himself still as she raised her sword, then rushed her, catching her by surprise. She reacted quickly, flicking his sword to one side and swinging her sword in a fast counterstrike. He reacted without thought, using his body weight to fall to the floor, letting the sword pass a whisper's breath above him and sweeping his legs to knock her to the floor.

She fell and twisted, dropping her sword to land on her hands, grabbing Kenneth and flipping him. The world spun, and Kenneth rolled and somehow managed to keep his blade as he spun to face her once more. She had retrieved her blade, and was facing him with more caution now, a look of concentration slowly melting away the previous disdain on her face.

Kenneth prepared himself again, his thoughts whirling as he assessed her every move. Heart pumping, he waited as Kali slowly approached him.

She struck, lightning quick, a rapid slice to his midsection that he barely blocked, and another to his head that he managed to duck. Backing up, he fell into the rhythm of blocking her strokes, slowly getting a feel for her fighting style. After a minute, he slapped her blade aside, and attacked.

He started by slashing at her sides, using the force of her own block to move his blade faster, abruptly changing his last swing towards her head into a thrust towards her midsection. She jumped backwards, slightly off balance for the first time he had seen, and he caught the hilt of her blade with his and twisted. Her sword fell with a clatter, and Kali stared cross-eyed at the blade point that was centered on her forehead.

Silence permeated the training room, with the sound of his heavy breathing sounding loud to Kenneth's own ears. He felt nearly as surprised as Kali looked, but felt invigorated despite the sweat that soaked his shirt. Instead of feeling tired, he felt more awake, and could still feel the adrenaline pumping through his veins.

He looked around to the shocked stares of Flammeth and Ellie, with Gabriel off to one side, nodding as if he had expected it to happen. He looked back to Kali, who had a dark, angry look.

Watching from the shadows, Saskia slipped away, unnoticed.

The heels on Nora's boots clicked on the flagstones as she strode down the walkway leading to the looming fortress, making a staccato tattoo that seemed loud in the early morning hours. She walked with a purposeful stride and a deadly grace that bespoke suppressed energy, like a coiled spring.

The guards at the gate saw her coming from a distance, but did not recognize her, nor would they. She was dressed in the armor of a lieutenant-general, high in the ranks of the Fallen, and her normally straight black hair was dyed blond and curled. She had also changed her skin with a spell, layering on a tan that added a darker cast to her skin.

She approached them with the dignity of a general, and presented them her identification card with a disdainful sneer, as if they were completely beneath her notice. It was all an act. She noticed every movement they made, and every weapon they held, her mind noting all escape routes and the easiest way to kill each of them.

They passed her through, and she continued walking towards the main keep, blending easily in with the crowd of people. Once near the keep, she stood in a dark corner, retrieving a vial from her belt. Unstopping the vial, she shook her hair, the dye draining from her hair into the bottle. She stoppered the vial, hair now straight and dark black again. Running her hands over her uniform, it changed back into her usual garb, and she checked to make sure all of her lethal weapons were in their proper places.

Whispering a spell, she tapped her boots with her fingers, and dark spikes shot out of the bottoms, and after flexing her fingers, out of her gloves as well. Running in a crouch, she jumped towards the Keep wall.

The jump took her over thirty feet in the air, and she landed, dark spikes sinking into the stone with a quiet hiss. She clung to the wall like a spider, unnoticed by the guards below. She climbed now, moving as quickly as she could, to the thirteenth floor.

Underneath the window, she stopped, listening. After carefully making sure she was secure, she closed her eyes, using her second sight to make sure there was no one in the storeroom.

Opening her eyes, she cautiously took out the window using her knife and crawled into the room. It was filled with chests, and smelled of old leather, with dust layering most of the chests. She replaced the window carefully and opened the door to the hallway outside.

It was also empty, as she knew it would be. She strode down the hallways, boots now making no sound, and paused at two large, ornate doors.

Throwing the doors open, she walked into the room. It was a large room, with several chairs and couches arranged for a sitting area in one corner, and a desk and small library in the opposite corner.

Lord Iephus stood in by the desk, holding a book in his hands, dressed in full military uniform. He didn't look up as she entered, and didn't need to. His savyl allowed him to feel the minds of others around him.

Nora walked to one of the couches and sat, pretending to lounge, and waited. Eventually, Iephus looked up.

"How did you manage to get up here?" he asked. She smiled, knowing that it irked him that she could so easily get past his defenses. She said nothing, smiling at him, never letting it touch her eyes, her mind carefully guarded.

He nodded, never really expecting an answer, and asked, "What have you found?"

"I followed his past to the Keep of Light, where he was held in one of the most secure dungeons," she said casually, enjoying his look of surprise as he realized she had broken into the Keep of Light.

"What did you find in his dungeon?" he inquired, rubbing his hands together. She smiled, and took out a scroll that was latched to her belt.

"I found this," she answered, handing him the scroll. He took it and unfurled it, staring at the Sign of the Fallen with intense eyes. "Naturally, it wasn't written on the scroll, so I moved it from the floor to the scroll so I could transport the exact sign from there to here."

That surprised him. Iephus's eyes shot up, boring into hers, and he questioned her in a quiet voice. "This is the Sign that he wrote himself?" Nora nodded, and Iephus smiled and laid the scroll on the desk. He turned to the bookshelves behind him, selecting a thick tome and setting it on the table with a soft thud. Opening it, he flipped through the pages until he came to a chapter filled with drawings of the same sign, each slightly different.

He studied the book for a long minute before laughing a deep, menacing chuckle. Snapping the book shut, he turned to look at Nora, a pleased smile on his face.

"You did well," he said, "very well. Lord Blaze was quite knowledgeable in the runes of old. The rune he inscribed still burns, so it indicates that he is, in fact, still alive and well. But there is more. The rune is attuned to him, therefore we can locate where he is."

Nora nodded, secretly fascinated. "Is my job done?" she asked, "or do you have further need for my services?"

"You will be paid for finding him as soon as I finish the locating spell. After that, you will go to his location, research his situation and report back to me. Then I will decide if it is possible to retrieve him." He looked at her, his eyes transparent windows to a twisted mind. "Of course, if we can retrieve him, do so immediately and without fail. I will pay you twice as much as your first job."

Nora smiled.

Kenneth woke at an abnormal sound, reaching to his side and grasping at air as he sprang out of bed and rushed the intruder. He found himself on the floor, both arms pinned, looking into Gabriel's face. After a moment, he quit struggling, and realized how foolish he must look.

"I had a hunch you would react this way," Gabriel said, "You slept with a sword at your side." Kenneth nodded, remembering trying to unsheathe a blade that wasn't there.

"What do you want me for?" Kenneth asked. Gabriel raised an eyebrow, and helped him up. Kenneth folded his arms. "You wouldn't wake me in the middle of the night just to see how I would react," he said, as if it were obvious.

Gabriel nodded. "I want you to go on patrol with me," he said, "I have armor and a uniform laid out for you in your personal armory." He walked to the empty closet and put his hand against the wall.

"Captain reopens this sector for re-admittance. Prepare to input data according to next entry." The wall glowed blue as runes spiraled outward, and Gabriel stepped back. "Put your hand to the center and speak your name," he instructed.

Kenneth walked to the closet, and did as Gabriel said, placing his hand in the center of the wall and saying his name. The wall flashed red for a moment, and then disappeared.

Kenneth walked through to a room and looked around in wonder. It had several uniforms of different kinds, one dark and camouflaged, one bright and official looking, and one that was similar to what Kali and Ellie had been wearing the night they had rescued him.

There were also two different suits of armor, metal and leather, both well kept. He walked up to them and noticed that behind them were three swords and several knives. He picked up one of the knives, weighing it in his hand as a shadow of a memory worked its way into his head.

He turned, facing a wooden wall and threw it, the knife spinning once before slamming into the wall with a solid *thunk*, where it stayed, quivering. He turned to Gabriel, who was leaning against a wall, looking unsurprised.

Gabriel walked to the knife, slid it out of the wall, and put it back on the stand. He turned to Kenneth, who shrugged, slightly embarrassed. "Try not to ruin the wall," Gabriel said, voice impassive.

Kenneth nodded, "Right," he said, slightly subdued. Gabriel went to the uniforms and unhooked the camouflaged one. Turning, he laid it on the table in the center of the room before facing Kenneth once again.

"You wear this uniform when scouting. It goes over the leathers, and is enchanted to help you blend into the background. When you are in battle, you will wear the leathers with the black, or the leathers covered with the metal, which would be in turn be covered by the tabard. It might look fancy, but it indicates that you are part of the Ranks of the Light, and you won't be attacked."

Kenneth nodded, and reached for the leathers, unhooking them and setting them next to the uniform. "I know how to put these on," he said.

"Good. Also know that when we return, you will have three sets of casual clothes set out for you. You will be required to keep your clothes, weapons, and armor clean, and will be held responsible if you injure anyone while using them. Dress how you want for tonight's scouting and report to me," Gabriel said before leaving.

Kenneth dressed in his leathers and uniform methodically, before briefly searched the room to find a baldric, a type of belt used for carrying swords. He attached the short sword to it, hanging it down his back. After checking to make sure he could unsheathe the sword easily, he belted on a long sword and several throwing knives to his waist, and put on a pair of leather boots, sheathing two more knives in the boots.

Kenneth finished with a pair of leather and chainmail gauntlets and met Gabriel in the top room. Gabriel checked over his equipment quickly, then stood back and nodded appreciatively.

Kenneth followed him out the door and into the night air, bracing himself for the cold. To his surprise, the August air was crisp but comfortable, and the slight breeze warm against his skin.

Gabriel turned to Kenneth. "We do several different circuits of the town at night. The different routes are rotated regularly, and are assigned to different night patrols. We are going to do circuit three."

Kenneth nodded and followed Gabriel as he jogged his way down the street, passing a car with a student talking on his cell phone. Focusing on the circuit, he kept up easily despite the added weight of the armor, and watched carefully to remember the pathways they took.

They traveled in silence for a minute, and eventually Kenneth asked quietly, "Why do you patrol?" as they turned a corner.

Gabriel answered just as quietly. "We have regular patrols for the general safety of the town mortals, but the real reason is to protect the town from demonic influence. The blades you carry are edged with silverlight, a powerfully enchanted metal that inflicts wounds on immortal beings. It will abolish magic, to a degree, and some types bolster your own magic."

They turned another corner, and Kenneth recognized the road that led to the school. They made their way down the road, the moon's light illuminating their surroundings.

Eventually they arrived at the school, and Gabriel stopped, looking up at the buildings. He sighed, turned as if to go, and abruptly froze. Kenneth turned and looked in the direction his eyes where facing, and saw the silhouette of a person walking slowly through the school grounds.

Gabriel breathed out slowly and spoke quickly to Kenneth. "This is why we patrol. Look carefully, and you will be able to see something hovering over her."

Kenneth squinted, and something in the light changed, and the figure was cloaked in darkness, a menacing shadow hovering above the person in the half-light.

The person walked closer, and Gabriel took Kenneth's arm and pulled him behind a pillar attached to the school, and breathed in his ear, "That's the girl who had a seizure during lunch." Kenneth nodded, and the girl walked closer, stepping into the moonlight.

Kenneth shivered as he observed her bloodshot eyes, vacant and staring as she walked, her form slumped as though her strings had been cut. The dark shadow above her was more visible as she approached them, and Kenneth felt Gabriel tense next to him.

The girl stumbled, falling to the ground, the dark shadow evaporating. Gabriel ran out from where they where hiding, Kenneth following close behind. They reached the girl in seconds, their swords ready, but there was no danger.

Gabriel knelt next to her, and shook her. She didn't move, and he quickly checked her pulse.

"She's alive," he said with relief, and he stood. "I can carry her, but what we really need right now is a little extra help," he said loudly.

Kenneth looked at him strangely, then jumped as a shape melded out of the shadows, forming the dark haired girl from earlier that day. She knelt by the girl, ignoring Kenneth's astonishment, and looked at Gabriel.

"The demon is not gone," she said. She had a quiet, lilting voice that fit her slim body.

"How can you tell?" Gabriel asked.

"I can isolate two fears that are emanating from her form. It probably is hiding somewhere in her mind," She answered.

Gabriel nodded. "Can you kill it?"

She smiled, white teeth gleaming in the moonlight. "Of course." She stood back, and Gabriel motioned for Kenneth to do likewise. Kenneth complied, giving himself a good fifteen feet between them. Gabriel followed, keeping his sword ready.

Saskia raised her hand towards the body, and it rose slowly off the ground, twitching and thrashing. Within seconds, the shadow was back, hovering over the convulsing form. It abandoned the body, the girl falling to the ground with a thump, and its wraithlike form attacked Saskia.

She stood her ground, unafraid as it came toward her, its ethereal form gliding across the ground with frightening speed. Finally she brought her hands together and closed her eyes.

Shadows drew themselves around her, swirling and pulsing. Terror emanated from her, and the shadow faltered, slowing. She opened her eyes, and they had transformed into pools of chaos. She parted her hands, slashing a clawed hand at the wraith.

It made a sound akin to screaming, a high-pitched grating noise as the shadows hurled toward it, wrapping around it and swirling madly. Then it simply ceased to exist.

She turned to where they were standing, Kenneth with his hands over his ears, terrified of the awesome display of power. She walked calmly to the body, and Gabriel helped her lift the girl.

Kenneth followed them both in silence as they returned to the church. He unveiled the entrance for them, pricking his finger against the thorn and saying the words to open the door. He fumbled a little with the words, flushing, but the door did open.

Gabriel laid the girl on the couch and stepped back. "She is only sleeping now. She will be fine," he said.

Kenneth nodded, watching Saskia out of the corner of his eye. Gabriel noticed.

"Kenneth, this is Saskia. She is the last Nephilim that stays here. I was going to mention her, but as you know, I got interrupted," Gabriel said.

Kenneth stilled his fears and put out his hand. "Nice to meet you," he said. She looked at his hand as if it were a viper, and gingerly took it.

Immediately there was a soft snapping sound, and Kenneth felt his mark come to life, shimmering over his skin. Startled, he looked at her, and she had a similar tattoo, starting at her wrist and wrapping around her shoulder.

He recognized it. "Fourth Captain, Regiment Three." Saskia had gone white, and he realized that he was still holding her hand. He let go, and the tattoos faded.

Gabriel cut in. "What happened? How do you know her rank?" Kenneth looked at him, confused.

Saskia answered, "He activated my mark of rank. Everyone is marked according to rank, and so he recognized the pattern." She looked at him, still exceptionally pale. "You *are* Lord Blaze."

Kenneth tried to speak, but Gabriel silenced him. "Quiet! I must explain something to the both of you." Kenneth grumbled but fell silent.

"Earlier today, Saskia arrived. You saw her." It wasn't a question, but Kenneth nodded anyway. "When she saw you, she immediately recognized your former self, and came to me. She has spent the last five years infiltrating the Fallen's ranks, gathering what information she could, occasionally returning to give us information."

Saskia nodded, confirming what he said as true. "I later wanted more confirmation on who you were, so I asked Gabriel to test you and to let me watch you spar. You proved who you are. Not only are you an excellent swordsman, but your savyl is the element of fire."

"Fire? What has that got to do with anything?" Kenneth interrupted.

"When you stepped outside today, you didn't feel cold, did you?" Saskia asked, ignoring his question. He shook his head, startled. "It is forty degrees Fahrenheit outside. Most people would feel quite chilled at that temperature, but you are fine in a sleeveless armor."

"I don't understand where this is going!" Kenneth burst in. "What does all this mean?"

"Lord Blaze was a tetrasavylus. He had three savylus in addition to his original one. He was born with the element of fire. Using a hellish ritual, he captured angels, one by one, and stripped them of their powers. Using their powers, he gained more savylus," Gabriel explained.

Saskia continued. "The element of fire is a physically draining element. It will drain your body heat to create the fire that you will into being. When he gained his first new savyl, he used it to 'never feel cold', thinking that it would give him unlimited power. Instead, he was unable to judge his power, and it was dangerous for him to use it without freezing himself. For his second, he chose to have extremely rapid body heat regeneration, and the inability to freeze. This helped increase his powers, but he was still unsatisfied. The last time he used the power to make the element of fire a mental power that drained his mental alertness instead of his body heat."

"That seems like a waste!" Kenneth said, "His first few times are pointless now!"

Saskia shook her head. "Even if he did the last change first, he would have followed with the next few. He needs those powers to wield the blade *Frost*, a powerful magic enhancer that grants the wielder many powers. It can also freeze you when you touch it, because of the magics woven into it."

Kenneth frowned. "So he needed the previous powers to prevent him from freezing himself while wielding *Frost*." Saskia nodded. "And you think I am him?"

She nodded again, and opened her mouth to speak, but was interrupted by the sleeping girl's groan. Everyone looked at the girl, and after a moment, Gabriel spoke.

"You should both go to bed. Don't speak to the others about this conversation. As far as they know, neither of you have anything to do with the Fallen. I will stay with the girl."

Kenneth nodded, and glanced at Saskia again, and froze, studying her dark eyes. They had flickered for a moment, flashing a scarlet red that made a shadow of memory rise in the depths of his mind. But try as he might, he couldn't recall where he had seen it before.

Dismissing it, he headed to his room to sleep.

Gabriel barely heard the door shut as Saskia and Kenneth left to sleep. He was staring at the girl sleeping quietly on the couch. Demonic activity in the form of possessions wasn't common; roughly one in every million people was possessed each year. It was rare that a town as small as this one had anyone possessed.

He turned as the door to the stairs opened, revealing an armored figure. Gabriel waved to him as he went out to patrol, silently praising Aaron for having such a dedicated child. Assured someone was on patrol, he walked swiftly down to the library and found Yigil.

As usual, she was reading. He had long ago gotten used to her reading without eyes. It still looked odd, however. She looked up as he entered, and he explained the situation, "We encountered a the girl on patrol. Saskia removed the demon, but I need to know where she lives." Yigil nodded, setting down the book.

They quickly made their way up to the top floor, and Yigil gazed at the child emotionlessly. "How did she invite the spirit in?" she asked, and despite her outward indifference, Gabriel heard tenderness in her voice.

"I'm not sure," he said, frowning, "I'm sure the possession happened during lunch, but it is possible that the possession occurred because the seizure weakened her resistance." Yigil nodded briskly, and waved a hand. A second later she nodded, and Gabriel lifted her easily. His savyl provided him with great strength. Coupled with the increase in strength that normal Nephilim had, lifting her body took next to no effort for him.

Yigil strode toward the door, Gabriel following close behind. Soon they were outside, Yigil leading the way through the town until they came to a small white house with blue shutters on the windows. The lights were off.

Yigil glanced at the girl, then back at the house before nodding confidently. "This is it," she said briskly.

"Nicely done," Gabriel complemented, but she shrugged it off.

"A simple tracking spell. A novice could have accomplished as much," she muttered, taking the girl from his arms. She laid out the girl as though there was an invisible table, leaving her sprawled several feet off the ground. Her silhouette flashed golden, and she faded.

"There," she said, nodding, "she will wake as though nothing happened." Gabriel nodded back to her.

"Shall we return?" he suggested.

"That would be—" Yigil began, and froze, nostrils flaring. She hissed, and Gabriel immediately brought his hands together, summoning his sword from his room with a thought. It flashed into his hands, frost covering it despite heat that it radiated from the distance it traveled, but Gabriel took no notice. He was to busy searching the surrounding landscape.

"Fool," Yigil muttered, and Gabriel looked at her strangely. She shook her head. "Not you. Me. I thought the girl was what reeked of demon, but this is a much stronger scent. Darkness and chaos, this is one of the *old* demons."

"Here?" Gabriel said, and Yigil nodded.

"We hunt." At her words she rippled, growing larger, wings bursting out of her back. They were black, streaked with gold that shimmered in the moonlight, their wingspan several times longer than her arms. With a powerful leap she jumped into the air, Gabriel following her from the ground, sprinting to keep up with her.

Seconds later, acrid smoke burned Gabriel's throat as they approached a flaming house. Firemen surrounded the roaring fire, attempting to douse the heat with hoses. Nothing seemed to be working, however.

Gabriel approached one of the men, keeping an eye on Yigil, who was now circling the house. He lowered the barriers on his mind, influencing the man to see him as a simple townsman.

"How long has the fire been ragin', sir?" he asked hesitantly, as though nervous.

The man glanced at him, his helmet under his arm. He looked exhausted. "Most of the day. I'm amazed the fire hasn't burned the house to the ground already. It's unnatural." He went back to examining the fire, and the waved goodbye to him as he was called back to duty.

Gabriel looked at the flames closely, noting the dark purple and black flames that were intermixed with the red and orange. *Hellfire,* he thought. There were few things more dangerous, but hellfire wasn't usually hot. It burned slowly, resistant to any attempt at smothering, and killed much faster than normal fire. Unlike normal fire, hellfire burned by drawing heat out of the object it touched, forcing it to spontaneously combust and freeze at the same time. If the object was alive, it also tainted them, forcing dark magic into their body like poison, slowly crippling and killing them even if they managed to smother the flames.

Yigil stopped circling and landed next to him, unseen to the firemen desperately spraying the fire. "I can't feel anything alive in the fire that's human. Something is still spewing flames though, but it's small. I'm guessing it's possessed a child."

Gabriel growled. "Two possessions in this small town, in this amount of time? How?" Yigil shook her head, and he continued. "We'll have to draw the demon out. We can't fight it while it's in there."

Yigil nodded, adjusting her blindfold. She radiated power, and Gabriel could feel his hair start to stand on end. Light coalesced in her hand, forming a sword, and she swooped off the ground. Hovering above the burning building, she reached out a hand and brought it back as though pulling a great weight.

With a great hiss, the fire went out. Surprised firemen stared in shock as the building slowly collapsed on itself, leaving nothing but ashes. They shut off their hoses, some of them coughing as a great cloud of ash pushed past them.

Eyes stinging, Gabriel walked carefully forward as the cloud cleared. Yigil's sword radiated barely enough light for him to make out the form of a small child. Darkness unattributed to the ash swirled around her, and she turned with a grace that defied the pudgy legs that held her up. She giggled, an innocent laugh that chilled Gabriel to the bone. He leveled his sword at her, and she glanced at him with black eyes.

A cruel smile curled up the side of her mouth, and she screamed, the noise like a razor, slicing at Gabriel's mind. He could hear the men behind him cry out in pain, and he clumsily blocked the mental attack. The scream cut off into a laugh as Yigil swooped, narrowly missing the child as she jumped to the side.

A second later, wings split the small girl's back, and the demon was airborne. Light sparked against dark as the monster summoned her own blade, formed from darkness and fire. Gabriel barely watched them as he ran to the nearest house and scaled it, kneeling on its roof. Demon fought angel in the sky, Yigil's face locked in a fierce concentration.

She was backing away under the onslaught, slowly getting closer to the building on which Gabriel crouched. Seconds later, Gabriel leapt with savyl-enhanced legs, slicing one of the demon's wings off at the joint.

They fell, Gabriel slapping the ground and rolling, the girl landing with a concussive thud that belied the small form. Yigil descended with terrible justice, ramming the sword into her chest. The monster screamed once, and then was still, wisps of smoke rising from empty eye sockets. It was over.

They glanced at each other, ash smeared and sweaty, before looking around. There was some serious cleaning up to do. "Good God," Gabriel muttered as he sheathed his sword, "Two in a night? What is happening?"

Service to God

Kenneth slept, dreams dark and troubled. His dreams where filled with warring shapes, battles and flying figures being cut from the sky, falling…falling…

Kenneth woke with a start, feeling as if he was also falling. He shook his head, trying to clear it of the images as he rolled out of bed.

Kenneth dragged himself to his closet. The last night's events left him with little real sleep, and he was still tired.

Placing his palm on the wall, he spoke his name, activating the enchantment that made the wall fall away, and walked through. After a short search, he found a small pile of clothes in the corner of the room. They were all dark colors, blues, blacks, and greens, and all fit him perfectly.

Walking to the wall with the weapons, he belted on a dagger, and strapped throwing knives onto his forearms. He checked himself in the mirror, making sure that the knives were hidden, before heading off to get breakfast.

Kenneth was unsurprised to find out that the room was empty, and after a short search of available food, he poured himself a bowl of Superwheats. It was early in the morning, with the kitchen clock's hands at five thirty.

Kenneth finished his bowl of cereal quickly, washed the dishes, and put them away. He walked to the sitting area curiously, and noted the girl from the night before was no longer there.

He shrugged and turned away, but stopped as something caught his eye. There was something underneath the coffee table, but it was blurred from his sight. Bending, he reached underneath and grabbed it.

It cleared as soon as he touched it, becoming a sheet of paper with angular writing inscribed on it. It read:

Lord Blaze

We understand your situation, and hope to get in touch with you soon. We are doing everything in our power to free you, but we will not be able to move for several weeks, due to your current situation. We have successfully secured your sword, and it waits for you in Nil'honderal.

This note will burn as soon as you release it.

Nora

Kenneth released a long breath and read the note again. *Well,* he thought, *this confirms their suspicions on who I am...* He hadn't actually believed them up to this point, but now it was obvious they were correct.

The only question is which side I'll choose, thought Kenneth. He released the note, and it vanished in a flash of fire, the smell of burned paper entering the air. He waved away the smoke and sat on the couch and thought.

After a few minutes, he shook his head and stood. His thoughts were taking him in circles. Walking to the door, he grasped the knob, and jumped back, startled, as the door opened.

The door swung to reveal a short, nervous looking man who wore a beret and had small, watery eyes. He also jumped back, noticing Kenneth standing on the other side. They stood, staring at each other for several seconds, until Kenneth stepped aside.

"Qui est ceci? Que veut-il?" Kenneth heard him mutter, and the man shuffled past him, his eyes probing the room nervously.

So this is Gimelli, Kenneth thought. He watched him for a couple more seconds, unsure what to do, as Gimelli poured himself a bowl of cereal and commenced eating. Kenneth shrugged, walked through the door, and closed it behind him. He jogged down the stairs into the training room, disturbed at the man's apparent insanity.

He did a short workout in the room to wake himself up thoroughly, before jogging back up the stairs. Gimelli was gone, replaced by an ash covered Gabriel.

Gabriel looked up at him as he entered, ignoring his curious look. "I returned the girl to her house. She will have no memory of what happened the past couple of days, but will otherwise be fine," he said. He motioned with his hand, and Kenneth followed him to the wall on the opposite side of the couch.

"Now would be a good time for a drill, and you need to know what this is for," he said, and he ran his hand down the wall, and a section of it disappeared. Inside was a small latch, and he pulled it.

Immediately a high pitch sound ripped into Kenneth's mind. It wasn't so much a sound as it was a thought, skipping the ears and going straight to the head. It was followed by Gabriel's voice saying, "emergency attack, entrance floor."

Gabriel turned to Kenneth. "This is located in every room of the hideout, and is only sounded to those who are registered members, so it will be soundless to intruders."

Kenneth nodded, his muscles still tensed. Gabriel stood against the wall, clearly waiting. Kenneth did not have to wait long to find out what he was waiting for. Within seconds, the door burst open, and four shapes blurred in, weapons ready. They scattered, finding advantageous positions around the room, and stopped.

Gabriel nodded his head. "You are clear to stand down," he said, and they all walked out of their hiding spots, Flammeth and Ellie sheathing weapons, and Kali scowling, hands empty. There was also another boy, short, with bright blue eyes and blonde hair that he assumed was Aelex. They all approached, looking curiously at Gabriel.

"That was a good drill," Gabriel stated, "But the reason I wanted you up here is a little more serious." He walked to the sitting area, and they followed, sitting in a circle around the table. Gabriel reached into his pocket, and pulled out a newspaper and threw it on the table.

The front cover was a picture of car crash, with the title: STUDENT'S NIGHT OUT TURNS TO NIGHT OF DISASTER. Underneath were the individual pictures of Flammeth, Kali, and Kenneth. Kali immediately snatched it up and read it aloud.

"Last night, a small Ford truck was found crashed off the side of a bridge. It fell twenty feet and struck a concrete roadblock and was smashed, killing three high school students at approximately three a.m. This terrible accident is still under examination." She looked up curiously at Gabriel.

He nodded. "You are now dead. Soon they will hold a funeral, and your 'parents' will move out of town, distraught. Meanwhile," he said, addressing all of them, "I want you three to be training in the Ranks of the Light. We travel there next Friday."

"This is so unfair!" Ellie interjected, "Why do they get to go but not me? I want to train to!" Gabriel looked at her, and Ellie colored, clearly embarrassed by her outburst.

"You can't join the army until you are sixteen. You know this. I don't expect to ever have to remind you again," Gabriel said, voice calm. Ellie nodded. "Good. Now, so you know, I have hired a personal trainer for you, since I will no longer have time to train you aside from my normal duties. Come, let us meet him."

He rose, and everyone followed him downstairs to the training room. As they walked, Gabriel spoke, "This man can train you in any weapon you desire, and I advise you to respect him. We have one week before you must leave to join the ranks, so I advise you to prepare yourself to the best of your abilities."

They reached the training room, and Kenneth looked around searching for the trainer. He saw no one though, and noticed everyone but Gabriel was also looking.

"Lesson one: never be surprised," came a soft lilting voice. Kenneth spun with the others, and jumped when he realized that the instructor was standing next to them.

He was an old man, leaning heavily on his cane, long white hair falling on his shoulders and dangling from his bushy eyebrows. He was slightly hunched, making him seem shorter than he would have been in his prime, and his body looked thin and frail.

After a moment of shocked silence, Ellie spoke scornfully. "You're my new instructor?" The old man nodded, taking no offense at her tone.

"I am Pariel, named after the angel who wards off evil. Thus I am brought here to teach, to show, and quite possibly to learn," he said, bowing to her. Ellie shook her head, and the man straightened.

"You do not believe that I am capable?" he asked her, his tone politely inquiring. He didn't wait for Ellie to answer, but instead hobbled his way to the center of the room, and turned, his beady eyes staring at them.

"Kali. I am told that you are excel in combat."

Kali nodded hesitantly, "I consider myself adequate."

The man laughed. "Well phrased, well phrased indeed! Adequate, yes, I also consider myself adequate. Come forth, young lady, and attack me."

Kali hesitated, and Kenneth could see how wary she had become. After underestimating him so recently, she was much more cautious when approaching a seemingly helpless foe.

She walked toward him slowly, her center of gravity perfectly balanced, until she was only a couple of yards away from him. The man still had not moved, and was looking at her, eyes calm.

"You are cautious. This is a good thing to learn," Pariel said. He shifted his feet slightly. "But to much caution is bad." He blurred, and Kali was on the floor, Pariel's staff at her neck, the man suddenly not frail or unsteady, his eyes gleaming.

He helped her off the floor. "Lesson two: never judge something by its appearance." He looked at Ellie, who colored for the second time that day and looked away in shame.

Pariel strode to the center of the room. "I can instruct you in any weapon in this room, as well as the art of hand to hand fighting, and I intend to teach you well. If you start to be lazy or obstinate, you will not learn, and therefore will not improve. To truly become a master at something, you have to want it with all of your being. Ellie, you stay here. The rest of you must talk with Gabriel about leaving for the army."

Kenneth followed the others to the top, where they talked about the specifics of the trip, before smoothing out the fine details over the period of several hours. After a short lunch break, Gabriel stood up.

"You are all free to go. Aelex, I want you to sleep now if you are going to continue to do our night watches. You cannot scout exhausted," he said.

Aelex yawned and stretched, speaking for the first time that day. "Gabriel, surely by now you know that I can do anything! Why, I feel as though I have had a week's sleep." Gabriel looked at him, eyes steady, and Aelex chuckled, "I know, I know. Just kidding." He looked at Kenneth. "New guy, eh? Haven't seen ya much yet. Been a little too busy sleepin', ya know? Seem like a nice kid though." He clicked his tongue and waved to him as he made his way through the doorway downstairs.

Kenneth watched him go, unsure whether he liked him or not. He looked back at the others, and saw them all staring at him.

"What?" He looked down. Wisps of smoke were curling off of his fingers, and a haze of heat surrounded his hand. He closed his fist, quenching the flame. "Sorry."

Gabriel cleared his throat, bringing their attention back to him. "I want today to be a rest day. Some of us did not sleep well last night, and the rest have been busy. Do what you will, but be ready to resume training tomorrow." Flammeth nodded and walked off, but Kali stayed. Kenneth was aware of her eyes as he slowly walked away.

Kenneth wandered about the floors for several minutes, unsure what to do. He eventually stopped at the training room, which was silent. Peeking in, he assumed that Ellie must have finished her lesson with the new trainer. He eased open the door, and quietly entered, shutting the door behind him with a soft click.

His steps echoed slightly as he walked across the room to the wall where the weapons were hung. Striding up to the wall, he carefully took down a long sword, its blade carefully blunted. He hefted it in his right hand, feeling the weight of the blade, feeling how *good,* how *right,* it felt in his hand.

Holding it with both hands, he lifted it into a ready position. Then he turned, swinging the blade in a murderous arc towards the person who was trying to sneak up from behind him.

There was a blur of motion, and Kenneth stopped his blade, its point facing Pariel, the new instructor.

"Lesson one," Kenneth said calmly, "never be surprised." The man chuckled, leaning on his staff, but Kenneth watched him carefully, never lowering the sword.

Pariel spoke, "You may lower your blade; I will not harm you." Kenneth nodded and planted the sword's point into the ground. The old man shuffled over to the wall with the weapons, taking down a sword of his own.

He carefully set his staff aside, swinging the sword with a practiced ease. "You wish to learn the sword?" Kenneth nodded. "Then we shall learn. What is your dominant sword arm?"

Kenneth frowned. He was currently holding it left handed, but he wrote right-handed. He swung the sword, shifted his hands, and swung again. Both felt normal.

"Let's assume that I am right-handed," Kenneth said. The man nodded, and shifted the grip on his own sword to his right hand.

"We shall fight until one of us dies, talk, and then fight again. Do not use your savyl, and I will not use mine." Kenneth nodded in acceptance, and Pariel raised his sword into ready position.

Kenneth felt confident; calm despite the master he was facing. He subconsciously shifted his own position to mirror his opponent's and attacked.

Pariel met his attack; his own sword leaping up to meet Kenneth's, the blades throwing up sparks where they met. Kenneth spun his sword off of his counterattack to his side, and used the momentum from Pariel's blade to cut at his legs.

The old man jumped with surprising agility and height, and Kenneth's blade slashed through empty air. Kenneth grunted in annoyance, wind whistling through his gritted teeth.

Backing up under the onslaught from the old man, he slapped away Pariel's blade several times, and found himself in another place.

The air was hot, but it was always hot in Xaphan, and sweat rolled down Kenneth's back as he faced off his opponent in the sparring mounds. It was Iephus, laughing, who faced him, moving with a speed and strength that belied his thin body. They spun and circled, slashing at each other with all their strength, trying to touch each other with their blades.

Iephus was setting up the Kildrian circle, a series of moves that disarmed the opponent. But Kenneth knew from the way his eyes moved and his muscles shifted, the way he barely changed his stance. He waited until he was about to strike, and then shifted the sword to his left hand in a smooth motion, placing it blade backwards, into an assassin's stance.

He spun with the attack, catching the flat of Iephus's blade between his long sword and the throwing knife sheath underneath his tunic. Twisting, he disarmed him, and used his opponent's blade as well as his own to place an X of sharpened death at his throat.

And then he was back, only to find what happened in his world of thought had taken place in the corporeal world as well. Pariel looked shocked, his own blade as well as Kenneth's forcing him to be still.

Kenneth lowered the swords carefully, and gave Pariel back his blade. The man took it unconsciously, his mind obviously elsewhere.

"Who taught you that sequence?" he snapped, coming back to himself. Kenneth shrugged, unsure how to answer.

"I kind of just made it up," he lied. Pariel shook his head in disbelief.

"Who taught you the blade?" Kenneth shook his head, unwilling to answer. The man shook his head and insisted, saying,

"You must tell me! Who was the man who had the privilege to teach you the way of the sword?"

"Bael," Kenneth said reluctantly.

Pariel sucked in his breath, clearly shocked. He took a step back, face paled. "Not a man at all. The leader of the demon armies?" Kenneth nodded. "You used to be in the Fallen Ranks. No, not only were you in the ranks, you were *high* in the ranks, to be trained by Bael himself! By the Lord! Does Gabriel know you are a convert?"

Kenneth looked at him quizzically, and opened his mouth to speak.

"Of course I know. We found out the day he arrived," Gabriel interrupted. Pariel and Kenneth both jumped. Gabriel was standing by the door, indicating that he had just entered. He strode over to them with his confident stride, and said, "No one else knows. This is why it is *imperative* that you train him privately. Not only in the sword, but any other weapon you can think of, as well as hand to hand combat."

Pariel nodded, regaining his composure. "Why do they not know?" he asked, genuinely curious.

Kenneth shrugged uncomfortably as Gabriel looked at him, clearly indicating that he should be the one to answer. "Because of this," he said, taking off his shirt. He let it fall to the ground, and willed his mark of rank to appear.

It started at his arms, like all marks, appearing like a snake coiling around his wrists, stretching its body towards his chest, and ending in swirls and jagged ends over his chest and face. It glowed a dark black, like the color of dried blood, and it pulsed, as if echoing his heartbeat.

To his surprise, with the mark came a surge of power, like someone had just given him a shot of adrenaline, heightening his senses and giving him strength.

Pariel was staring, mouth open, astonishment clearly written on his face. Kenneth let it fade, feeling the power drain from his body.

"Good God," he said softly, "you were the Semiaza, the Nephilim leader in the Ranks of the Fallen." It wasn't a question, but Kenneth nodded. "Why did you leave them?"

Kenneth hesitated, looking at Gabriel. Gabriel sighed. "It is a complicated story. For now, you know what you need to know. I would like to talk to Kenneth alone." Pariel nodded, snatched up his staff, and disappeared in a blur of motion.

"How does he do that?" Kenneth asked curiously.

"His savyl allows him to slow time nearly to the point of stopping. To him, everyone else seems to slow down," Gabriel answered. He looked at Kenneth. "You know much more than you did yesterday." It wasn't a question.

Kenneth hesitated, wondering how much he should tell Gabriel. He picked up the swords, placing them on the wall to give him time to think. Eventually, he spoke.

"I remember training. Almost all of it, I'm sure. I think the army won't be able to help me much there." Kenneth turned and faced Gabriel, who seemed unconcerned. "I also remember how to do random things."

"Like how to summon your mark of rank?" asked Gabriel.

"Exactly. That, and I *know* things, things I don't really know where they came from. I feel as though only part of a memory has come through, the part where I gained knowledge, and not the actual memory itself."

Gabriel nodded thoughtfully. "I wouldn't worry about the training in the army. They will quickly recognize that they have nothing to teach you, and move you to something more worth your time." Kenneth nodded. "I want to know one more thing before I allow you to leave." Kenneth looked at him, unsure what to think. "How old are you?"

Kenneth laughed. It seemed such an odd question, even though he now knew that older Nephilim could pass as younger humans because of the way they aged. Nephilim lived much longer than humans. "I don't know," he answered honestly. "I'm physically around sixteen or seventeen, but I grew up never knowing my parents or when I was born. I didn't even know the days of the week until I joined the army and was taught the calendar."

Gabriel nodded as though he had expected it. "So you guess around seventeen?"

"I guess," Kenneth said, unsure why it mattered.

Gabriel frowned thoughtfully. "Then you are very close in age to everyone else here," he mused quietly.

"How old is everyone else?" Kenneth wondered.

"Ellie is twelve, Flammeth is nineteen, and Aelex and Kali are seventeen," Gabriel answered absently. "Now go, rest. You have a long week ahead of you."

Kenneth's sword felt like lead. Pariel had awakened him at three in the morning by softly opening the door and throwing several knives at him—their edges carefully blunted. Only Kenneth's extreme reflexes and years of being in danger had prevented him from being 'killed'.

Pariel had commanded him to meet him in the sparring room in less than ten minutes. Kenneth had carefully dressed, grabbed a sparring sword from his room, and headed into the training center.

He had been immediately attacked when walking into the room, and had been fighting constantly for nearly an hour now. Pariel didn't underestimate him this time, and had managed to block all advances that Kenneth made towards him.

Kenneth backed up quickly as Pariel advanced, swinging his blade from side to side with soft sounds of cutting air. Despite the hour and the exercise, he seemed perfectly fine.

Their swords sparked as they clashed against each other, and Kenneth backed closer to the wall behind him. Pariel came at him quickly, hoping to pin him.

Kenneth batted back several strokes, his sweat running freely. His back pressed against the wall, and Pariel's attack increased.

Kenneth growled and slashed hard, left and right, briefly driving him back. Using the time, he flipped, feet hitting against the wall. Pushing off with the last of his strength, he flew at Pariel, driving him to the ground and knocking his sword away.

Pariel looked at the sword at his throat and laughed a deep, hearty chuckle. Kenneth carefully touched it to his throat before rolling off of him. He got up, hands on knees, exhausted.

"How are you not tired?" Kenneth complained as Pariel got to his feet.

"My savyl allows me to manipulate time. I'm not tired now, but in a few minutes, my body will relive what we just did, tiring out my body as if we were fighting still. It's quite useful."

Kenneth frowned. "I thought you said if I did not use my savyl, you would not use yours."

Pariel grinned. "That was last battle. No such stipulation was made for this battle."

Kenneth grunted in annoyance. "I see." He walked to the wall and replaced the sword from where he had removed it the night previously.

Walking to the center of the room, he sat himself on the floor and began to stretch his burning muscles.

"Explain to me how exactly Nephilim tire," he said. He still didn't remember some tidbits of information. Pariel nodded in deference.

"Very well. Nephilim, as you know, are generally stronger than humans. The divine section of DNA that we possess gives us a variety powers as well as greater strength. Depending on the savylus a person has, we can usually calculate the approximate strength difference between them and normal people. It isn't perfect, but it works for general cases."

"Nephilim in general are about one and a half times stronger than the normal human. Savyl or not, this is usually the case. When a Nephilim has a savyl, the strength normally increases as well. If you have two, it increases again, and so on. This is why I, for example, am not normally as strong as you are."

Kenneth nodded. "Where did you learn to fight?" The question was simple curiosity. He had only ever fought one person who could draw out a fight like the one he had just fought.

Pariel grinned. "I was apprenticed to the Exalted himself, many years before he was appointed. He trained me well, although I will have to admit I have God-given talent."

Kenneth had to agree. He got up, finished with stretching, and bade Pariel a brief farewell to eat breakfast.

After breakfast, with a recently awakened Flammeth and Kali, Yigil informed him that she would be teaching him until lunch.

He followed her down into the library, where she stopped in a cleared space. She turned to face him, and lifted one of her hands, bringing it palm up towards the ceiling.

Immediately runes spiraled out from her, spraying against the borders of the circle that she cleared. When she lowered her hand, the runes faded slightly, and began to slowly circle them.

"What do you know of how a savyl works?" she asked.

Kenneth frowned. "A savyl is based off of a Nephilim's divine DNA strand," he said, recalling his recent discussion with Pariel, "strengthening the bearer and granting him or her a specific quality in magic."

Yigil nodded. "Almost. The savyl does not grant a specific magic. It instead grants extended magic of one region that they possess, giving them greater control and power in one type of magic. This is key in your instruction. Everyone can do what you do with your savyl, but your savyl grants you immense control over that section of magic, and great strength in that area."

"Each Nephilim has a baseline of magical power. This is the limit of all of their magics, save their savyl. If that baseline is high, the person can use other magics, such as spinning a spell, or performing a ritual. As you might know, your baseline is high. Therefore we will learn not only how to use your savylus to their greatest effect, but also how to spin enchantments and spells to do what you wish with them."

She raised her hand again, and the runes brightened. "When I step out of this circle, you will immediately be attacked with magic from all sides. Without moving, you must destroy my spells before they reach you. If they touch you, they will give you an unpleasant shock. When you have been hit three times, we will stop. Begin."

Kenneth immediately closed his eyes, instinctively knowing that it would help him locate the sources of energy that would be her spells. He felt one off to his right within seconds, and he blasted it apart with one of his own, barely realizing that he already knew how to spin his own spells.

The exercise continued for some time, slowly growing in intensity until Kenneth's concentration faltered, and he was shocked three times within a second, ending the exercise.

He opened his eyes, muscles still shivering from the electricity. Yigil merely nodded to him, and said, "I am finished with you. Do you have any questions, or shall we depart to meet again tomorrow?"

Kenneth thought for a second. "How does Flammeth's savyl work? Can he turn into *anything,* or only other humans?"

Yigil seemed pleased. "A good question. Flammeth's ability allows him to turn into anything, save for two requirements. He has to know the anatomical structure of the organism that he turns into, and the organism has to be capable of thought. Otherwise it doesn't work. It is not an exact replica, however. His transformation will look exactly the same, but the organism will weigh exactly the same as he does in his normal form."

Kenneth nodded, intrigued. "Can he transform individual parts of himself?"

Yigil sniffed. "Yes. That is why he has that infernal hair color and earrings. How he managed to give himself earrings and have them actually be part of his body is beyond me, however. He is quite unique."

Kenneth grinned. Unique certainly described Flammeth. Thanking, Yigil, he headed off to lunch.

Forbidden Magics

When evening rolled around, Kenneth was exhausted. He had been awake for nearly fifteen hours, most of the time fighting or performing magic. After lunch he had met with Aaron to get measurements for a better suit of armor. When they were finished, Aaron told him he would probably be finished the day before he left.

When he had returned upstairs, Ellie was sitting with Kali and Flammeth, chatting aimlessly about school. He was tempted briefly to sit with them, but exhaustion and hunger won over, and he settled for eating a bowl of cereal instead.

When he was finished he headed down to his room to sleep, but paused at the doorframe. The room looked normal, but something seemed different.

Kenneth walked in carefully, cautious not to touch anything. Walking to his bed, he inspected it closely, and was rewarded when he noticed that the bed had been shifted slightly to the left, leaving a slight dent in the carpet where it had been.

Turning, he regarded the rest of the room. Objects that he had left out looked like they were still there at first glance, but were slightly shifted the second time he looked. He turned to his closet and opened the door by speaking his name. It was unchanged, even after close examination.

Suddenly awake, Kenneth scaled the stairs quietly, and was about to open the door when he heard Flammeth speaking. On a hunch, Kenneth stopped at the door and listened.

"I don't know why you don't like him! So he beat you in a sword fight! That isn't grounds to hate someone," came Flammeth's voice.

Kali sighed. "It's not that. Yes I'm a little sore from him beating me, but he did it *during his second time ever holding a sword.* You don't just fight like that. It takes training. And don't be an idiot and say that he might be talented. You're smarter than that."

Flammeth grunted and muttered something under his breath, causing Kenneth's ears to strain to try to catch what he said. "I'm not stupid, its obvious that he's fought with the sword before. But what if he takes fencing lessons? They do that in the mundane world sometimes, you know."

Kenneth could almost hear Kali shake her head. "And the throwing knives he carries everywhere? I suppose he learned how to throw those as well? It's kind of convenient, don't you think? He shows up here, supposedly innocent in the ways of Nephilim, and yet he knows how we fight, how to react in a dangerous situation, and how to use his power, even if it is 'subconscious'. And have you noticed how scarred his arms are? Not many mortals get cut in a way that it leaves scars like that, and not in that number."

Kenneth glanced at his arms, fists clenched, his scars barely visible in the gloom. Flammeth grunted again, sounding annoyed. "Okay, okay. I get your point. But don't you think that Gabriel would have noticed all of this as well? I mean, seriously, he's one of the smartest people in the army. And you of all people should know how suspicious he is when it comes to strangers."

Kali made a noncommittal sound. "Then why has he done nothing about it?

"Maybe Gabriel has, and we don't know about it," Flammeth replied.

"Fine, but it doesn't mean I have to trust Kenneth. And nothing you do will convince me that he is safe."

Kenneth backed down the stairs slowly, sure she had searched his room. It was a good thing he had nothing of his past, else Kali might not have stopped at searching his room. Judging by the venom in her voice when she said she didn't trust him, she might have killed him as well.

He returned to his room, locking the door and setting his alarm for two in the morning—an hour before Pariel expected him to wake. That would give him six hours of sleep.

Fully armored, he fell asleep holding his sword.

Kenneth's alarm awakened him with its buzz, and he rolled out of bed silently, shutting of the alarm as he passed by it.

Unlocking his door, he carefully opened it with his body behind it the entire time, before carefully walking into the hallway.

The hall was empty, and Kenneth's breathing was loud in his own ears. He tread softly on the carpet, walking to the stairs and making his way to the kitchen.

When he opened the door, he found Aelex sitting at one of the chairs at the table, calmly eating an apple. He merely nodded, mouth full, as Kenneth walked in.

Aelex chewed and swallowed before saying, "You're up early." When Kenneth only nodded, Aelex grinned. "You know, if you keep spending all your time around me talking, it's going to be awfully hard for me to tell you about my incredibly handsome self," he said with mock seriousness, and Kenneth found himself smiling as well. He decided he liked Aelex.

"I spend most of my time practicing to be a skilled orator," Kenneth said, sitting at the table. He took an orange, carefully peeling it with one of his knives.

Aelex smiled. "I can tell! Great diction, a good vocabulary, you've got it all! The face could use some work, but we can't do much about that." Kenneth looked at him with amusement, but Aelex only winked at him and took another bite out of his apple.

"Fine. If my face needs some work, so be it. At least I do not have to go to great lengths to hide my inferior intelligence by insulting other people's appearances," Kenneth said with a straight face.

Aelex mimed taking a knife out of his chest. "Cold! Oh so cold! The stab wound is deep, see? Very well, Mr. Superior Intelligence, Mr. Self-Dubbed Beauty departs to sleep in a soft, warm bed. I would say good night, but alas, night is over. You cockalorum." And having had the last word, he ducked out the door, humming merrily to himself.

Kenneth watched him go, half wondering if he would ever meet anyone else quite like Aelex. It was the oddest blend of insults and wit he had ever seen. He seemed to assume that everyone found him funny, and therefore was his best friend.

He finished his orange in silence, and picked up an apple, bouncing it on his palm. He cut it absentmindedly, carefully wiping the blade afterwards.

His musings were cut off by the sounds of steps approaching the door leading outside. He looked up at the same time Saskia entered. She flinched, clearly startled. They awkwardly stood, unsure what to say to each other, until Saskia finely broke eye contact and grabbed an apple, albeit a little more hastily than her normal grace in movement allowed.

He watched her curiously. Now that he knew more of her past she seemed more human and less frightening. It seemed odd that she was more afraid of him than he was of her.

She delicately peeled the apple, an action that caught Kenneth off guard. It wasn't that he thought the action was unusual, but the normalness of it seemed out of place. They had both been in Hell itself, and yet they sat here, peeling and slicing apples to eat.

Something must have changed in his face, because she glanced up and asked quietly, "Thinking about Hell?" At his nod, she sighed and set down the peeler, the apple finished.

"It's not always pleasant, is it?" she asked, now slicing the apple into quarters. "The experience, I mean. In some ways, it's beneficial. Growing up in hell makes us stronger, mentally and physically. It gives us survival instincts that others hold up as great skill, when they don't realize that really it was learn or die." The final word was punctuated by the last cut of her apple, scoring the table with the knife. She absently wiped the table and took a bite of the apple.

Kenneth looked at her in surprise. "You grew up in Hell too?"

She nodded. "The outskirts. I wasn't born there, but I spent a good portion of my teenage years in Girideal."

Kenneth nodded. The word was now familiar to him. The outskirts of hell were divided into cities, or cults, each with their own demonic culture and dangerous way of life. Girideal was one of the more dangerous cults.

She cleaned her knife absently. "Where were you raised?" she asked.

"I was born in Xaphan. Nasty place."

Saskia raised her eyebrows. Xaphan meant 'scream' in the demonic tongue. Not many children were born there, and fewer survived. Xaphan compared to Girideal was a wolf compared to a puppy.

"Pleasant," she muttered. Kenneth checked the clock. It read ten minutes until three. He rose, scraping his small pile of orange peels into his hand, and threw them into the trash.

"I suppose I'd better get to training," he said quietly, and Saskia chuckled.

"Starting to wish that Pariel didn't know who you were?" she asked.

Kenneth chuckled ruefully. "It would make things a little easier, yes," he said with some amusement. He turned to go, but paused as a thought occurred to him.

"You can read people's fears?" he asked.

"Yes," she answered, wary.

"What is my greatest fear?"

There was a pause. Eventually, she asked, "Why do you want to know?"

He shrugged. It was mainly curiosity. "I want to know."

She shook her head. "I can't tell you a fear if you don't know it yourself. Otherwise you aren't afraid of it."

He nodded. It made sense. He gave a short wave to her and headed down the stairs into the training room. He opened the door cautiously, his memories of being attacked the previous morning still vivid in his mind.

The room was empty. Kenneth walked slowly to the center, his footsteps echoing slightly. He turned slowly, searching the room for anyone who would be hiding, but he still found no one.

There was a soft click as the door opened, and Kenneth whirled, knives flying to his fingers, and Kali yelped as a knife *thunked* into the doorframe beside her.

Kali frowned at him. "What the hell! Do you always try to kill people?"

Suddenly glad he decided to throw a warning shot first, Kenneth blushed, apologizing. "Sorry," he said quickly, "I thought you were Pariel."

"He does have good reason to be wary," Pariel stated, walking in behind her. "I ambushed him the first time he walked in here. Let's just say his training is a little more... intense than it normally would be."

Kali snorted, reaching to pull the knife out of the wall. After a moment of pulling, she ignored it and stalked in the room.

Nothing you do will convince me that he is safe. The words rang in his ears as he yanked the knife out of the doorframe and slid it back in his sheath. He turned back to Pariel, unsettled.

"I brought Kali here this morning to help with your hand-to-hand fighting lesson. Her savyl allows gives her a great advantage when it comes to martial arts of various types, and therefore will give you a good example to follow, or a good partner to fight, depending on how good of a fighter you are," Pariel explained. "No weapons should be necessary for today's lesson."

Kenneth nodded, removing the variety of sharp objects that he had hidden around his body, creating a small mound off to one side. He also removed as much of his armor as he could—he needed to be as light and maneuverable as possible.

When he turned back to them, he took a step, and, almost as an afterthought, removed his shoes. That would give him better balance.

Pariel nodded in approval. "We will begin with several warm ups and strength training exercises to wake up our bodies and help our technique. I believe both of you to be past the basics, so we will begin with something a little more advanced."

Kenneth soon found himself doing some of the strangest things he had ever imagined himself doing, such as a one-handed handstand that evolved into a Shoulder-Lock Hip Throw, a move used to flip an opponent who wields a knife.

Kali executed each of the 'warm-ups' with ease, balancing perfectly as she shifted from one form to the next. He couldn't help but notice how steady she was, her form never wavering even when she did the hardest exercises.

Eventually they finished, and Pariel stood from where he had been instructing them on the floor. "Good. Now you will fight. I want to see how well you hold up against her. You will lose, of course, but I want to see how long you can keep fighting."

Thanks for the vote of confidence Kenneth thought. He readied himself, one foot forward, the second one back and tilted slightly to the side, his weight perfectly in his center of gravity. They watched each other for several seconds, each attempting to find the best way to defeat the other.

With a sudden decisiveness, Kali walked toward him with a deliberate pace. When she got within six feet of him, she paused before leaping for a flying kick at his head.

Kenneth rolled to the side, cursing the fact he had still managed to underestimate her abilities. She landed perfectly, turning to unleash a flurry of fists, knees, elbows, and kicks.

Kenneth backed up frantically, blocking strikes that seemed to come from every direction. As he blocked he assessed the situation. She was faster than him, and probably more skilled than he was. There was no way that he could knock her off balance—her savyl saw to that.

He was stronger than her though. That was an advantage that he was sure of. He started getting into the rhythm of the fight, short gasps erupting from his mouth as his lungs demanded air. As he fell into rhythm, he became less frantic, more calculating, and much more dangerous.

He began hitting her as she attacked him, throwing his blocking arm or leg against hers as she struck. It hurt him, but he knew it hurt her far more. She subconsciously punched slower, automatically trying to save herself from experiencing pain, and he quickly seized the opportunity.

He ducked to the side and struck with an open palm at her temple, intending to stun her, or knock her out. He underestimated her reaction timing. The world spun as she dodged, grabbed his arm, and spun herself around him, flipping him and landing with him pinned on the floor.

They were both breathing hard, sweat pouring, and Kenneth mentally shrugged. It looked like Pariel's assessment of his skill in hand-to-hand combat was accurate. Kali rolled off of him, and Kenneth stood, his back mildly aching from landing on it.

Kali walked over to Pariel, who was clapping slowly. "Well done, Kali, that was no easy fight. We will continue our lesson after lunch. For now, I will ask you to please leave us. Your friends should be about ready to awaken."

Kali bowed, shot Kenneth an unreadable glance and left with a slight limp. Maybe he had hit her a little harder than he had thought.

"How long did I last?" Kenneth asked. Time always seemed to move differently when he was fighting.

"About four minutes. A lengthy fight, especially against an opponent of skill," Pariel mused, "Perhaps you should spar with her more often." Kenneth's heart sank slightly. He had been hoping this would be the only time.

Pariel shrugged. "We will see. For now, you should join the others." Kenneth nodded and headed out the door to eat a second breakfast.

Gabriel frowned. Gimelli had informed him that he had received a message last night. While this was not odd, the message itself was unusual, indicating that he needed to be in the town square at noon. It was one of the town's most populated areas, and he was naturally concerned. He had guards placed at every entrance and exit, and several more on rooftops.

People rushed around him, and he briefly wondered what he was waiting for. Several people attempted to sell him a variety of foods, but he always declined. He paced slowly, a fountain burbling quietly next to him.

"Mister? Would you like a newspaper?" came a small child's voice, and Gabriel turned. A small Japanese boy looked up at him, holding a stack of newspapers in his hands.

Gabriel opened his mouth to politely decline, and then paused, his mouth still open. Those eyes...they had seen ages come and go. He should know when his mind was being manipulated; he could do it to others. But the touch was so subtle he had almost missed it.

He cleared his mind of the influence with a thought, and stepped back, his mouth snapping shut. His eyes narrowed. "A newspaper." His voice was carefully neutral.

"Indeed." This time the voice was deeper, rich and cultured, and it issued from a moderately tall young man with dirty-blonde hair and blue eyes. "Newspapers." His voice was also neutral, though an underlying hum of amusement could be heard.

"And why do I need these?" Gabriel asked, taking them. He didn't ask the man his name. He had met him once before, and heard many more things about him.

"Research them. It will help. Also, be warned. I have been watching the boy too. He is much more dangerous than you think, and you were quite right in guessing that he is being tracked. By a *good* friend of both of us. I think you know her."

"Nora? How?" Gabriel said in disbelief. The man shook his head.

"To tell you would disturb too many strands of time. And trust me, right now it looks like a web made of finest silk. To touch even one string disturbs the rest. Even what I've said is dangerous. But watch carefully." The man turned to go.

"Wait!" Gabriel said quickly, and the man paused.

"I am listening."

"What are you doing right now?"

The man turned, his brilliant blue eyes flashing in the sunlight.

"Watching," he said with a smile. And then he was gone.

Kenneth ate breakfast with the others, enjoying their company. There was something about being with them that lightened his day. Even Kali's glowering didn't bother him as much.

He finished cleaning his dishes and left the room, unsure what to do. He wandered the halls, stopping by to briefly watch Aaron pound away on his armor. Eventually he found himself walking into the training room.

To his surprise, Gabriel was in the room. His shirt was off, and his muscles gleamed with sweat as his bound hair bounced to the rhythm of his exercise. He had his massive greatsword, his blade moving in a blur of sharpened steel as he spun and slashed at imaginary foes.

Kenneth got the feeling that he had never actually seen Gabriel fight before. Watching him dance and spin to a deadly song that he could only hear, it was clear that even when fighting Kali he had held back for reasons unspoken. The deadly grace that was being displayed now would wipe her out in seconds.

Gabriel slashed through the air with a final stroke, freezing as the phantasmal blow fell. He turned and looked at Kenneth, his face still locked in the deadly ferocity of his training, and Kenneth once again found himself in another time and place.

Gabriel, in gleaming armor, fought with a man whose armor seemed to suck in light, their blades flashing as they hummed through the air. Kenneth watched them from an awkward spot in the ceiling.

They ducked and spun, and Kenneth knew they weren't just sparring. They were doing everything they could to kill each other.

He smiled. Somehow, this man's death was good. Something told him that if he died, it would benefit him more than Gabriel could possibly know. So he waited, and watched.

Abruptly the man faltered, his scream ending in a bubbling sound as Gabriel sliced off his hand before slashing a final stroke through his throat. The man fell to the ground, blood gushing from him in spurts.

Gabriel froze, his eyes rising to where Kenneth hid. Kenneth stayed still, knowing that movement would betray that he was there. Gabriel's eyes slid away, and Kenneth breathed again.

And then he was back, with Gabriel sheathing his sword and walking to a wall. He grabbed a towel and mopped his face and turned to Kenneth. "Did you want something?" He scooped up a water bottle from beside what appeared to be a stack of newspapers and took a drink.

Kenneth shrugged, the memory still swirling. Why was he so happy that Gabriel killed someone? "No, sorry. I was wandering, and found myself here."

Gabriel nodded, lowering the bottle. "I find myself in here when I need to think. It seems to be happening a lot more recently." Kenneth shrugged again, unsure what to say.

Gabriel glanced at the clock. "You should be getting to your lesson with Yigil. It starts soon." Kenneth nodded, but hesitated as Gabriel frowned.

"One more thing. There is a peculiar section of this fortress where you will encounter a strange dead end. Saskia stays in that wing. The code is 2249." Gabriel nodded in finality as he ended his statement.

"Why are you telling me this?" Kenneth asked.

Gabriel looked at him with sad eyes, their silver shining like polished metal. "Because she needs a friend, even if she won't admit it to herself. And you, like her, have problems fitting in."

Kenneth thought about Kali, and how he never saw her during the day. He nodded, and left Gabriel in the training room, heading towards the library. As he entered, a multitude of fumes hit his nose, and he coughed, waving away the light mist that covered the room.

He walked briskly to the back, careful not to breathe in too deeply, and noticed Yigil standing over glass bottles the size of test tubes. He peered at them, noticing their odd colors and how some were sparking ferociously.

"Potions?" he asked. She nodded, taking a small pinch of something at her waist and dropping it into the vial in front of her. As the powder was absorbed, the potion went from a glistening black to a bright, lively blue.

She looked up at him. "Today we will study potions. But first: What are potions?" She asked.

Kenneth smiled, happy his memories were clear for once. "A potion is a mixture of magically resonating objects, usually in liquid form, that cause the magic inside of a person to be manipulated in a certain way."

Yigil looked surprised. "Very good. It sounded like you read that straight from a textbook. But yes, each of these potions are mixed with several objects, such as Daeva blood, that resonate with magic in a certain way. Alone, they don't do much. Mixed together, the various ingredients create a combined reaction that can do many beneficial things. All potions are dangerous, however, and most are extremely expensive to make." She swept her hand across the vials on her desk. "Each of these is a known potion that has certain effects. Tomorrow, I want you to be able to tell me what they do. Call it a homework assignment of sorts." Kenneth nodded, running his eyes once more over the potions to lock them in his mind.

"I will now give you time to search the library. You can do anything to the potions except destroy or drink them," Yigil said, her hand now gesturing to the vast library. "I expect you will be able to find what you need." Kenneth nodded, walking towards the library, and started searching.

After a half an hour, he had accumulated a good stack of books on a small desk, and was leafing through a manual on how to properly mix potions. Beside the book was another full of divining incantations, most of them written in Latin.

He glanced at the book, running his eye over a useful looking incantation, and then stopped. He opened the book wider, peering carefully at the binding inside. Satisfied, he picked up the book and walked to where Yigil was carefully repairing a decrepit scroll.

She looked up as he approached. "You have a question." It was a statement, but Kenneth nodded anyway, despite the face that she was blind. She acted so much like she could see it was easy to forget.

"This book has had pages removed from it," he said, laying the book on her desk, "I wondered if you had removed them to prevent me from using the information from them for my potions research." Yigil quietly picked up the book, lightly running her hand across the pages.

"Not for your research," She said quietly. "I removed the pages so that Flammeth and the others would not stumble across it in their research. Some knowledge is forbidden, and for good reason."

"Forbidden? Like what?" Kenneth said, guessing he wouldn't get an answer. He was right.

She sniffed. "Like I would tell you," she said, giving the book back to him. "It's forbidden for a reason. Some types of magic can consume you, leaving you to its mercy. Dark magics, magics that aren't easily controlled. I would advise you to stay away from them."

"Like raising the dead?" Kenneth asked. She stiffened.

"That is impossible," she snapped, "Many people have tried, trust me. While demons can inhabit dead bodies, giving birth to the tales of zombies and undead of old, no one can truly be brought back to full life without the full power of God."

"What about trading lives?" Kenneth wondered as something flickered in his memories.

"What?" Yigil said, caught off guard.

"Trading lives," Kenneth said, "One person sacrifices their life to restore another. That would satisfy the energy required, right?"

"It is untested." Yigil said, tight lipped, "And I am done talking about this infernal subject. Go back to your research."

Kenneth shrugged, walking back amongst the shelves. He returned the book, and turned his head slightly as he heard the quiet click of the door. He had thought he had seen someone in the shadows of the library, but hadn't been sure. The shadow had been small, suggesting a feminine form. Was Kali spying on him still?

He shrugged and went back to labeling the potions. At this rate, he wouldn't have to tell her tomorrow. He'd finish tonight.

Fear's Touch

"You are scouting with Saskia tonight," Gabriel informed him. Kenneth nodded, his mouth full of food. They were gathered around the table in the kitchen, Kali and Ellie engaged in a small food fight with grapes, with Flammeth absently trying to spear his strawberries with a spoon, his mind clearly elsewhere. Aelex had woken up, and was calmly slurping a smoothie and throwing grapes at Ellie when she wasn't looking.

"What time?" Kenneth asked, swirling the water in his glass.

"Second shift. Midnight to four," Gabriel said, laying down his fork. Kenneth nodded again, swallowing a big gulp of water. "Pariel told me that tomorrow you will be training with the others. He has a particular exercise in mind for all of you."

Ellie looked up from dodging a grape. "What exercise is it?"

Gabriel smiled at her. "He didn't say."

"Lame!" Flammeth pronounced, coming back to earth. He looked in confusion at his mutilated strawberries and shrugged, scooping their remains onto his spoon and depositing them into his mouth.

Gabriel shrugged, his posture indicating that he didn't tell Pariel what to do. He did, of course, but the methods Pariel used were up to him. Gabriel stood. "I am going to talk to Yigil. Don't stay up too late. Sleeping in the day before the day before is as important as the night before." He smiled and left through the door that led to the library.

His reminder caught Kenneth by surprise. It was Wednesday night. They were leaving to be inducted into the army on Friday. The week had flown by, and Kenneth didn't feel anything like the boy who had been dragged into the fortress after being attacked by a drunk. Guilty memories of his past pressed on him, and he angrily shoved them away as he stood up.

"I'll let Saskia know she's on patrol tonight," he muttered, and Flammeth shot him a sympathetic look. He probably thought he was dreading patrolling with Saskia, not running away from memories of the past.

He walked down the stairs slowly, remembering his conversation with Gabriel. *There is a peculiar section of this fortress where you will encounter a strange dead end. Saskia stays in that wing. The code is 2249.* Kenneth opened the door that led to the hallway that Aaron worked in and explored the various turnoffs.

At one point he turned, and the hallway ended quite abruptly. Against the back wall was a table with a vase of flowers sitting innocently on top. Kenneth approached it, looking carefully around it. Nothing.

With a sudden thought, he opened the drawer that was embedded into the table and smiled. The bottom of the drawer had a small keypad installed in it. He quickly tapped 2249 into the keypad, and heard a small click. Closing the drawer, he stepped through the section of the wall that had opened and closed it behind him. He was now in a hallway similar to the one he had left.

He strode down the hallways quietly, his footsteps muffled by the carpet that covered the wood floors. He paused at several doorways, unsure of where Saskia would be, but finally located her when he heard a faint sound of metal hitting wood.

Ah, he thought, *so this is where she practices.* He had wondered when he had never seen her in the training room. He walked over to the door that the sound was coming from and knocked quietly.

The sound within the room paused, and he heard, "Come in Gabriel." Kenneth opened the door and walked in. It was a fairly large room of wood and bamboo, with several varieties of weapons on the walls. She sat cross-legged in the center with her back facing him, throwing knives buried point-first into the wood around her. Others stuck in the wall in front of her.

"I'm not exactly Gabriel, but I'll come in anyway," he joked. She turned, surprised.

"Oh," she said, startled, "I didn't know you knew how to get to this area."

Kenneth shook his head. "I didn't. Gabriel wanted me to tell you that you are on patrol with me tonight. Second shift."

Saskia nodded, picking up a knife and throwing it at the wall with more force than necessary. It stuck, quivering, in the wall. At this, Kenneth noticed that while she was sitting in a position that looked relaxed, every muscle in her body was tense.

"Are you ok?" Kenneth asked before he could stop himself. She glanced at him and threw another knife, not watching it. It stuck beside the first.

"Why?" Now that he had noticed, he could tell that her voice was slightly strained.

"I don't know," he said, unsure where he was going, "you just seem...tense," he finished lamely.

She snatched up another knife. "Do I?" she muttered, throwing the knife. It struck one of the knives already in the wall, screeching and throwing sparks. Kenneth flinched.

She turned to him, ignoring the knife as it clattered across the ground. "Do you ever...Are you..." she started, and then she stopped. "Damn," she said quietly. She scrubbed at her eyes, and Kenneth realized she was crying, tears leaking out despite her efforts to keep them back.

He stood there awkwardly, unsure what to do, and Saskia sighed, closing her eyes and collecting herself.

"Are you ever afraid of yourself?" she asked him quietly. Kenneth frowned.

"I didn't, before," he said, "but now... I sometimes get scared, wondering if I will return to who I was before. It feels like there are two of me, each fighting for who I am. The part of me that was evil, cruel, and cold, and the part of me that has only known what I've experienced here. The terrifying part is I don't know who will win when I regain all my memories."

Saskia opened her eyes again, her eyes slightly red. "I scare myself." She sounded tired. Kenneth frowned.

"Your savyl is fear… You are afraid of fear?" he asked. She shook her head.

"I fear myself. What I could do with my power. Any fear you have at the moment, I can bring to life. Irrational fears? Those are the worst. They stupefy a person, making them incapable of doing anything but dying. Very, very few people are able to master their fears, and fewer than that have no fears."

"But that isn't the worst. Spiritual savylus use emotion. Ellie is lucky. She got a happy emotion, like compassion. I got stuck with fear. She gets to feel sorry for someone when they are hurt to heal them, but I have to feel terrified in order to kill people. It's horrible. And so effective. I can kill people with a glance." She looked at Kenneth through slanted eyes, gauging his reaction.

Kenneth shrugged self-consciously, unsure what to say. "It's good that you aren't power hungry, I guess." Saskia looked at him for several seconds, and for a moment Kenneth was afraid he'd said the wrong thing.

"You're not…afraid of me?" she asked hesitantly. Kenneth chuckled in spite of himself.

"I thought you could tell my fears. Of course not. If you wanted me dead, I'd probably be dead by now." She gave a small laugh and wiped the rest of the tears from her cheeks.

"I try not to read fears of…friends," she said eventually. She looked relieved. "It feels too much like I'm invading their privacy." Kenneth nodded, slightly relieved himself. It was still a little disconcerting to know that someone knew all of your fears.

She sat again amidst her knives. He tossed her the knife that had skittered across the floor towards him, and she caught it easily, flipping it and sending it spinning towards the wall with a flick.

"See you on patrol," Kenneth said, heading towards the door.

"Wait!" Saskia said quickly, and Kenneth paused, glancing back.

"Yeah?" he asked.

"Thanks. Just… Thanks," she muttered. She turned and sent another knife spinning towards the wall.

Kenneth smiled, Gabriel's words coming back to him. *She needs a friend, even if even if she won't admit it to herself.*

"No problem," he said, before leaving to get in a little sleep before patrol.

Gabriel picked up the stack of newspapers for the third time in two minutes, flipping through the titles. They were all frighteningly similar, each containing a story about a strange event that had happened to an individual. Each mentioned demonic involvement, some joking, others mentioning rumors, and a few stating it right out.

He sighed. First Kenneth, now this… Events were starting to move quickly. If he wasn't careful they would begin to outpace him. He set them on his desk again and fingered his sword at his waist.

A knock sounded at the door, and Gabriel called, "Come in." The door opened, revealing Gimelli. He shuffled in, eyes darting, and walked over to the desk.

"Let me guess," Gabriel mused, "All over the world, people are encountering strange occurrences, going insane, and randomly having seizures, leading to rumors of demonic involvement."

Gimelli looked shocked. "Yes," he said, his voice thick with his French accent, "How did you know?" Gabriel merely flicked a hand to the table. Gimelli scanned the titles and returned his gaze to Gabriel.

"Reports are clear. Other outposts have had increased demonic involvement all over the world. There have even been reports of a couple Fallen Angels seen." Gimelli's watery gaze was steady, but his hands constantly were moving, rubbing themselves against each other unconsciously.

Gabriel shivered slightly. Fallen Angels were much more dangerous than demons. Demons were merely the souls of powerful Nephilim that sacrificed their life to the devil to become more powerful. Fallen Angels were exactly what their name implied:

angels that fell from heaven in the Great Fall shortly after mankind was created.

"Get Yigil. I need advice," he commanded, and Gimelli nodded, shuffling out. Gabriel looked at the newspapers, his mind swirling. Something was brewing, and he didn't like it.

Kenneth turned his head as Saskia walked into the room. Aelex had returned a couple of minutes ago, grabbing an apple and mumbling good night before yawning his way down to where he slept. He had waited patiently in a chair by the table, confident that Saskia would eventually arrive.

She was dressed in her usual black, her scouting armor layering over her body, blending her form into the background, making her impossible to see if Kenneth didn't concentrate. He was dressed similarly, although he carried two swords, one on his back and one on his hip. She only had one in addition to her knives.

He stood, and they silently walked out into the open air. Kenneth breathed in deeply. He hadn't realized how much he'd felt cooped up in there. He glanced at Saskia. She appeared to have recovered from their earlier meeting.

"It's good to be outdoors," she said quietly, stretching in the moonlight. "The others complain when they have to patrol, but it's not all that bad."

Kenneth agreed. The night was never cold to him, and the air was light in his lungs. "I still don't know the routes," he admitted.

Saskia's smile gleamed in the moonlight. "That's pitiful," she teased.

Kenneth raised an eyebrow. "Other things demanded my attention. Like not letting Pariel kill me, for example." She mirrored his expression, raising her eyebrow as well.

"Then keep up!" she laughed, and her form blurred as she ran. Kenneth stood for a moment, surprised, before pounding after her. He was faster than her, but her armor made her hard to track, even in the moonlight.

Unexpectedly she veered off the road, nimbly jumping from the top of a car onto a deck on the second story of a building. Using an excellent display of balance, she ran along the deck's rail for a second before leaping onto the roof. He saw a flash of her smile before she continued on.

Kenneth grunted in irritation, running up the car and leaping onto the deck she had left moments before. *You're not the only one with good balance* he thought as he leapt from the rail onto the roof. He could see her leaping from rooftop to rooftop several houses ahead of him, and set off after her, careful not to slip on the dew covered shingles.

It wasn't long before he had caught up with her. She skidded to a halt, and he slowed, turning back to where she had stopped.

"Caught you," he said, but she grinned devilishly at him.

"Not yet!" she said. She let herself fall backward, flipping once and landing on her feet on the flagstones below. Kenneth laughed, and realized he was having the most fun he'd had since he'd arrived in Montana.

He jumped after her as she ran again, grunting slightly as he hit the flagstones below. He raced after her, sharply turning a corner as she ducked into an alleyway.

A flash of silver passed by his face, and he ducked, all of his senses sharpened as his body prepared to fight, but there was only Saskia, holding another knife.

"You lose." She said, smiling innocently. He shook his head in disbelief, picking up the knife she'd thrown.

He handed it back to her. "I lose," he conceded. She took the knife from him, wiping it briefly on her sleeve to remove the dew, and sheathed it. She glanced at him, and he realized all he was doing was watching her.

He coughed. "The route? Still don't know it, unfortunately. And we are supposed to be patrolling."

She blushed and strode out of the alleyway, jogging down the sidewalk. He followed her, watching as the city passed the night. It was remarkably peaceful. He kept up with her easily, despite wearing armor.

Hours passed in companionable silence before Kenneth eventually asked, "Would you be willing to train me?"

She looked at him like he was crazy. "Me, train you?" The thought seemed to amuse her. "You could defeat me in any weapon I choose, pummel me to death in hand-to-hand combat, and burn me to crisp on a whim, and you want me to train you?"

Kenneth was adamant. "Yes."

She stopped. "Why?" The humor in her voice was gone, replaced by curiosity.

"It wouldn't be normal training. You mentioned earlier that only a handful of people could face their own fears. I want to be able to overcome my fear," Kenneth said quietly.

Saskia shivered. "Oh God," she mumbled, "You want me to force you to experience your worst fears?"

Kenneth looked at her. "Yes."

She began jogging again. "You're stronger than I thought," she told him. He looked at her, confused, and she elaborated. "Mentally, I mean. I knew that you'd have to be pretty tough, to live with Iephus twenty-four-seven, but I never would have thought that you would voluntarily put yourself in a situation to experience your worst fears."

Kenneth frowned. "It'll make me better." It seemed simple to him.

Saskia shivered. "Still," she muttered. "Fine. I'll train you. But in return, you'll train me too. Obviously most of this will be in the army, but I think you'll be bored there anyway."

Kenneth agreed. It didn't mean that he wasn't looking forward to the army though.

They slowed as they approached the cathedral, and Saskia pricked her finger and whispered the words, allowing them access to the door. They walked in, and Kenneth sat down at the chair he had been sitting in while waiting for Saskia. Jogging for several hours wasn't exactly a walk in the park.

Saskia sat across from him, reminding him of an earlier time. "Apple?" he inquired, grinning.

Saskia's lips twitched. "No, thanks," she answered.

He shrugged. "Are you going to be in the exercise with Pariel tomorrow?" he asked.

She shook her head. "I don't train around Kali and the others." Kenneth nodded in understanding.

"Why are they so afraid of you?" he asked.

She shrugged guiltily. "I let them. I've never exactly encouraged them to get to know me. I couldn't exactly tell them I was in the Fallen's Ranks as well, right? They would eventually figure it out. It's safer for them to stay away from me, be afraid, and be safe." She caught Kenneth's surprised glance and said quietly, "I do like them. I just had an…unfortunate ending with the last person who became my friend."

"Dead?" Kenneth asked gently. She nodded, looking off to one side.

"They approached him, trying to get him to join the Fallen. He refused," she whispered.

Kenneth nodded. Refusal meant death. It was not swift, either. "I'm glad I don't have to go through that," he said, attempting to divert her thoughts, "can you imagine what that'd be like? Oh hey! Join the army. You've already joined? Then who are you? Unholy Lucifer! You're the Samiaza!"

Saskia chuckled hoarsely, and Kenneth stood, joking demeanor vanishing. "C'mon," he said gently, "Let's get to bed. Some of us have an early day tomorrow."

She nodded and stood. "Sleep. Last time I slept seems like a distant dream."

Kenneth grunted in agreement. When he finally reached his room, he barely had time to lock his door before he had passed out on his bed.

The morning's exercise ended up being an obstacle course with several stages. They were told they needed to wear their armor during the test. "You won't get a choice when the time comes," Pariel had said to them. They each went through it separately, so that they couldn't use each other's techniques to get through the obstacles.

When Kenneth entered the training room, the floor was cleared, with everything in the room lining the walls. Aelex and Flammeth had already gone; they stood off to one side, laughing with each other and watching him. The obstacle course spanned the length of the room, and, in some areas, reached up toward the ceiling as well.

He walked toward it slowly. The first section was a series of tall poles, each varying in degrees of thickness, balanced on the ground. The second was a rope, reaching all the way up to the ceiling. Near the rope was a small ledge, which led to a suspiciously padded hall. After the hall was a drop to a cushion below, and the last obstacle was an odd looking stone.

"I'm hoping you can guess what you must do to pass each obstacle. Get past the poles, climb the rope, get through the hall, jump down to the cushion, and I'll explain the last one when you get there. Any questions?" Pariel's voice echoed slightly in the room from where he stood on the other side. Kenneth shook his head, readying himself.

"Then...Go!" Pariel shouted. Immediately Kenneth stepped carefully on a pole. It was balanced precariously, wobbling beneath his foot as he fought to keep his balance.

He took another step, and then they were sliding out from underneath him. All caution thrown to the wind, he hopped as quickly as he could from one pole to another as they fell, barely making it to the rope.

He swung gently on the rope as the poles fell, listening to the cheering from Aelex and Flammeth in the corner. He was laughing, he realized with a start. Smiling, he pulled himself up the rope.

It didn't take him long to reach the ledge, despite the height. His enhanced muscles could easily take the weight of him, even with the practice armor that was strapped to his body.

As he eased himself onto the ledge, he looked carefully at the padded corridor. It was obviously rigged, but Kenneth couldn't figure out how. He walked through it slowly, tension building as he walked five feet, and then ten.

He saw flicker of movement out of the corner of his eye, and he reacted instinctively. Looking back, he wouldn't even remember why he reacted the way he did. A piece of foam shot straight into the air, causing him to shift slightly. Almost immediately, his brain recognized it as not threatening, and he noticed a small shift in movement on his opposite side. He turned that way and ducked as a panel of the wall exploded violently toward him.

He felt it graze the hair on his head, and he froze, eyes darting, waiting for another. Nothing happened, and he slowly stood from his crouch. The original piece of foam was to make him turn towards it, preventing him from seeing the one across from it. Clever. Very clever.

Nothing else attacked him as he finished the last few feet of the hall. He briefly looked down at the cushion, smaller now because of his height, and jumped. He had never been bothered by heights.

The cushion enveloped him, and he rolled out of it. Flammeth and Aelex were clapping, chuckling at something one of them had said. They were cut off as Pariel addressed him.

"The last part of the obstacle course is mental," he said, steepling his fingers, "You must overcome yourself. Touch the stone when you are ready."

Kenneth looked at the stone. It was as tall as he was, and shined an obsidian black that mirrored the room in dark tones. He approached the obelisk and carefully placed his hand on the cold surface. Nothing happened.

He looked at Pariel in confusion, and then jumped as the room faded, revealing a listless, black landscape that extended as far as the eye could see. He turned. Standing before him was a man terrifying to behold, armored in red and blue flames, seemingly frozen in time.

At his side was a sword that radiated cold like a fire would radiate heat, glowing a soft white that added strange contrast to the barren land they stood in. Fingers gripped the sword's hilt, unsheathing it with a loud ring. The temperature dropped.

Kenneth backed up as frost crackled around his feet. "Lord Blaze." The words came out like a curse. Kenneth could see him smile behind his beautiful helm.

"Of course." The man seemed amused. His voice was hard, cold like the sword he carried.

White puffs of breath could be seen now, and the air seemed like it would shatter from cold. "Then you know that I am you. There is no need for us to fight."

The man laughed, a harsh, cruel chuckle. "You are weak. Petty. I will rule. You, on the other hand, will merely fall." He walked toward Kenneth in a slow tread.

Kenneth continued backing up, carefully stepping so as not to fall on the ice that now covered the ground. It was so cold. "You realize that this is all in my thoughts, right?"

Lord Blaze paused. Then he swept out a hand, blasting freezing air at Kenneth, knocking him off his feet. When Kenneth's sight cleared he was standing above him, sword at his throat. "You of all people should know that what happens in one's thoughts is far more dangerous than real life." He swung the sword.

Kenneth jerked back from the stone, his sword clattering to the ground as he fell. He lay gasping on the ground for several seconds, before pulling himself up with Pariel's help.

"Your memories are your greatest enemy. You are torn, your mind separated into two people, each fighting to be the real Kenneth. You must master yourself, else you will be destroyed," Pariel whispered as he led him to where Aelex and Flammeth were standing. Kenneth nodded, still shaking.

"You okay?" Flammeth asked as Pariel left. "You're really pale."

"I'm fine," Kenneth said shortly.

Flammeth raised an eyebrow. "I'm guessing you don't get along with yourself."

Kenneth shrugged, slowing his breathing. "No. I don't," he said, and that was the end of it.

Kali walked in wearing a strange armor. They were each required to wear the armor that they would normally battle in, but Kenneth had never seen armor like the kind she wore. It was exceptionally light around the torso, but had heavy plate lining the outside of her arms and hands. He filed away the armor in his head as Kali was told the same directions that they all had received.

She passed the first two obstacles easily, lightly jumping from pole to pole, and climbing the rope quickly. The corridor was her downfall. She reacted so well to the first cushion that she had turned her body so that the second was completely behind her. It caught her in the middle of her back, throwing her against the padded wall.

Flammeth chuckled as he heard her swearing. "That was satisfying. She will hate him for that," he commented, and they shared a laugh. She recovered quickly, however, and soon had jumped down to the cushion.

Kenneth watched her as the last section of the obstacle course was explained to her. She seemed completely calm, approaching the stone with a small smile. She stayed that way for several seconds before lowering her hand. Pariel nodded to her, and she joined them.

"How did you guys do?" she asked, and Aelex laughed.

"I was amazing of course!" he said, and Flammeth rolled his eyes.

"He biffed on the first obstacle," he explained.

Aelex huffed. "So I did. But I did it stylishly, see? And I totally got past the rest. Easy."

Kali shook her head with amusement. "How'd you do, Flammeth?"

Flammeth opened his mouth to answer, but was cut off by Pariel. "Quiet please! Ellie is coming in."

They turned as Ellie entered. She received the instructions in silence, and ran a quick eye over the obstacles. Hopping lightly, she passed over the forest of poles with a grace reminiscent of Kali and jumped to grab the rope.

Flammeth nudged Aelex. "That makes everyone but you!" he stage whispered. They shared a laugh as Ellie started climbing. Kenneth could see as soon as she began that she wasn't going to make it to the top. About fifteen feet up the rope she paused, arms shaking, and they cheered her on from the sidelines. She smiled at them tiredly, and attempted to continue, but her arms gave out.

There was a small yelp, and she fell into the net below. Kali helped her out of it. "You gave it your best shot. Do you want to continue?" she asked her.

Ellie shook her head. "I'm too tired. I wouldn't be able to make it anyway." Kali nodded, and led her over to the group, where they congratulated her attempt.

Pariel allowed them to talk for a couple seconds, then commanded their attention by clearing his throat. "Some of you may have noticed there was something unique about this obstacle course," he said, and Aelex immediately nodded. The others looked at him in surprise, and he elaborated with Pariel's permission.

"Each obstacle was made with one of us in mind, to show us our greatest weakness," he explained, and Pariel nodded happily.

"That is exactly right. Aelex's was the poles, Ellie the rope climb. Kali's was the hallway, and Flammeth's the jump. And last, but of course not least, was Kenneth's. The seer stone."

Kali shot Kenneth a look, and he could only guess what thoughts lay behind it. His attention was quickly brought back to Pariel, however.

"You are dismissed for the day. Good luck in the army! Remember your training!" he said, and they left the training room in an excited bunch.

Kenneth turned to Flammeth as they headed to an early lunch. "The jump?" he inquired.

Flammeth grimaced. "I'm scared of heights," he confessed. "They terrify me. I got up there, looked down, and froze. I can't move. It's bad," he explained. Kenneth nodded in sympathy, and sat at the table.

They ate quickly, chatting about random things. As Kenneth put the last couple dishes away, he frowned and wondered aloud, "What do we have next?"

Aelex answered him. "I think Yigil is teaching us geography."

Flammeth snorted. "Geography? We learn that at school. Why would she waste time on that?"

"Maybe because humans don't know geography in comparison to multiple worlds?" Kali suggested innocently, and Flammeth paused.

"An excellent point," he said with a bow. Kenneth frowned. Multiple worlds? His memories hadn't returned that thoroughly yet. He followed them as they headed down to the library.

Yigil was waiting there for them. She directed them to sit at a table, and spoke. "Tomorrow you will travel with Gabriel to a fort on the barrier that separates Earth from Hell. Contrary to the belief of mankind, Earth is not quite a sphere. When observed with eyes that see beyond the fifth dimension, it is clear that there is a path that connects the two planes that are called Earth and Hell. This passage we call the Pérasma."

She paused, allowing her explanation to sink in, and then waved her hand. A perfect model of Earth appeared in front of her, spinning slowly on its axis. "The Pérasma can only be accessed in certain areas of the world, where time and space cross perfectly. The fabric of time and space is not flat, but instead like a badly folded cloth, crossing over itself with wrinkles and stretched areas across the universe." The earth distorted, stretching in some places, and compressing in others, making a bizarre orb.

"To access the plane, it is necessary to travel to an area where the time-space fabric is thin enough to pass through it entirely. There are several such places in the world." She dropped her hand, and the orb disappeared.

Aelex frowned. "Can you explain that in English?" He shrugged as Yigil snorted and crossed her arms. "Sorry, buth I can't envision the world past a sphere," he muttered.

"The world isn't round, but is instead oddly shaped. We can use the odd shape to travel to the passage that descends into Hell. Easy enough for you?" Yigil snapped, before taking a calming breath.

Aelex gave a nod and a sheepish grin. "Good," Yigil sighed. "Now we will go over what is expected of you when you join the army."

Kenneth sighed. This was going to be boring.

A Temporal Shift

Kenneth gave up on sleeping at nearly one in the morning. Every time he closed his eyes, nightmares consumed him. He went down to the training room, its large expanse silent and looming. He briefly considered working out, but discarded the idea in favor of trying to conserve energy for when they traveled to the fort.

Instead he sat in a corner, enjoying the quiet. The darkness was far from scary to him. Instead it was comforting, like a blanket that hid his unquiet mind.

Some time passed before the quiet click of the door jerked him from his thoughts. His eyes probed the darkness, and he recognized Saskia walking quietly. She stopped in the center of the room, her eyes almost closed in the half-light.

She stood there for a second, before turning around and leaving the room. Kenneth shook his head. Was she sleep walking? He chuckled to himself.

Hours later he woke, his head against the wall. He shook himself and stood, looking at the clock on the wall. It was half past seven. He headed for breakfast, and then stopped, realizing he wasn't hungry.

Deciding he should see if his armor was ready, he headed up the stairs and into the corridor that led to Aaron's workplace. Carefully covering his ears, he walked through the door.

He unstopped his ears to silence. The room was empty, the fire cold. On the table, however, was a set of armor. He walked over to the table, examining the armor and feeling its weight.

"Ah, so you've come to get your armor," Aaron's deep voice startled Kenneth, and Aaron laughed as he jumped. "It's only me," he joked, as if his bulk wasn't intimidating at all.

Kenneth calmed himself. "Is it finished?" he asked. Aaron nodded.

"Do you know how to put it on?" he inquired, and Kenneth hesitated.

"I know how to put on normal armor, but this… doesn't look like normal armor," he said. Aaron smiled.

"Quite right," he said, "This is one of a kind. Gabriel asked me to design armor that would be much heavier than normal armor. In order to give the proper range of motion for fighting, I had to modify it slightly. Putting it on will be similar, however. Let's try it out."

He helped Kenneth put on the armor, and Kenneth quickly understood what he had meant by heavier armor. The plates were much thicker than normal armor, making the armor nearly half again as heavy as the usual armor he had been wearing.

"Why did Gabriel ask you to make the armor so thick?" he asked, and Aaron nodded like he had guessed the question would come.

"He explained to me that your strength was much greater than a normal Nephilim, and that you'd be able to move in the plate fast enough to fight. He also mentioned that he expected the plate would absorb better," He explained, fastening the breastplate's straps on Kenneth's back.

"Absorb what?" Kenneth said.

Aaron shrugged. "I don't know." Kenneth frowned, but let it drop. He turned, examining himself in the mirror on the wall. It was an excellent set of armor. At the thought, another question rose.

"Did you design Kali's armor as well?" he asked. He saw Aaron nod in the mirror, and turned.

"I did indeed. She was a great experiment," he said, smiling at the memory. When Kenneth asked him to explain the armor's design, he shook his head. "You'll find out today," he said with a grin.

Kenneth left his armor on. They would be leaving soon anyway. He briefly visited his room, arming himself with various knives and his swords before heading toward the library to ask a question.

The library was empty, but Kenneth could hear voices speaking in the back room. Heading over to the room, he pushed open the door.

"There are more, sir. And they're getting more frequent and more deadly," Gimelli said, handing a sheaf of what looked like newspapers to Gabriel. Gabriel took them and looked up, seeing Kenneth.

"Ah, Kenneth. Gimelli, thank you. You are dismissed," he said. He looked up at Kenneth "I see you acquired your armor."

Kenneth nodded. He glanced at the stack of papers. Why did he want newspapers? "I have a question," he said.

Gabriel raised an eyebrow, "Is that so?"

Kenneth shrugged. He did ask questions frequently. "What, exactly, is Yigil?"

Gabriel frowned and sat. "A good question... She is an angel."

Kenneth frowned. "I thought so, but... her eyes..." When he didn't continue, Gabriel sighed.

"Her past is her past. We will not discuss what is hers to divulge. For now, it is time to leave. We have a long way to travel." Kenneth nodded, and followed him out of the room and up to the top room. Everyone but Saskia was gathered there, each wearing their armor and weapons as well as their pack of clothes. He had little time to wonder where she was, however, before Gabriel opened the door leading outside.

"Stay close to me and don't get lost," he said before walking out and not looking back.

Aelex followed quickly, and Kenneth hefted his pack and stayed close behind. They walked through the streets of the city, no one seeming to notice that they were wearing armor and weapons.

Eventually they came to the city park, and Gabriel strode through the tollgate and led them into the small park's wooded area. In the center was a massive tree that split into three trunks at the bottom. It was covered in graffiti, the initials of the years of lovers carved into the trunk.

Gabriel stopped and turned to face them. Kenneth stood, perplexed, and looked at the rest of the group. They seemed confused as well.

"We are about to travel to the fort of Güderam. This will be your home for the next few months, if not years. You are no longer under my orders *nor are you under my protection.* Do not come running to me with your problems. I will not help you," Gabriel said, his voice firm.

Aelex raised his hand, and Kenneth hid a smile. It was, in a sense, a polite way to ask to talk, but everything Aelex did seemed to make a mockery of the person he was talking to.

Gabriel raised an eyebrow. "Yes?" he asked.

"How, exactly, are we going to travel there?" asked Aelex. "It might be me, but I don't see any fort or ready method of travel." Kenneth agreed, but didn't voice his opinion aloud.

Gabriel chuckled. "Your 'method of travel' is right behind me." All eyes went to the enormous tree. "This tree was grown and maintained for one purpose. It acts as a way between worlds, or a temporal shift. It will allow us to travel to the Pérasma." He walked up to the tree and placed his hand over an enormous carved heart, and whispered, "Qui diligit Deum, hic inquirit." It sounded Latin to Kenneth, but he didn't quite get the meaning.

The tree shivered, and the graffiti warped and distorted, changing into runes of power that glowed with a faint white light. The runes detached themselves from the tree, and began swirling around, leaving soft trails of the white light behind them. The tree shook again, and the three trunks bent at the center, revealing a small opening in between them.

Gabriel, smiling at their awe-struck looks, picked up his pack, stepped into the tree, and vanished.

Aelex was the first to follow, shouldering his bag immediately and vanishing right behind him. Kenneth looked at Kali and Flammeth briefly, before making up his mind and walked to the center of the tree.

The moment his foot touched the center of the tree, the world lurched and spun, turning a light bluish color. He felt as though he was falling through empty air, all sense of direction lost.

Everything flashed white, and he hit the ground, hard, and staggered, trying to regain his balance.

A hand caught him, and Kenneth looked up. It was Aelex, with a wry grin on his face. Kenneth thanked him and stood.

"You did better than I did," Aelex laughed, "I fell flat on my face! Gabriel didn't even have time to steady me. Nope, I just went *down*." Kenneth laughed with him and looked around.

He was standing on a white marble floor, the same tree behind him on soft green grass. As he looked up, he saw that he was in a large temple, with tall columns lining the walls. Gabriel was standing several feet away, his beefy arms folded.

There was a slight popping noise, and Flammeth appeared several feet away, laughing and staggering. Aelex moved quickly to stabilize him, but it was to late. Flammeth toppled forwards and landed on the marble floor, hard.

He lay there, gasping through his chuckles, before accepting Aelex's help up. "That," he declared, "was the best rollercoaster ride that I've ever been on!"

There was another slight pop, and Kali appeared, took one step for balance, and then stood rock still. She looked up, noticed everyone staring at her, and snapped, "What?"

Flammeth merely shook his head, little snorts of laughter still slipping out.

They followed Gabriel outside, and Kenneth looked around in astonishment. They were standing between two mountain ranges, their peaks reaching into the sky and dusted with snow. But what astonished Kenneth was the land on either side of the mountains.

To his left, the grass was green and lush, with trees and animals loping lazily through the grass. The sun shone brightly, and the sight held peace.

But to his right the ground was barren, hard red earth cracked open from heat. The sky was dark, not with clouds, but with a black ethereal mist that covered the sky. Occasional flashes of red lightning flickered through the darkness.

Beneath him lay a city, people rushing through the streets, militia marching on the walls of the city, and marketplaces filled with people bartering for goods.

Gabriel turned, and took in the city with a sweep of his arm. "This is Güderam, the fort junction between the borders of Earth and Hell. This is your home for the next couple of months." Aelex nodded, face determined, and Flammeth and Kali stood, tense and ready. Kenneth simply nodded, unsure as to what to do.

Gabriel gazed at them for a couple more seconds before continuing. "The city is on the border between the bridge that connects *Hell* to Earth," he repeated, making sure they understood, "This place is dangerous, and you must treat it with caution. This is not a training exercise, nor is it a game. You could die here." He looked at them sharply, making sure they received his point. "Now come, or else we will be late for inspection." He turned and led them into the city

They walked for a short while, Gabriel leading them confidently through the winding streets of the city until the street ended outside of a training area. For the first time, there was open space, occupied by two large barracks and a sparring field right next to one of the two city walls.

"Welcome to Regiment Three," Gabriel said as he led them to a small group of what looked to be new recruits.

Kenneth and the others hesitantly joined them, and waited, wondering what would happen. They didn't have to wait long. Soon a monster of a man walked out of the barracks and joined them. He was massive, head and shoulders taller than Gabriel, and just as bulky.

"All right! Lets get started, shall we?" came a slightly high-pitched voice, and Kenneth jumped. Beside the giant stood a slender man, his body dwarfed in comparison. Kenneth had been so focused on the enormity of the first man he hadn't seen the second.

The recruits broke out into whispers, their awed silence broken, and the large man brought two hands the size of shields together in a deafening clap.

"Quiet," he grumbled into the stunned silence that followed. No one moved.

The slender man cleared his throat and continued, "My name is Asa, but you will call me Captain. We will be testing you in alphabetical order by last name. You will first spar with Geb here, and then we will test to see if you have a savyl. If you have already been tested, state the result. A warning: you will not be allowed to use your savylus during the spar. And don't think you can slip it by me. I can negate your savylus with mine."

A murmur went up at that, but was quickly silenced when Geb cracked his knuckles.

Asa pulled out a clipboard and a pen. "Hana Alden." A tall, willowy girl made her way out of the small group and walked toward him. She nodded to him shyly and looked up at Geb, who dwarfed her.

"Choice of weapon?" he asked, voice like gravel.

"I normally fight with a rapier, but I'd like to use a long sword to fight for this spar." Her voice was nervous but steady. Geb nodded and handed her a long sword from a rack in the arena and pulled out a massive sword that Kenneth recognized as a greatsword. It was nearly as tall as the man who wielded it.

Hana circled around him slowly before attacking with sudden certainty. They clashed for several minutes, but it was obvious that Geb was holding back. After a while, he casually disarmed her and touched the blade briefly to her throat.

"Very good," he stated. She nodded, out of breath, and walked to Captain Asa, who was writing on his clipboard. After a moment, he looked up.

"Have you been tested?" he asked.

She nodded. "Negative."

He nodded, understanding, and wrote a bit more. "Jared Derr."

A young man swaggered forward. He sneered up at Geb, and said, "long sword" in a slow drawl.

Geb handed him the long sword, and they began to duel. He did better than Hana, but the end result was the same.

"Very good," Geb said, with the same exact tone as he disarmed and 'killed' him.

Jared smirked and walked over to Captain Asa. He saluted with the air of mockery.

"Tested sir," he said in his slow drawl. "Disavylus of Strength and Speed." When he said this, several people looked shocked, and a susurration ran through those watching. Kenneth frowned. It seemed that disavylus were much more rare than he thought.

Jared's smirk deepened, and he presided over their astonishment with an arrogance that made Kenneth immediately dislike him.

Jared stepped back, joining a group that clearly knew each other. His friends congratulated him, and another recruit followed, and Kenneth soon found himself in a sort of trance, half paying attention, and half daydreaming as the rest of the recruits took their turn.

Eventually, they called "Kali Ross", and he snapped out of his reverie. She walked forward with her graceful stride, and spoke quietly with Captain Asa.

He listened with a quiet intensity, before saying, "Yes, General Griffith informed me of your peculiarity. I have encountered something similar to this before. My powers only block your talents that affect objects outside of your own body."

Kali nodded, relieved, and walked to Geb, whose immensity made her look like a child.

"Weapon of choice?" he said in his grumbling voice. In response, she kicked off her shoes and readied her hands, her strange armor gleaming in the sunlight. Geb looked surprised, but Captain Asa waved him on.

He raised his greatsword, his eyebrows furrowed, and attacked with a murderous horizontal swing. There was a gasp as Kali leaped into the air, the blade whisking beneath her, landing deftly onto Geb's blade hand. He immediately moved as if to swat her off, but she flipped over his hand and planted both her feet into his forehead.

Geb fell with a great percussive hit, and Kali flipped again, this time backward, landing deftly beside him, and lowered her arms. As he lay there stunned, she calmly walked to Captain Asa and stated, "Tested. Savyl of Motion."

Kenneth nodded, his suspicions confirmed. The armor was to protect her arms and legs if she was to block a weapon with them.

She walked back to the group, and there was a couple seconds of silence before Captain Asa cleared his throat and said, "Kenneth."

Kenneth walked forward amidst mutters, and someone said loudly, "Kenneth who? What? Did no one want to own up to birthing this wretch?"

Kenneth turned and saw that it was Jared, laughing with his buddies, and his dislike for him increased.

Ignoring him, he approached Geb and said quietly, "Long sword please." Geb nodded and handed him the long sword. Kenneth gripped it tightly, feeling the balance of the blade. It was well made, the leather on the hilt barely worn from use.

He swung it from side to side several times, feeling its weight, trying to ignore the stares that he was receiving. He looked up, and past Geb stood Gabriel, eyes watching intently. He was clearly interested in the spar.

Kenneth focused on Geb and let his body settle into the windsinger's stance, his muscles relaxed, with his grip on the sword loose but firm.

Geb came at him cautiously, perturbed by his earlier defeat. Kenneth circled with him for a couple seconds before attacking.

His swing was purely to get the spar started. It was aimed low, and Geb's greatsword swung quickly to parry it. They moved to and fro, almost dancing as Kenneth dodged the enormous blade and Geb tried to hit him.

Kenneth's pulse was up, and his mind was racing. The greatsword had many advantages, but maneuverability was not one of them. Its enormity made it awkward and hard to use quickly. Ducking and weaving through his swings, he worked his way closer to his opponent, where it would be the most difficult for Geb to block. With sudden decisiveness and lightning speed, he lashed out, cutting strokes to the right and left. His warded blade hit Geb's arms with a weird smacking sound before thrusting forward into his chest.

His sword bounced off the warding, but the effect was the same. He stood back, and realized he was soaked with sweat. He had lost track of time during the spar, but he saw that Geb was also breathing hard, rubbing his now-bruised arms.

He walked over to Captain Asa, and noticed the absolute silence that covered the spar field, and that several soldiers had stopped to watch. He turned to Captain Asa, who, eyebrows raised, asked, "And what is your savyl?"

Kenneth looked around, uncertain how to answer. Eventually he shrugged and said, "Fire."

"And what do you mean by that?" Jared asked.

Captain Asa cut him off. "That's quite enough out of you." He addressed the recruits. "There is a fourth, rare type of savylus called an elementalist. They wield one of six elements: fire, water, earth, air, light, or dark. Kenneth, would you care to demonstrate your element of fire for us?"

Kenneth shrugged, tired. The last night hadn't given him enough rest. He walked over to the edge of the yard, where a log lay. He picked it up and moved it to the center of the yard, where no one stood. Then he jogged back to the group.

"I don't see how this has anything to do with—" Jared began, but cut off into a yelp as the log exploded into splinters and fire, spraying them all in blackened sawdust. The remainder flared, giving off intense heat that could be felt from nearly fifteen feet away. Startled, Jared stumbled backward and fell to the ground, staring in shock at the smoldering wreck that used to be a log.

Kenneth allowed himself a tired smile.

Training in Darkness

Flammeth and Kenneth walked amidst sparring warriors and training recruits, voicing their opinions of the past day's events. The sun beat down on them with a ferocious heat, and the ground was hard, cracked clay—a result of being so close to Hell. Heat waves wafted up the smell of sweat as the soldiers trained.

The day had been hard, but bearable. Their regime was strict, and discipline hard. They were awakened before dawn, and set to running around the city. They then had training in an assortment of weapons until breakfast. Following breakfast were lessons in tactics, and fighting theory, an hour until lunch to rest before heading to hand-to-hand training followed after eating.

Kenneth would have enjoyed it more if everyone hadn't ignored him. He had expected to be accepted after he had managed to defeat Geb. Instead, everyone was either jealous or too afraid to go against Jared's wishes and befriend him.

As it was, Flammeth and Aelex were the only ones who cared to speak with him, and so Kenneth and Flammeth walked in their free hour, wearing the uniform of a 3rd private, the lowest rank in the regiment.

They crossed into the 4th Regiment's section, a mirror to their own barracks, Flammeth complaining how they made him transform out of his signature green hair.

"I just don't understand," he declared, one finger pointed in the air, "how they can do something so *unfashionable!*"

Kenneth rolled his eyes. It was probably the fourth time he had heard the complaint that day.

"You know, I think short, brown hair suits you. I think you should keep it," he said, his face completely deadpan.

Flammeth looked at him, scandalized. "How can you say that? Do you not understand—" He broke off as Kenneth began laughing. "I see, Mr. Sarcasm," he huffed. "But I don't think this is a matter to be laughed at so easily. This is serious!"

Kenneth chuckled. "Oh get over it. At least they didn't make you get rid of your earrings." Flammeth's hands shot to his golden loops, his face concerned.

"Do you think they'd do it?" he whispered, mortified. At Kenneth's nod, he exhaled slowly, fingering his earrings.

Movement caught Kenneth's eye, and he looked toward the edge of the training yard. He frowned, sure he'd seen something. He glanced away, and then immediately looked again.

Shadows seemed to obscure the figure, but as Kenneth focused, he mentally stripped them away. It was Saskia, standing, a thin sword in hand, regarding those who were training.

He turned to point her out to Flammeth, but stopped, squinting his eyes. She was wearing the uniform for a 3rd Captain. He wondered why she was already such a high rank.

"Earth to Kenneth, Earth to Kenneth, do you copy? I am going to punch you in Three…Two…" Kenneth turned and caught Flammeth's fist as he lazily went to punch him on the arm.

"What's going on man? You were staring at nothing over there," Flammeth said, with one eyebrow raised.

"I was looking at…" Kenneth began, and then stopped. Saskia was gone. "Never mind," he muttered, "Lets get back for training."

Training was difficult, as usual. Afterward, Kenneth walked alone down the streets the city. He bought himself a hot mug of cider and wandered aimlessly, soaking up the business and flow of the people.

Night slowly fell, and Kenneth found himself on the wall facing the descent to hell, sitting quietly.

Some time passed before he realized he was being watched. He stood and turned, resting his hand on his sword at his waist and spoke loudly into the quiet of the night. "You can come out now."

There was a surprised intake of breath and Saskia stepped out of the shadows, her dark eyes glittering in the moonlight.

Kenneth relaxed and sat back down. "Why were you watching me?"

Saskia shrugged. "I was curious. You don't act at all like…" She hesitated, glancing around, "how you used to."

Kenneth smiled. "I don't really remember how I acted, so it's rather difficult to act that way," he said laughingly.

Saskia smiled in response. "I guess…" she said, sitting cross-legged across from him. Wind blew, bringing the smoky scent of the barren lands below.

A thought occurred to him. "You said you met me as my previous self?"

Saskia shook her head. "I never said so, but yes, I met him on several occasions."

Kenneth frowned. "Then how did I act?" he asked, remembering his battle with his thoughts during the obstacle course.

Saskia sighed. "Lord Blaze was a cruel man. He delighted in pain, and was powerful and intelligent. He acted kindly to few, and showed mercy to less. When I met him, it was only to receive orders. He would always issue the orders, sometimes not explaining why I was to do what was ordered, and leave. We never spoke more than that."

Kenneth nodded slowly. "You don't think of me as Lord Blaze." It was a statement, but she took it as a question.

"You don't act like him, and you look different, so it's hard to," she answered.

"I don't look like him? How does that make sense?" Kenneth said, confused.

Saskia frowned at him. "Lord Blaze carried a weapon called *Frost.* It was one of eight great blades forged, and allows for the user to access frost magic as well as amplifying their own powers. Using these powers, Lord Blaze created a suit of armor out of *crystintillas,* or frozen flames. It not only looked impressive, but it was also deadly. *Crystintillas* is almost impenetrable, and when cracked it creates a small burst of fire. So to break his armor you had to be resistant to fire like he was. He wore this suit at all times. You don't have the armor."

Kenneth nodded, remembering the armor's crystalline beauty. It did make sense. "You didn't like him?" he asked.

Saskia looked him in the eye, the moonlight making her dark eyes shine silver. "I hated him, and everything he stood for. Know this: if you return to being Lord Blaze in truth, and forsake the way of the light, *I will kill you.*" Her voice shook, and she stood. She hesitated a moment, and then left, the darkness clinging to her form as she slipped into the night, leaving Kenneth with his troubled thoughts and a surprising sadness.

"Tell me. Why is this taking so long? It has been nearly two weeks since you have located him, and still he remains where he is." Iephus's voice was carefully controlled, but Nora could sense the anger in his frame. He stood in an aggressive stance, one hand on the hilt of his sword, his eyes flashing.

"I can't remove him from the army without them suspecting something. He is fooling them well—they all think he doesn't remember anything from his past. He will be safe so long as he keeps up his charade. Meanwhile, he will learn about them while they attempt to change his heart," Nora said. She was leaning against a wall, her ease a mask that covered her fear.

Iephus growled. "We don't need to know their ways. We need to wipe them out. I am getting impatient, Nora. I think you are losing your touch," he said threateningly. She shook her head. Now was not the time to mock him. Not when he was like this.

"You know I am the best," she said. "It will take but a while longer. I am nearly in the perfect position to remove him. Give me time."

Iephus turned, walking to the nearest window. The darkness of the city lay beneath him, flickers of light indicating areas that were lit by torches. Darkness and fire.

"You have three days. Take any longer, and I will kill you." His voice was deadly quiet. Nora swallowed, her mouth dry. She had no doubt that he could.

"Go. Now." She bowed at his command and left, rattled for the first time in nearly a century. Where had her composure gone?

"Get it together," she snarled at herself, startling a guard that was patrolling the hall. He looked at her, and she glared at him, her red eyes gleaming.

He jumped back, hitting the wall. She ignored him. She had more important people to kill.

"Yesterday you were introduced to the weapons that you can fight with in the army." The speaker was a tall, black-haired woman with tanned skin and well defined muscles in her arms and legs. Her uniform indicated she was a Corporal. "Today you will decide which weapon you will learn how to use. If you have trained with a specific weapon in the past, I would highly advise you to continue with that weapon."

Kenneth stood with Aelex and Flammeth, Kali standing off to one side, arms folded. The rest of the recruits were clumped in several groups. At the corporal's gesture, they walked forward.

"All who wish to learn the sword, come with me," commanded the lady. "Those who wish to learn the ranged weaponry, go with Corporal Bradley," she said, indicating a tall man with a powerful looking bow. "Those who wish to learn the battle ax or war hammer, go with Corporal Han." This time she pointed to a heavyset man holding a hammer with the head the size of a large chest.

They split themselves accordingly, Kenneth following her along with Flammeth, Aelex, Kali, and several others, including, much to his dislike, Jarrod and his friends. They jogged to one side of the training grounds, and stopped by a rack holding wooden swords.

The corporal turned to speak to them. "My name is Corporal Luna. You will address me as Corporal, and no differently. My job is to train you in the sword, not be your friend." Her gaze rested briefly on Jarrod before taking in the rest of them. "Today we will learn the basics of the sword."

Kenneth sighed as she passed out the swords, teaching them the proper way to hold the sword. She droned on for some time, showing them several stances before she split them into groups to spar.

"Who here has trained in the sword previously?" she inquired, and hands were raised. Jarrod was among them. "If you have trained in the sword, step behind me."

She paired up the beginners, setting them to spar, before turning around to organize the more learned fighters. "Who thinks they are capable, and who thinks they are advanced? Tell me as I point to you, as well as your name," she stated.

Few people identified themselves as advanced. Kenneth, Kali, Jarrod, and a bulky boy with blonde hair were singled out for a second time. The others were set to spar, and Corporal Luna turned to them. "So you think you are advanced? I hope you weren't being prideful. We will see how advanced you actually are shortly."

Kenneth nodded. This was familiar. The army was filling in gaps of his memories from his early training, replacing random knowledge with the lessons were he had learned the knowledge.

Jarrod smirked as he was paired up against Kenneth. He twirled his sword, and Kenneth sighed inwardly. Sword twirling was so flashy and useless. He glanced over at Kali. The blonde boy looked confident; he thought he since he was facing a girl he would have an advantage. Kenneth almost felt sorry for him.

He returned his gaze back to Jarrod. Jarrod was already in his stance. Kenneth glanced at his feet and shook his head at his arrogance. He was in giant stance. Obviously he believed Kenneth to be far inferior.

Kenneth didn't budge from his position, his feet slightly apart, sword hanging by his side. When Jarrod didn't attack him he raised an eyebrow.

"Are we going to fight anytime soon?" he asked, and Jarrod sneered.

"Don't you want to get in a stance?" Jarrod said, and when Kenneth didn't move he smirked again. "Suit yourself."

He rushed Kenneth, and Kenneth stepped to the right, leaning back and tripping him. Jarrod rolled, coming to his feet, facing Kenneth with an angry look.

"Never attack someone with giant stance unless they are smaller, weaker, and faster than you. Unless you can overwhelm them in an instant, the stance is a disadvantage," Kenneth instructed.

Jarrod reddened, shifted into windsinger's stance, and attacked again. This time Kenneth brought his sword up, the wood swords clacking together as he blocked the blow. He blocked twice more, then slid the sword down to Jarrod's cross guard. He took a step forward, locking his sword against Jarrod's before twisting the sword down and stomping on it.

The wood flexed and shattered, and Jarrod jumped back in surprise. "You can't do that!" he shouted, and heads turned. Someone sniggered.

"An enemy soldier wouldn't have stopped at your sword," Kenneth stated quietly, and Jarrod opened his mouth angrily.

"Quiet!" Corporal Luna snapped, and he snapped his mouth shut. "Your partner is correct. You would be dead." She turned to Kenneth. "On the other hand, we only have so many sparring swords. Try not to break them, will you?"

Kenneth saluted. "Yes corporal."

"Good then. Recruit, grab a fresh sword. And don't assume your enemy is a worse fighter than yourself. You'll get yourself killed." The corporal walked away, leaving Jarrod sputtering in anger.

He turned to Kenneth. "You'll pay for this." He whirled around before Kenneth could reply, stomping off to snatch a sword. Kenneth watched him go impassively.

When sparring had finished the sun was high in the sky. They took a break for lunch, some groaning about blisters, others chatting excitedly about what they had learned.

Kenneth sat with his group under a tree, eating silently while the others talked. Flammeth was congratulating Kali for never losing against her partner, and Aelex was making fun of the corporal.

He leaned against the tree, his thoughts sinking into dark memories surfaced by their training. He was so immersed in his thoughts that when Aelex threw an apple at him he reacted violently, slicing the apple in half with a dagger.

Shocked faces greeted him when he realized what he had done. "Sorry," he muttered, "I…" he looked down as he noticed they weren't looking at him. He had been drawing in the dirt with the dagger. He hadn't drawn a picture, but instead a sign. A very dangerous sign.

"What is that?" Flammeth asked quietly, and Kenneth shook his head, unwilling to answer.

"That's the Sign of the Fallen," Kali hissed, and as one they tensed, drawing back from him.

"Wait," he said desperately, "I can explain!" He swiped his hand over the mark in the ground, and they looked at him silently.

"Go on," Aelex said, all laughter gone from his blue eyes.

"I was born and raised in Hell. I'm a convert. I swear to you, I am not part of the Fallen any longer. Yigil can attest to that. She read my memories herself. Why else do you think Gabriel didn't kill me?" he said desperately, and he could see their thoughts churning.

Flammeth was the first to speak. "It does make sense. It all does. Your skill with the sword, the training separate from the rest of us…" He trailed off, looking at Kali.

She was gazing at him with a flat stare. "You were born and raised in Hell, huh? And you converted?"

Kenneth nodded. "I am not your enemy. I promise."

She shook her head. There was a moment of silence, and then she sighed. "I apologize. I was distrustful and hateful toward you. I didn't know the whole story."

Kenneth was shocked. By the looks on the other's faces, they weren't expecting this either. "Well, you did have good reason to suspect..." He said weakly.

"I know," Kali said. "I still think you're dangerous. Just... on accident." She glanced over with a sad look, so quick Kenneth nearly didn't catch it. He followed her look to Saskia, sitting alone across the field, eating. Maybe Kali knew more about Saskia than he thought.

"Guys? Try not to tell everyone, okay?" Kenneth said, "People don't like converts."

Flammeth saluted. "Your secret is safe with me, sir." Kenneth rolled his eyes. Aelex chimed in as well, and he looked at Kali. She nodded slowly, and Kenneth sighed in relief.

"Time to go train," Aelex interjected as a bell was rung. They got up, brushing crumbs off themselves, and jogged over to Corporal Luna.

"It is time for your close combat training. This will follow lunch everyday. Previously you were told the fighting theory, now you will meet your instructor."

A hairy man stepped forward. He was tall, his defined muscles gleaming in the sunlight. "My name is Ryan. I will be your instructor. Do not mind protocol, I don't like being called 'corporal'. Ryan does fine."

He walked forward, examining the recruits. "Who has close combat training?" he asked, following their earlier training session's structure. Hands once again shot into the air, but one did not fall when he continued. He trailed off, looking in confusion.

Kali did not lower her hand. He continued to look at her, but she didn't back down. Eventually he crossed his arms. "Well? What do you have to say that is so important?"

Kali lowered her hand. "I don't need to be in this class, sir. I request to test out of it."

Ryan looked at her and laughed. "Girl, I'd take this session and not get killed in your first battle."

Kali was adamant. "I will not get killed. I request to test out of this. I will have better use of my time learning something else."

Ryan folded his arms. He wasn't laughing now. "You want to test out, eh? You know what the test is? You have to defeat me in hand-to-hand combat, girly." He looked huge compared to her, but Kenneth was well aware of her skill.

In response, Kali kicked off her shoes, readying herself. Those who had been with her during testing stepped back away speedily. They'd seen what she could do.

Ryan shrugged and raised hands into position. "Whenever your ready, girly." Kali walked forward with a sure stride, until she was only a couple feet away from him. Then she rushed him.

Despite his surprise at her ferocity, he quickly recovered. He was a good fighter, there was no doubt. He held her off for nearly a minute until he threw a punch at her. She grabbed on to his arm as it passed by her, pulling herself across his body, swinging around his neck with her legs, and toppling him.

Kenneth chuckled. She had taken him out with the same move a couple days ago. Corporal Luna stepped forward. "I believe that would indicate that she was right. She would waste her time in this class. Come on, recruit."

Kali saluted and jogged off with her, leaving Ryan on the ground. He rolled to his feet and stood, an irritated look on his face. "Anyone else feel the need to test out?" When no one said anything, he nodded sharply. "Good. We will begin."

They trained until dinner, and Kenneth welcomed the warm soup and bread. He was hungrier than he could remember in a long time. They gathered their food, and found Kali sitting on a bench a little ways away.

She glanced up at them as they joined her, a small smile on her face. There was silence for a second before Aelex chuckled and said, "Did you see the look on his face when she took him out? Priceless!" They dissolved into laughter, and Kenneth took a bite of bread dunked in soup.

"What did you do after you tested out?" he asked curiously.

Kali lowered her bowl. "Corporal Luna took me to a ranged weapon's course. She said it would give me a good advantage to be able to fight with both the sword and the bow." Kenneth nodded in agreement.

"Why didn't you test out? You could have probably made it," she asked Kenneth, and he shrugged.

"I thought of trying, but if I failed after what you'd done to him, he would have disliked me thoroughly. I didn't want to have an instructor that could make my life hell," he said. There was a sudden quiet, and he looked up from his soup. "What?"

"What's it like?" Flammeth asked. "Hell, I mean."

Kenneth shivered. "Not pleasant."

Aelex rolled his eyes. "Don't go into detail or anything." Kali gave him a sharp look, but Kenneth cut her off.

"It's fine. If they want to know, its fine," he repeated. He rubbed his eyes. "I was raised in a city where if you didn't kill, you'd die of starvation. It wasn't easy for people to survive, but children... They almost never survived. We roamed in packs, protecting each other, never really trusting anyone. At night we would never get sleep. You don't sleep at night, not with..." He broke off, shuddering.

They were looking at him, pity in their eyes. He didn't want pity.

"I'm finished," he muttered, suddenly not hungry. He stood, setting his bowl down. He walked out into the city, leaving the barracks behind.

He had barely entered the streets of the city before he stopped. "Following me again?"

"How do you do that?" came the irritated voice. Saskia stepped out of the shadow of a building, annoyed about her failure at staying hidden.

Kenneth chuckled. "All magic leaves an energy field. When you use your power to obscure yourself with shadow, it leaves traces. I only had to figure out what they felt like."

Saskia harrumphed. "Oh, so now you're an Opseer?" Opseers could see all forms of magic in their energetic base. Kenneth shook his head.

"Not quite. I can't see the energy, only feel it. But it is a unique feeling," explained Kenneth.

"Well then. Where are you going?" she asked.

"I don't know," Kenneth answered honestly. She squinted at him and shrugged.

"Okay," she said, and they wandered the city together. It was large, with shops crowded together on the streets, and people walking from one area to the next. They passed pubs full of soldiers drinking their nightly beer, and shops full of people bartering for goods. Other areas of the city were quieter, the streets dark, houses full of people sleeping.

They eventually passed a pub where Saskia stopped him. "We should stop here," she told him. "It's nice." Kenneth nodded.

"Okay," he said agreeably, and they entered. The bartender looked up as she entered and smiled at her.

"Captain. It is good to see you on this fine night," he said pleasantly. He glanced at Kenneth. "Will he be with you?"

She nodded, and the bartender turned, pulling a small lever disguised as a tap. A section of the wall slid open behind him, and

Kenneth followed Saskia through. It opened up into another bar, brightly lit and slightly crowded.

Kenneth followed her to an empty table. "Why the back room?" he asked quietly.

Saskia sat, crossing her legs. "This bar back here is only for converts. People from hell who want to spend time with others who won't look at them differently." Kenneth nodded, remembering the looks of sympathy and pity that he had been given when he had explained to them what hell had been like.

"I don't blame them," he said as the waiter approached them.

"Good evening sir, good evening captain," he said cheerfully. "What may I get you? Our daily special for today is the Hell's Bite. It's a mixture of vodka, rum, ghost peppers, and a single cherry."

Kenneth raised an eyebrow. "That sounds deadly."

The waiter chuckled. "It's knocked three people out so far tonight. None of them could taste anything when they woke up."

Saskia shook her head. "I'll have my usual." The waiter nodded and turned to Kenneth.

"And you sir?"

"I'll have a hot chocolate, if you have it," Kenneth said, and the waiter nodded.

"As you wish sir." He left, weaving through the tables as a man took a sip of a shot of clear liquid with a floating cherry and sprayed it on his laughing friends, beating his chest and coughing.

Kenneth watched in mild amusement and looked at Saskia. "Do you come here often?" he asked.

"It's the only pub that I go to. None of the others let me in. They're too afraid that I'll scare away their customers." She shrugged as the waiter returned. "None of them have lemonade like here, either," she added as he slid her a strawberry lemonade.

Kenneth took his hot chocolate and thanked the waiter. He sipped it. It was superb. He glanced around the room again.

"Do you still want to train with me?" She asked him, and Kenneth turned his attention back to her. He nodded, and she sat back, sighing. "Okay. I found a place we can train, but we'll have to do it at night."

Kenneth shrugged. He didn't mind. "When will we start?"

"Tonight, if that's fine with you," she said, and Kenneth nodded, slurping his drink. His gaze fell upon a group of men arguing in the corner. They had obviously been in their drink, and the argument was starting to get heated.

Kenneth flagged the waiter as he passed by to alert him, but he was too late. Glass shattered as one of them stood and flung his drink to the floor, yelling. He lunged at the man sitting across from him before reeling backward in shock as something silver flashed by his face.

Kenneth slammed his other knife on the table, leaving it quivering in the wood. "I would advise you to calm yourself," he said quietly, and the man looked at him with bloodshot eyes.

"Y-you're right," he slurred, and sat. His bleary eyes focused on the knife in the table. "I'll pay for the table."

The bartender appeared as if from nowhere. "You bet you will, Logan. That's the third time this week you've tried to start a fight. One more and I'll have to throw you out." The bartender looked at Kenneth. "Thank you sir, for acting quickly. That could've been messy." He handed him his other knife, and Kenneth sheathed them, thanking him.

Saskia tapped him on the shoulder. "Now would be a good time to leave," she said, and Kenneth agreed. He attempted to pay for their drinks, but the bartender refused, saying he had earned his cup.

They wandered back into the night, and Kenneth followed Saskia as she led him the base of the eastern mountain. They climbed a short way, pausing at a small ledge. Saskia carefully squeezed between two boulders and disappeared. Kenneth approached the crack and copied the action, following her into a widening cave.

He blinked in the darkness and held out a hand. It sparked to life, flames covering his hand, illuminating the cavern. It was large, with stalactites and stalagmites around the edges. He focused, and the flames condensed into a ball. With another thought, he sent the burning orb hovering just below the ceiling.

"Nice," Saskia commented. He grinned.

"You found it," he pointed out, and she grinned back. She walked to the other side of the cavern and turned to face him.

"We'll start out with minor fears today," she said, and Kenneth nodded. "I won't tell you which ones I'll bring to life, but I won't let them kill you either. They will hurt you if you're not careful though."

"Pleasant," Kenneth muttered.

"You were the one who wanted to do this," Saskia pointed out. She closed her eyes and raised a hand, breathing slowly.

"What is the matter with you?" she said after several seconds had passed. Kenneth looked at her in confusion as she opened her eyes again. "Don't you have any *minor* fears?" He shrugged.

"I never saw any reason to be afraid of something I can overcome," he stated, and Saskia shook her head.

"We'll have to start larger then. Good God, I didn't know these still existed," she whispered, and the room darkened, a pool of shadow appearing between her and Kenneth.

He immediately drew his sword. Its coalescing shape confirmed his suspicion of what it was.

"Daimoniki Pórmi," he growled, and it sounded like a curse. They were known in the Greek legends as Furies. It grew to full size, slightly larger than a man, with bat-like wings and brown fur covering its body. It's red eyes bled malevolence.

He attacked it immediately, but was driven back by its claws. He ducked a swipe and slashed at its overly long fingers, but the daimon was too quick. It skittered back, its wings flapping, releasing a horrible stench.

Kenneth coughed, the foul smell hitting his nose, and the daimon struck, swiping a spiked tail at his face. Kenneth rolled out of the way, carefully avoiding being impaled by a stalagmite.

An idea struck him. He dodged another slash by the monster and threw out a hand towards the ceiling. A concussive explosion sounded, and stalactites fell, impaling the Fury. It screamed and withered, slowly collapsing on itself until it vanished into flame.

He turned to Saskia. "How'd I do?"

Captain in the Light

Saskia watched in wonder as Kenneth left the cave. She had never seen anyone respond to fear like he did. Every fear she conjured from his mind that should have left him cowering he had attacked immediately. Only one of the four fears she had brought to life had defeated him. It was that fear that scared her the most. His fear of Lord Blaze.

That same fear also gave her hope, whispering in her mind that there could be a chance that he would win out eventually, and stay as Kenneth forever. But she didn't dare hope in fear that she would be betrayed. She didn't want to fall for a man who—She suppressed the line of thought before it continued.

Get control of yourself, Saskia, she thought, *He won't ever notice you beyond what you are—a killer.* But still that hope flickered, resisting her attempts to put it out.

She left the cave under the cover of darkness, the moon covered by the ethereal mist that darkened Hell's sky. They had decided to leave separately to not raise suspicion about the area of town. She moved like a wraith, ghosting her way through the town back to the barracks where she was quartered.

She had her own room. No one had volunteered to room with her, and the person they had assigned threatened to resign. She told herself she didn't mind, but it sounded empty, even to her.

She started a fire, warming the room. Despite the heat of the day, it got extremely cold at night, similar to desert conditions. Sparks flared and caught, and soon the room warmed considerably.

A knock sounded on her door, and she froze. It opened, as she knew it would, and she kneeled, careful not to look up. He never wanted her to see his face. He was careful. But she always felt his fears, always in the same pattern. *Pain* and then *fire*, followed by *death*. And last was his worst fear, a fear that she herself had felt while spying among the Fallen. It made sense that Fallen spies in the Ranks of the Light would feel it as well. The fear of being discovered. She would find this pattern in a man in the army eventually, and these visits and her orders from the Fallen would end.

Kenneth hit the padded pole with his sparring sword with a solid *thud*, feeling the shock shiver up his arms. Four days had passed since he had first come to the army, and he stood, training with his group in the morning, sweating and grunting as he worked.

Corporal Luna was currently supervising them. She watched closely, never allowing anyone to slack off, but seemed to enjoy helping the recruits learn how to use the sword.

She called break, and Kenneth stood down, sword point first in the dirt, breathing lightly. He looked over at Corporal Luna, waiting for the minute's rest to end.

Corporal Luna prepared to give the order to resume, but was interrupted by a courier. They spoke quietly, and the courier left. Corporal Luna turned and addressed the recruits.

"I am needed for a brief time. You may rest until I return." There was a small cheer at their good fortune. She smiled and jogged off.

Kenneth watched her go, aware of everyone else sitting or laying down, stretching muscles and catching their breath. He was starting to bore of the sword exercises. He was by far the most advanced in his class, and they were learning the basics that he had mastered years ago. The only thing that remained interesting was his nightly training sessions with Saskia. Their mutual training sessions were the only thing he looked forward to.

Picking up his practice sword, he walked to the spar pole and hit it. Hard.

The wood shuddered, the shock of the blow shivering up his arm. Aware of the others watching him, he swung again, a brutal two-handed blow.

The wood flexed and shattered, sending splinters flying in all directions, leaving him with a hilt and half a foot of broken wood protruding from it.

"Hey! What are you doing?" came the call. It was Captain Asa, supervising the field.

Kenneth turned to him, face impassive. "What does it look like?" The captain spluttered. Kenneth tossed him the sword. "Here, I don't need this."

The captain caught it, looking bewildered. "What?"

Kenneth looked him in the eye, deliberately speaking slowly. "I don't need that."

Captain Asa flushed angrily. "You're a soldier. Of course you need a sword."

"That's not a sword. That's a stick. Tell me. Why have I not been promoted to a more advanced class or rank?" Kenneth's voice was calm and controlled. Nothing indicated that he was angry.

"Don't take that tone with me, recruit!" The captain said, face getting redder. Kenneth merely raised an eyebrow, and the captain coughed, flustered.

"Is there a problem here?" Corporal Luna said as she returned, her long legs carrying her quickly to the situation.

Captain Asa turned. "This recruit destroyed his sword and disobeyed orders!"

Kenneth frowned. "Actually, you didn't order me to do anything. I just asked a question."

He sputtered. "You still destroyed your sword!"

"Be quiet! Both of you!" Corporal Luna said sternly. They both fell silent despite her lower rank, and she looked hard at the two of them before continuing. She turned to Kenneth. "What was your question?"

"Why have I not been promoted to a more advanced class or rank?" Kenneth repeated. "You know I'm wasting my time down here."

She frowned. "Everyone is required to train for several weeks in the lowest rank of the army before being promoted."

Kenneth looked at her. "That's your only reason?" he challenged.

She hesitated, and then sighed. "We also evaluate how well you follow orders and work well with others."

Kenneth smiled grimly. "Your assessment is finished. I don't work well with others. They work well with me." He turned, and walked off, leaving everyone staring after him in astonishment.

"Your report is quite... original, Corporal." The person speaking was an older man sitting at a table, with graying hair and lean muscles hidden in his general's uniform.

"Yes sir," she replied.

"What in the blazes are we going to do with this boy? He has half the recruits riled up and who knows how many more!" interjected another soldier, his uniform bearing the stripes of a Lieutenant General. There were several men around the table, ranging in rank from Second Captain to First General, sitting in their end of day council.

"Well we obviously can't promote him," said one of the generals, "otherwise everyone will think that if they protest their rank, they will get a promotion!" There was a murmur of assent.

The First General stood, silencing them. "Don't be a fool Jacob. The boy is right. He is being wasted as a recruit. I've seen him fight. He's one of the best in the army." Jacob blanched, then muttered quietly under his breath. The general continued, "We will promote him to a Fourth Captain."

The council sat in a shocked silence for several seconds. "What?" Came the strangled question from the group.

The general raised an eyebrow. "The boy said so himself. He doesn't work well with others: they work well with him. He has had past military experience. Some of you don't know this, and I apologize because that is all you will know, all you *need* to know. He will do better in this position. As for the others, we will treat them the same, and soon they will expect nothing to come of their position."

The general turned away, dismissing the gathered men. He sighed, his face grim. "I just hope I don't have to kill him in the end." Only Luna heard him, and she didn't think she was meant to.

Ash drifted in the air, caught in the updraft of the fire, and then fell, slowly settling itself on Kenneth's head. He brushed it off absently, watching the fire as his thoughts reviewed the past day. He was sitting cross-legged on a ledge he had found in the mountainside. It provided a good view of the entire city, and was a fairly easy climb.

The fire burned close by, its color reflecting the orange and red of the sunset. It burned cheerfully, casting a flickering light in a circle as light faded into night.

Kenneth hadn't returned to any future classes. He had gone back to the barracks, packed up his meager supplies and belongings, and moved to the ledge, building the fire out of boredom. Waiting.

"You look ready for battle." Kenneth didn't move, despite not seeing the speaker. He hadn't had anywhere to place his weapons, so he had strapped on all his gear, similar to when he had first arrived, and put his army uniform in a simple sack.

"It depends on what you consider a battle," he replied. He turned his head, watching as Saskia sat beside him. She too, was dressed in full battle regalia. He raised an eyebrow. "What are you fighting?"

She smiled, but didn't answer. "You really upset them." Her voice didn't indicate what she thought of the matter.

"I meant to. They needed upsetting." Kenneth shifted, watching the fire dance on the logs. It was cooler now that the sun had fallen beneath the horizon, the night air tainted with the acrid smell of smoke.

There was a silence as they both watched the fire. "They're going to promote you." Saskia said eventually.

"I know," said Kenneth.

She frowned at him. "How?"

"I knew this would be reported to the person who promotes people. It's not a corporal's decision to promote people; they only recommend the person to their superiors. Therefore it would be taken to someone of high rank and authority. This person would be warned who I was." Kenneth paused.

"So?" Saskia prompted.

"So this person would be the one who ordered them to assess how well I work with others. That would be the only feasible reason why I had not been promoted to the next rank. So I told him." He chuckled.

"Told him what?" Saskia inquired.

"I don't work well with others. They work well with me," Kenneth quoted. "It's a line from a famous general when he was questioned about on how he managed to keep such discipline in his army. He should know the quote, General David is well known. I was saying that I don't work with others, I tell them what to do." Kenneth smiled. "He was bound to understand. He knew I was right, so I effectively forced him to promote me."

Saskia looked at him appraisingly. "How long did it take you to figure all that out?"

Kenneth shrugged. "About ten seconds." At her shocked look, he said, "Remember, I used to be in his position. I know what people request of him, and how he would need to react in certain situations."

Saskia nodded slowly. It made sense. "Even so, I'm impressed." Kenneth looked startled at her admission.

She ignored his look and stood. "We should probably go back."

Kenneth nodded reluctantly and reached towards the fire. He breathed it in with a sigh, and the flames faded briefly and reappeared in his hand, lighting their way.

"Cool," Saskia said appreciatively, "but I can do better." And in saying so, she faded into darkness, leaving only her smile, and then nothing.

Kenneth was guided to the captain's quarters, where he slept a dreamless sleep. He woke as he always did, right before dawn, and dressed in his new uniform that was laid on the floor, strapping his knives underneath his sleeves and his long sword to his belt.

Walking out of the barracks, he jogged over to the general's building. Finding him among his small entourage, he saluted, fist to shoulder, before speaking to the gray-haired man.

"Sir. I appreciate your quick response. What are my daily duties as a Fourth Captain?" One of the officers with the general tried to respond, but the general held up his hand, examining Kenneth with sharp eyes.

He raised his eyebrows, amused. "So you are the boy who knows too much. I am General Burns," When Kenneth didn't respond, he turned to his aide and selected a map, gesturing for Kenneth to come closer.

Spreading the map on the table, the general sat down across from Kenneth. "Tell me," he said, "How would you better defend our position?"

Kenneth frowned looking at the map. It was of the city, with all the fortifications marked. The major roads were all straight lines, providing easy visibility for fighting in the city itself, and the walls of the city ran from one side of the mountain range to the other. Unless armies could climb mountains, they would choose the wall.

He sat down across from the general and picked up a pencil. "If I may?" he inquired.

"Be my guest."

Kenneth started sketching on the map, talking while he worked.

"The mountains on either side of the city provide for an excellent impasse, but they could be used for more. If you had teams dig slightly in the rock to make ledges, you could build wooden fortifications for archers to attack the enemy as they approached." He finished drawing and labeling the area, and moved on to another section.

"Over here, the wall and it's trench will work well to prevent the enemy from advancing over the wall, but if you dig underneath the grounds behind that in large circles and temporarily brace the ground to prevent collapse from usual use, an enemy army would be too much weight. Or you could put explosives down there to blow when they approach. It could take out a regiment or more per section."

Burns nodded, looking intently at the drawings. "Anything else?"

Kenneth shrugged. "Destroy the wall behind you and use it to fortify this one. It only provides the enemy defense against you when they take the city."

The general chuckled. "The wall behind us is so old, if they tried to use it, it would just collapse. Nor will they get that far."

"Why the tactical questions, General?" Kenneth asked, although he thought he knew the answer.

Burns sighed. "I have a feeling we will be in a major battle here shortly. The Fields of Hell have been too quiet lately, and the sky grows dark with evil. It is always better to be prepared for nothing than to not be prepared for disaster when it strikes." He rolled up the map and set it on a shelf, and dismissed the surrounding officers. When they had left, he addressed Kenneth.

"You asked what your duties were? From now on, I want you to oversee the reinforcement of our defenses."

Kenneth looked up at him in shock. "Are you sure that's wise?" The general raised an eyebrow. "Surely you know who I was, and you're still putting me in charge of your defenses?"

The general hesitated. "I've considered those same thoughts all night. But I figure if you're going to betray us, it doesn't matter.

Besides, if you're going to know something, I want to know what it is." And in saying so, he walked inside his building.

Kenneth shrugged and went off to start working.

Explosions

Sophie made her way down the grade school hallways, books in hand, to her locker. She was humming a little tune and had a small smile as she opened her locker, her mind elsewhere.

Her thoughts where directed towards Jackson, a new kid that had recently moved from Washington to their town in Montana.

She blushed when she thought of how cute he was, with his buzzed blond hair and green eyes that seemed to sparkle when he looked at her. At the thought of him in her next class, she brushed her dyed, red hair out of her pale eyes. She was almost in high school; surely her parents would let her accept if he asked her out.

The tone that precluded an announcement buzzed, and Sophie looked up, curious.

The frantic secretary's voice sounded over the intercom, "All students report to—" but was cut off by a terrifying crack of gunshot, and then silence.

Sophie screamed, and wasn't the only one. All around her, students ran to the nearest classroom for safety. Her books were dropped, forgotten in the haste to get to safety.

She turned the corner and ran into Ellie, and they both tumbled over. Wiping her black hair out of her purple eyes, Ellie stood.

Wait, Sophie thought, *purple eyes? Since when have they been purple?* There was no time, though.

Shots rang out again, and Sophie heard screaming, and a horrendous pain in her thigh. She fell again, nearly knocking Ellie over again.

From the ground she saw, through a haze of pain, Ellie running toward the direction of the shots. She tried to call out, to warn her, as she ran, but her voice failed her.

The hallway was nearly empty now, save for the injured or dead lying scattered on the ground. The shooter, a tall man with a shock of brown hair stood with a bemused expression on his face as Ellie approached.

"Release this man!" Ellie yelled, and Sophie groaned in pain, wondering if she was hallucinating. Blood seeped through her fingers as she clutched her thigh, creating a sticky pool around where she lay.

The shooter laughed, pointing his gun at her, and said one word: "Never." His voice sounded like screams forced into a word, and his eyes gleamed red. He pulled the trigger.

Ellie charged him as he looked at his gun in confusion, wondering why it hadn't fired. He dodged out of the way at the last second, dropping the gun and holding his arm where she had cut him with her knife.

"You're Nephilim!" he hissed, and then the knife kissed his throat and he fell, thrashing, to the ground.

Sophie was sure she was dying, the world growing dark as she saw Ellie step away from the corpse.

In the shadow that covered the world, she saw Ellie walk to the center of the hallway, surrounded by those in pain and dying. She knelt, and inhaled sharply, for a brief second surrounded by a nimbus of light.

Sophie's pain washed away, the blood flow slowing, and then stopping as the world returned to its normal color. She shook herself, looking at her now uninjured leg.

Out of the corner of her eye, she saw Ellie stagger and fall. Sophie got up, slightly unsteady, and made her way past shocked and now uninjured students to Ellie.

Ellie groaned, and pushed herself up to one knee, swaying, her face pale.

Sophie found herself staring in wonder, unsure what to say. "How did you do that?" She found herself stammering. Ellie looked at her and sighed, shaking her head.

"I was never here, understand?" Sophie looked at her, confused, and called after her as she ran.

"Where are you going?"

She never got an answer.

Kenneth made his way past the barracks and training field to a small building that was painted the courier's white. He shouldered his way inside the crowded room, looking for a spare man. After a moment, he walked to an open booth. Inside was a sergeant of high rank. His lapel indicated he was first-class.

Kenneth leaned in so the man could hear his orders. "I need every unassigned fire and earth elementalist to meet at the front gate, as well as a mining crew and a group of engineers and carpenters. They are to report there immediately."

The man squinted up at him. "I know you. You're that insolent kid who thinks he can waltz his way to the top ranks. Forget it kid. I'm not following your orders." He grunted and moved to turn away, but Kenneth caught his arm. He had met this man before, he was sure. In the bar, spewing his drink on his friends.

"When you converted, did they not advance your rank to what you were in the Fallen after they had made sure you were actually on their side?" Kenneth hissed, catching the man by surprise.

The sergeant turned back to him, his beady eyes looking Kenneth up and down. "A convert, eh? How do I know you aren't lying, boy?" Kenneth extended his hand, and the man took it.

Kenneth activated their rank with a soft snapping sound that was reminiscent of an electrical shock. The other man's mark sparked to life, as well as Kenneth's own, but only to their eyes.

The sergeant's mark swirled around his hand and up to his elbow, indicating he had been a third-class Sergeant before he had left the Fallen. As he looked at Kenneth, his jaw dropped. Kenneth's mark spread across the entirety of his body in a terrifyingly beautiful tattoo that pulsed with magic.

The sergeant released Kenneth's hand like it was a viper and grabbed a sheet of paper. "Elementalists, you said? And miners with engineers and woodworkers?" Kenneth nodded, and the sergeant saluted. "Right away sir. Anything else I can do?"

Kenneth shook his head, and the man scurried off. It appeared he had intimidated the man a little more than he had meant to. He shrugged and left the building, heading toward the gate. It was not long before a small group had gathered there.

Kenneth drew their attention to him with a small explosion of fire, quieting them instantly. "General Burns has instructed me to better fortify our defenses. Any person that is a woodworker or engineer, you must review these designs and see if you can translate them into the mountain." He handed the sheaf of papers he had drawn up the previous night to a sturdy man carrying a theodolite, tripods, and other surveying and carpentry equipment.

"Those who are miners or elementalists, you and I will be hollowing out the area underneath the fields of Hell," he said, gesturing behind him. "I will need the miners and earth elementalists to find a good entrance area, as well as make the decisions on what rock to take out. We are attempting to make an area that we can force to collapse when the enemy draws too close." Heads nodded, and a young man with golden eyes stepped forward.

"What will the fire elementalists be doing, sir?" he asked, saluting.

Kenneth smiled. "What we do best, of course. We will be blowing things up." A small cheer went up at that, and the young man thanked him with a flash of a grin. Kenneth then showed them how to make magical explosives that didn't constantly draw on their energy, and would be activated when a specific magical pulse was sent out.

The group set off excitedly, the earth elementalists and miners already arguing on where to start, and the fire elementalists shooting sparks at each other.

"Captain Kenneth?" called a voice, and Kenneth turned.

"Saskia!" Kenneth said in surprise as she informally saluted him, fist over heart. "You're a higher rank than me, you don't need to salute me!"

She laughed. "I know, but it was fun." She walked over to him, watching the group walk into the distance. "How are things going?"

Kenneth shrugged. "They've barely started." At her nod he looked at her. "Did you need something?"

She nodded. "I wanted to let you know that I'm free tonight, if you want to practice again."

Kenneth smiled. "Good. I want to try something new. When shall I meet you there?"

Saskia twirled her black hair around her finger. "Around twenty-one hundred I think," she said. Kenneth saluted sharply, a slight smile on his face.

"At your command, so do I obey," he said with mock seriousness. As she left, he turned back to his workers. Soon explosions echoed through the fortress, shaking the earth as they hollowed out the ground.

Nora was sweating freely, dark beads rolling down her face and soaking her shiny black hair. She licked her lips nervously, hands clasped behind her back to stop them from fiddling.

Lord Iephus paced in front of her, ignoring the guards that stood on either side of her. He looked completely calm, but urgency could be seen in his steps. He stopped abruptly, turning to face her.

"You request more time. I've given you time. Three days, in fact. And still you sit here, telling me that you are nearly there, nearly in position. I think you're lying," His voice was carefully controlled, but madness burned in his eyes.

"I do not lie." Hundreds of years of training kept her voice steady and her composure sure, but inside she was a tempest. "I need but twenty-seven more hours. Barely more than a day."

Lord Iephus's eyes glittered like the black armor that he wore. "Is that so? And why should I believe you? Give me one reason not to kill you right now." His voice was like shattered ice.

Desperately, Nora carefully lowered the barrier in her mind that prevented him from seeing her thoughts, unveiling a single memory, thought, and idea. She could feel him read it immediately, and suddenly he was calm.

"So she proved more difficult than you thought. You need more time to break her," Iephus mused. "Why not kill her?"

"She loves him. Even though she is a traitor, she will join the Fallen to stay with him," Nora explained.

Iephus nodded slowly. "How do you know for sure?"

Nora smiled a razor smile. She was back in control. "The strongest chains are always forged by love."

She could see that he agreed. He turned away from her, pulling a rope that hung by his desk. "Very well. You will have your twenty-seven hours," he said, and she smiled. Victory.

"But," he continued, and her smile faded, "You will stay here." At her confused look, he elaborated. "Not all of you, of course. Your mind will be free, as only you know how." A servant appeared, and he turned. "Ah. Inform the Draekos that we have someone for them," he commanded.

Nora was screaming before their pale, lifeless hands even touched her.

"This is the entrance?" General Burns asked, and Kenneth nodded.

"One of a couple. This was the first we opened, however," he informed him, and the general nodded, examining it thoughtfully before entering into the cave. They walked down a narrow staircase for several seconds before it opened up into an enormous cavern.

"Darkness and chaos," the general muttered, "You've only been at this a single day, and you've got it this big?" The cavern extended nearly a mile in every direction, and was about one hundred feet in height. Large columns of stone supported the ceiling, and the ground was even and smooth.

"Its amazing what miners can do with earth elementalists, sir. We also had the fire elementalists use their powers to explode large sections of rock at a time," Kenneth said. "We placed charges in every column. At a certain magical frequency, every charge will go off, collapsing the land above us."

The general shook his head. "This is deadly. What we needed, but deadly. I pity those poor fools when they attack us in large force. Continue your work. If my mental math is correct, you have only a couple miles left before the entire entrance is hollow." Kenneth nodded, and they left the cave.

He left the general after asking his leave, and checked the time. It was nearly nine. Perfect. He jogged through the city toward the cavern that Saskia had shown him several days before.

He hadn't gone far before he realized he was being followed, and not by Saskia. He turned an unnecessary corner, and spotted the group. He thought he recognized them, but it was too dark to be sure.

He turned another corner and swore. Two men were coming down the street, and they didn't look like they wanted to let him pass. He glanced behind him, and the group had caught up to him. They must have run.

He walked toward the two on the other side of the alley slowly. It wasn't long before he confirmed who they were. "Really Jarrod?" he asked loudly, and one of them jerked. "You couldn't beat me during the day, so you attack me at night?"

Jarrod stepped forward. "This isn't revenge. This is putting you in your rightful place. Who do you think you are, demanding to be elevated in rank?" he challenged, and Kenneth didn't answer.

Jarrod unsheathed his sword, and Kenneth mirrored his action, praying he wouldn't have to kill him. "You don't want to do this," he warned him, "I don't want to hurt you."

Jarrod laughed. "The only one who is going to hurt at the end of this is you." He walked forward, sword raised, and then retched and fell to his knees.

"I don't think so," came Saskia's voice, and all of a sudden Jarrod and his friends were running from something Kenneth couldn't see. They rounded the corner, and Kenneth turned to face her.

"That was good timing. I thought I was going to have to kill him," Kenneth told her. She nodded.

"Thankfully it didn't come to that," she said, and he followed her as they traveled to the cave.

"What brought you into my spat with Jarrod?" Kenneth asked as they walked.

"You were late," she said, causing him to glance at his watch. "I came to formally reprimand you."

Kenneth raised an eyebrow. "Indeed?" Saskia nodded. "Well then, I hope being attacked was excuse enough for being late."

She chuckled. "You don't have a very good history with alleyways anyway."

Kenneth thought of Richard. "Agreed," he muttered.

They entered the cave, Kenneth throwing his ball of fire to illuminate the cavern. They resumed their previous stance, facing each other across the rocky expanse. "You said you wanted to try something new?" Saskia prompted.

"Oh yeah," Kenneth said, remembering his idea. "Start with a…less intense fear." She nodded, and he readied himself. She closed her eyes, and brought one of his fears to life.

He squinted, and…there! He could only see the edges of the magic, but it was definitely there. He ignored the coalescing shape in front of him and felt at the magic with his mind. It was like an intricate web, spidering across between him and her.

Now came the chance. What if he changed it? He gingerly released power into the web, altering it slightly.

The daemon that had appeared vanished in fire, causing both him and Saskia to jump back, startled. She looked at him in shock. "How did you do that?" she said, thoroughly unnerved.

Kenneth shook his head. "I'm not sure," he lied, "Can we try another?"

She nodded, throwing out her hand. This time frost filled the room. He knew what was coming. Only one thing he feared involved cold. The web was back, slightly different, humming with power.

Again there was the web, intertwining the two of them, pulsing around Lord Blaze's body. He took a step forward, and Kenneth took a step back, feeling at the web. It was connected to him in several areas. What if he cut it off him?

The web snapped back as he severed the lines of energy that connected to him, spinning and reversing themselves. Suddenly it was not Lord Blaze, but Kenneth, lying on the ground, dying from a wound in the neck.

Kenneth looked at himself, and then back at the Kenneth dying on the floor, and finally at Saskia. She ended the spell almost immediately, her face extremely pale. She sat, her legs unsteady. Kenneth walked forward and sat beside her.

"I think we're done for tonight," he said quietly, and she nodded, trembling. He looked at the area were he had lain, dying. "That was your fear," he said wonderingly. She nodded again.

"I thought I had killed you. Then I realized the spell was still activated," she whispered. "How did you...I've never..." Her voice trailed off.

"I'm not quite an Opseer," Kenneth explained, "but I can feel magic in its energetic base. I cut your magic off of me, so it reversed itself. I didn't realize what would happen." She nodded, controlling herself with deep breaths. After a moment she stood, wobbling a little, and walked outside. He followed her, concerned.

She sat on the ledge overlooking the city, and he joined her. To his surprise, she leaned against him. "Your freezing!" he exclaimed softly, and he put his arm around her. Holding his hand out, he exhaled slowly, and flames spiraled off his arm and hovered, burning in front of the two of them.

"Thanks," Saskia whispered, and he smiled at her.

"We should probably get back. The night lasts only so long, and we need sleep," he said reluctantly. Saskia shivered.

"Sleep," she muttered, her eyes haunted. "I haven't slept well since we left Montana." Kenneth nodded.

"Nightmares?" he asked. She nodded. "Same here. Always about Hell. We're too close to it." He gazed into the distance, where lightning flickered across dark sky.

He didn't mention his most recent nightmare. It was always the same, ready whenever he closed his eyes. Of Lord Blaze regaining control of his body in truth, killing his newfound friends and forsaking love. He felt himself grow cold at the thought, and Saskia stirred beside him.

"What's wrong?" she asked, pulling away from him.

"Nothing," he lied, "I'm fine." She sniffed. "We should head back anyway."

"I'm not moving until you tell me what's bothering you," she said stubbornly.

Kenneth smiled a sad smile, watching the flickering flames hovering in front of them. "Then stay," he said quietly. She leaned back into him, and he replaced his arm around her.

They stayed that way until dawn came.

The Knife of Betrayal

Kenneth was surveying the work of the carpenters as they attempted to wedge the wooden palisades to the sheer walls of the mountain.

It looked as though it would work. He gave them permission to test one, and walked on, intending to refill his canteen. It was a hot day, and the sun beat down on everyone harshly. The infirmaries had several come in because of dehydration, and there had been a statement released about drinking water.

For Kenneth, it felt amazing. The heat seemed to energize and invigorate him. He wasn't even sweating. The underground work was even hotter, and the fire elementalists were working with a passion, empowered by the heat that smothered everyone else.

Filling his canteen, he stoppered it and turned.

"Saskia," he noted, "what brings you here?"

She raised an eyebrow. "Maybe I am seeking to refill my water, as you just did."

"Ah, but yours is already full," he said, grinning, "I saw you fill it not twenty minutes ago when I was talking to the general."

She smiled. "Your skills of observation remain unparalleled. General Burns asked me to show you something that he said 'might give them a stumble'. He told me where it was, but I'm as curious as you are to what it is. Shall we travel?"

Kenneth nodded and followed her as she made her way to the front gates. There, Kali, Flammeth, and Aelex were waiting.

Saskia answered his question before he asked it. "General Burns thought that their particular savylus would help. Again, I don't know why."

Kenneth greeted them, shaking Flammeth's hand, and getting pulled into a back pounding hug by Aelex. Kenneth stepped back, feeling rumpled, and nodded to Kali, who was watching, arms folded.

He froze unexpectedly, noticing a soldier in the background watching him. He was leaned up against the wall, clearly resting, his spear lying beside him. Nothing was abnormal about him; he was mildly short, and had blonde hair and bright blue eyes, but Kenneth felt as though he had seen him before.

Saskia coughed. He turned to her, mind back in the present, looking slightly abashed. They set off at a light jog, rounding the side of the mountains to an area below a ledge.

"It's on the ledge," Saskia called, and started climbing. Kenneth shrugged and joined her. It wasn't a hard climb, and they made it to the top in less than a minute.

It was a small ledge, barely ten feet in length, but abnormally flat. He looked around it and frowned, wondering what it could be used for. It was too far from their defenses to be used for an archer's outpost.

He turned to Saskia and opened his mouth to ask a question, but paused. Her normally dark colored eyes were a bright scarlet red.

"What's the matter with your eyes?" he said suspiciously.

She turned away from him and pointed at Kali. *"Necto."* Ropes appeared and wrapped themselves around Kali. She yelped and struggled, falling over.

Flammeth looked at her in shock before growling, his voice deepening, his body growing larger, hands morphing into paws, fur sprouting, until he was an ice tiger in all its strength.

"Desiit" Saskia snapped, and there was a popping sound, and Flammeth fell to the ground, stunned, his normal self once more.

Turning, she thrust her hand forward, fingers splayed, and said, *"Caedo."* as Aelex charged at her, sword raised. He stumbled and fell to his knees, looking up at her in disbelief. Blood fountained from his mouth, and he collapsed.

Kenneth watched in horror as a person he had just begun to trust systematically incapacitated his friends. This was not the magic of fear. This was dark magic, magic he knew that he had next to no chance in overcoming in his current state.

Running, he launched himself off the ledge, slapping the ground and rolling to break his fall. He ran, heart pounding, and he heard Saskia shout something at him. He glanced behind him, and threw out a hand towards the mountain.

The temperature around him dropped, the few water molecules in the air freezing as heat rushed into him, and then washed from his fingers into the rock, melting it behind him. It fountained from the side of the mountain, leaving a pool of spreading magma nearly fifty feet in diameter underneath the ledge, preventing her from following him.

He continued to run, his armor crackling as crystals of ice fell off of him and melted. He now understood what Gabriel had meant about his armor absorbing better. With the amount of heat he had transferred, a thinner suit of armor would have melted. As it was, the one he was wearing had come close.

He continued running back towards the gates, but hadn't gone far before a scraping sound was made behind him and he whirled, ready. Something flashed past his face, and he fell, head ringing, to the ground. He rolled, throwing a knife at his attacker.

It was a bad throw. Saskia flinched as it slammed into her temple, hilt first. Her red eyes flickered, briefly flashing brown. She struggled to raise an arm.

"Don't be a fool," she hissed, and darkness enclosed him.

Kenneth sat up, holding his head. He was by a fire; its cheerful flames were dancing on the floor of a cave.

"He wakes," came a strangely accented voice, and Kenneth turned. It was Saskia, standing at the entrance to the cave.

He tried to summon fire, but it was like dipping himself in sludge, sickening him. He retched and sat back, gasping.

"I wouldn't do that. We gave you a potion that prevents you from using your savylus." She walked over to him and sat across from him, cross-legged, like so many other times.

He looked at her with hatred. "What have you done?"

"Saskia has done nothing," She said, looking up at him with scarlet eyes.

His eyes narrowed. "Nora," he hissed.

Nora nodded, amused. "She didn't know what she was doing. She does now, unfortunately, so she can prevent me from doing anything she doesn't want, but it is still I who controls who is on the surface."

She blinked, and her eyes faded to a dark brown. "Kenneth!" Saskia said, accent gone.

"Kenneth, I'm so sorry!" she started again, her eyes shining with unshed tears, but Kenneth shook his head and silenced her.

"What is done is done. You were not under control of yourself. How much control do you have now?"

Saskia sat back. "I can stop her from doing anything I want her to. I just needed to know she was there. Your knife brought me back enough to eventually regain control." She gestured to a bruise on the side of her head.

Kenneth nodded. "I would like to speak with her." She nodded, and blinked again, eyes once more filled with red.

"You would speak with me, hmm? Tell me *Lord Blaze*, how much do you remember?" The lilting voice was back.

Kenneth grimaced, unwilling to answer.

"You don't remember anything? We thought you were acting. Pity, else my plan would have worked perfectly." Nora seemed almost amused by the thought.

He looked at her. "Why have you possessed Saskia?"

She sighed. "It's quite simple, actually. I was ordered to retrieve you by a mutual friend. When I located where you were, I took control of this girl's body to find out how I could get you out of there. That was annoyingly tedious. She is so good with her mind. When the time came, I attempted return you to the Fallen, but you resisted."

"I might not have if you hadn't attacked my friends!"

She clucked. "Really. Well I was ordered to bring some of them as well. Besides, they would have been the first to notice that you were gone. I couldn't have that…"

Kenneth shook his head in anger. "Well you can leave Saskia now."

"No, actually I can't. You see, Iephus has stolen my original body," Nora almost succeeded in hiding the tension that she felt.

Kenneth sat back. "What?" he said, startled.

"He stole my body and placed an enchantment on it that prevents me from returning. He will only release it when you return."

Kenneth's face was grim. "Then we will return. But only to release my friends and obtain your body."

Nora tried to speak, but Kenneth interrupted her.

"No arguments. You are not in an area to bargain. Clearly Saskia has control over you now, since I am not currently in the Fallen Ranks." She subsided, and Kenneth continued. "You told me my sword is at Nil'honderal."

"I did," she answered warily.

"We are going to retrieve it."

"It will not be easy," she warned.

"I expected that. We will leave in the morning."

When morning dawned, Kenneth was already awake, packed and ready. He had made a quick run into the city during the night, changing into his scouting armor and retrieving the rest of his weapons. He had two knives up his sleeves, and one at his belt, opposite his dagger, and a sword belted at his left side and on a baldric across his back.

Saskia woke as the sun rose, just as Kenneth moved to wake her. She glanced up, brown eyes taking in his form.

"Got enough sharp edges?" she asked wryly, but Kenneth could sense the sadness that enveloped her.

He grunted and handed her what he retrieved from her rooms.

She smiled humorlessly as he turned his back, allowing her to change into her armor and weapons. She had a long sword and several knives, but otherwise was weaponless.

When she had finished changing, they left the cave. Its entrance came out facing the Plains of Hell, about fifty feet from the ground.

When they reached the bottom, he turned to Saskia. "Nora, I believe you can take us there using transdimensional location."

"Now how did you know I could do that?" she asked, eyes burning to scarlet.

Kenneth raised an eyebrow. "I guessed."

She chuckled, realizing she had been manipulated into admitting she had that skill.

"Hold on tight, this isn't pleasant," She warned, grabbing on to his arm. He gripped her forearm tightly, almost hard enough to hurt.

She seemed to twist away from him, her form wavering on the edge of perception, and then disappearing. He redoubled his grip, and the world disappeared into darkness.

He felt nothing, thought nothing, knew nothing. He *was* nothing. Endless time passed.

A thought broke through. A name. Kenneth. His name.

Feeling returned in a rush of prickles, bringing the awareness of his hand, tightly gripping something. Another hand.

Sight returned. Then full awareness crashed into Kenneth, and he released Saskia's hand, and fell to his knees.

He stood, unsteady, and promptly threw up.

"Gross," Nora remarked. He ignored her, and wiped his mouth on his sleeve.

He raised his eyes, taking in the change of terrain. They were in a small grove of dying trees, the stench of rotting leaves suffusing the air.

The sky was an angry red, with black clouds streaking across its expanse. Kenneth turned, and through the dying branches he could see black spires winding towards the sky.

They headed towards the spires with a silent grace, making their way carefully through the forest. It took them less than ten minutes before they were at the edge of a clearing.

The area was almost a perfect circle surrounded by dead and dying trees, and crackling brown grass. In the center was a cathedral, its walls and turrets covered in sinister runes and statues. It was, Kenneth thought with a quiet amusement, quiet as a grave.

"It's a damned cathedral," Saskia whispered. He nodded. "I've only heard of them."

Kenneth grimaced. "Four hundred years ago, six hundred and sixty six people committed suicide in this building to empower it with darkly divine powers. Their dead bodies and other powers of the shadow protect the many magical artifacts it contains."

Saskia shivered. "How do we get in?"

"We knock," Kenneth answered, and he strode out of the forest, all attempts of hiding gone. He ignored Saskia as she hissed at him to stop, and walked to the front doors.

The doors were massive; nearly fifteen feet tall, made of thick steel, and imbued with spells and enchantments of protection.

Reaching towards the center, Kenneth took hold of a skull knocker, and brought it down, hard.

The skull made a sharp pealing sound that lingered in the air for too long, and mist coalesced around the cathedral.

Kenneth turned, and watched as the mist slowly swirled and merged into men and women in robes, each with a bloody stab wound over their heart. Their eyes were closed.

Kenneth allowed his mark of rank to appear, its form snaking over his body. Reveling in the power that came with it, he stepped forward, speaking with authority.

"I claim right of passage according to the order of the Semiaza. I claim right of passage for what is rightfully mine. I claim passage under the name of the Fallen Star, whom I serve." His voice echoed eerily in the darkness.

There was a soft susurration amongst the dead and they faded with the wind, blowing away into the night. Kenneth turned towards the doors as the swung open silently, and entered the darkness within.

Into the Land of Fire

Gabriel frowned. "What do you mean, missing?" He was standing, his arms clasped behind his back, his large sword belted to his waist.

Gimelli shrugged. "They are no longer in Güderam. None of them. They left to do something—my informant wouldn't get any closer to hear what though. They were on the side near hell. Bad for birds. They didn't return, and now it's been over a day. The army should start searching for them soon, but my dispatch should return shortly with more news." Despite his cringing demeanor, his voice was strong, his French accent slurring his speech slightly.

Gabriel nodded thoughtfully. "Very well. You are dismissed. Thank you for the news." Gimelli merely nodded, shuffling out of the room, muttering to himself in French.

"This is dire news," Yigil said, stepping out of the shadows as he closed the door.

Gabriel nodded. "I wish I knew if he has betrayed us. Ken—*Lord Blaze* could be deadly with the inside information that he now knows. If—" He froze, looking up at Yigil.

She nodded. "He's here. And not alone."

Less than a minute later, Gabriel walked into the upper room.

Kenneth turned. "Ah, Gabriel. I was wondering where you'd be."

Gabriel eyes probed the room. "If Saskia wasn't here with you now, you would be in a great deal of trouble." He walked to the center, pulled up a chair and sat at the table. "Explain," he said.

Kenneth sat as well, and motioned for Saskia to sit. "We may be here a while." He said.

"You will hear an explanation, but not from me," Kenneth said, and held up a hand to forestall him. "Nora, if you would."

Gabriel turned, eyes narrowing. "Nora?" he hissed.

Saskia's brown eyes burned to a scarlet red. "Sorry Gabby, but I'm to old for you."

He growled, a menacing sound. "Be glad Yigil does not know you're here."

Kenneth frowned. "Why would..." His face cleared. "Ah. Of course. She is Shalbriri."

Gabriel swung to face him. "She no longer goes by that name."

"Or that gender apparently. He was looking quite masculine when I left," Nora broke in.

Kenneth silenced everyone with the crack of his palm on the table. "You are not stupid Nora. Angels have no gender. Now explain why you and I are here, and why I am not trying to kill you right now."

Nora shrugged. "I actually don't know why we are precisely *here*, but I will explain how we got into this situation." She pointed at Kenneth. "I was sent to retrieve his location. When I found him, I was told to retrieve him."

"And your 'orders' were from whom?" Gabriel inquired, although he was sure he knew the answer.

"Iephus, of course," Nora answered. "Anyway, I was also told that if I could capture Kali and Flammeth, I would be rewarded. Since Aelex was their closest friend between the two of them, he had to be neutralized so he wouldn't immediately notice they were missing."

"Neutralized?" Gabriel said menacingly.

Kenneth looked sad. "He's dead," he said quietly.

Gabriel shook his head despondently. "Continue."

Nora nodded. "It all went swimmingly, except for one thing. He actually does not have all his memories. Therefore he did not willingly come with me like I thought he would."

Kenneth coughed. "You seem to have skipped over the part where Iephus stole your body and you took possession of Saskia."

Nora bared her teeth. "I try not to dwell on it."

Gabriel's eyes narrowed at Kenneth's. "We need to talk. Alone."

Kenneth looked at Nora. "I need Saskia now." She nodded, scarlet eyes fading.

"Saskia, would you be so kind as to guard the perimeter while Gabriel and I speak alone?"

Saskia nodded. "Certainly."

Gabriel watched her go. When she was gone, he turned to face Kenneth, fingers steepled in front of him.

"I think I know what your wondering," Kenneth said quietly.

Gabriel raised an eyebrow. "Oh?" was all he said.

"How much do I remember?" Kenneth asked. At Gabriel's nod, he elaborated. "I remember bits and pieces of everything. I know all of my training, even if I do not remember every instance of training. But the major portion I don't remember is being Semiaza."

"But that's still probably not what you're wondering. How much do I remember of Gabriel of the Second Light, First General of the Legion of the Light, a member of the Raguel Core, Personal Guard, Advisor, and friend to the Exalted himself? The man who earned a medal of heroism for saving the Exalted's life, and who, for some reason, has managed to tick off the Fallen Ranks so much they have a standing reward for his death, but I don't know why? And all before you turned twenty-five, I might add."

Gabriel shrugged. "The past is the past."

Kenneth shook his head. "Why would you be here, in this little hole of a city, protecting it from the occasional demon on rampage, instead of fulfilling your duty in an army?"

Gabriel shook his head. "I do not see why it matters."

"Then let me say two words to change your mind. Temporal shift." Gabriel's face didn't change.

They sat, staring at each other, neither breaking eye contact, until eventually Gabriel sighed and stood.

"Follow me," He said. He led Kenneth down the stairs to the library. Opening the door, he led him to where he had been once before, while being interrogated by Yigil.

He closed the door and turned. "What tipped you off?" he asked.

Kenneth smiled. "I guessed." It wasn't entirely true. He had come to the conclusion shortly after visiting the damned cathedral.

"That's a hell of a guess." Gabriel grumbled. "Fine," he said, "I was granted the ability of creating a planar passage within the grounds of this city. We chose this city *because* it is a hole, and no one would suspect. It is also in an area where the world borders are thin. I chose the tree to try to throw you off, but I guess it didn't matter. Now, since you brought this up, you want to go somewhere. Because some friends of ours have recently been captured, I can guess where."

Kenneth nodded, his face like stone. "Hell. The Fallen Fortress."

Gabriel shook his head in disbelief. "And how are you going to get them out?"

Kenneth's smile was razor sharp. "I've got some ideas," he said, laying a hand on the sword at his waist.

Gabriel shook his head. "Ideas aren't going to cut it."

"Then what about this?" Kenneth said, and he unsheathed a sword at his waist.

Its hilt and scabbard were wrapped in leather, but the blade gave off a soft blue glow, filling the room with its luminescence. Its blade was inscribed with runes, swirling, repeating the same word over and over.

"*Frost*," Gabriel breathed, eyes wide.

Kenneth sheathed it and the light disappeared. "Wrapped in leather, it should look like a normal sword until I need it. And yes, I do remember how to use it."

Gabriel shook his head in disbelief. "How did you get it? Where did you get it?"

"Saskia and I took a visit to Nil'honderal."

Gabriel frowned. "The damned cathedral? You just walked in and took it? Are you insane?"

Kenneth shrugged. "Does it matter?"

Gabriel looked to the side. "Nora and Saskia is going with you?" Kenneth nodded. "Don't trust them. Saskia will still be under the influence of Nora, and I think you remember plenty about Nora." Kenneth nodded again in agreement.

"I can take you to the gates. Even that will be dangerous."

"I live for dangerous."

Father Nathaniel was cleaning up the church after Saturday evening mass when he heard the church doors open. It was not uncommon for people to come in after services and ask questions, so he thought nothing of it. He merely finished putting out the candles and went to greet whoever had entered.

It was a small family, the parents leading a slender girl down the aisle, maybe fourteen years old. He greeted them with a wave and walked toward them. As he got closer he noticed the girl wasn't slim, she was *skinny*. Clothes hung loosely on her frame, and her arms and legs were devoid of any fat, and had little muscle.

Tearing his eyes away from the girl, he listened to the father, who was speaking in broken English.

"Mi hija, she is not well," he said, gesturing to his daughter. Father Nathaniel had to agree.

"I am not a doctor," he started, but the man interrupted him.

"No es medico, sí. We saw doctors. They no help. She be sick in the spirit," he said, gesturing wildly.

"How—" Father Nathaniel began, and stopped as the girl looked up, eyes boring into his.

"Él no gusta lo aqui. Irámos!" she said slowly, rising to a shout on the last word.

The man looked strained. "No."

The girl shook her head and repeated, "Irámos!"

The man looked at Nathaniel imploringly. "Padre, por favor, take the demon out of her. It is killing her."

Father Nathaniel stared in disbelief. "I'm not an exorcist, but I can give her a blessing..." He said weakly.

The man nodded vigorously. "Blessing, sí. Do this thing."

"Bring her before the altar," Father Nathaniel said, and he went back to grab his blessing bucket full of holy water.

When he returned, the girl was standing before the altar, looking at the ground, her parents on either side of her.

He walked down the first couple of steps and brought out the holy water.

"Do you understand English?" he asked the girl quietly. She nodded, never raising her head.

"Then you know what I say, when I bless you, in the name of the Father," he said, sprinkling holy water on her, but his voice faltered as she wrenched backward, her voice deepening as she swore.

"Él no gusta eso," she said, squinting up at him. *He does not like that.* Nathaniel felt goose bumps ripple up his arms. She seemed unable to look at him, and as he prepared to continue, he noticed it was not him, but the crucifix on his chest that she was unable to gaze at.

He continued with the blessing, and she hissed the second and the third time the water touched her, but did not move.

The father thanked him, and they left, looking hopeful.

Turning, he fell before the cross and prayed.

The world flashed white, and Kenneth hit the ground with force, bringing him to one knee.

He stood as heat washed over him, strengthening him, revitalizing him.

There was a pop, and Saskia appeared beside him. He caught her as she nearly fell, and when she had righted herself, he turned and surveyed the land.

"Holy, Mother of God," Saskia whispered quietly.

Kenneth agreed. The Fallen's capital fortress was massive, extending as far as the eye could see. The keep in the center rose with black spires into the clouds, and men in black armor strode around the forbidding walls, keeping watch.

There was a shout, and Kenneth nodded. They were in the middle of the road, easily spotted. The fact that they had appeared out of nowhere made it rather suspicious.

He turned to Saskia. "Say nothing until I get him to take us somewhere private." She nodded, nervous. He had instructed Nora earlier to not surface unless he asked her to.

A soldier approached. "State your names and business."

Kenneth looked at the man's rank. He was a simple private. It would not do.

"I will only speak to your sergeant. Until you bring us to him, I will say nothing. Attempt to attack us, and we will kill you for your stupidity."

The man paled as he caught a glimpse of Kenneth's face. "Yes milord," he muttered, bowing slightly, and led them into the city. He brought them through the walls into a small tower. They went up a flight of stairs, and stopped at a door.

The soldier knocked and let them in.

"What in the blazes—?" came a voice, and a bearded man turned. His eyes took in Kenneth and Saskia's hooded forms, and he said, "Gavin, what are you doing?"

Kenneth turned. "Leave us. Tell no one what you've done." The soldier nodded and left, closing the door.

"What are you doing, ordering around my soldiers?" the man demanded.

Kenneth flipped back his hood, revealing his face.

The man gasped and fell to one knee. "My Lord Blaze! We thought you were dead!"

Kenneth nodded. "I am dead. You never met me. In fact, no one ever came through the gates at this time." The man nodded several times.

"What will you do?" the man asked, curious, and then at Kenneth's stare he blanched and mumbled, "Forgive me, my lord."

They left the man, still kneeling, Kenneth pulling his hood back up to hide his face.

"Won't we be conspicuous with our hoods up?" Saskia asked quietly.

"No. There are many fiends here ugly enough to hide their faces in public. We will be noticed, but not questioned," Kenneth answered, just as quietly.

They exited the tower, walking slowly down the street. As he had predicted, few people noticed them, and they slipped through the crowd with little resistance. It was nearing night, and Kenneth led them to a back alleyway.

"Night lasts for sixteen hours here," he explained, "in this, we have the advantage."

Using numerous handholds on the walls of the alleyway, they scaled a building.

The massive Keep loomed above them, countless flashes of fire illuminating the dark clouds around it.

"They'll have put them in the dungeons," he said quietly. "We have to break into the Keep."

Saskia laughed quietly. "That's all?"

Kenneth turned toward her and shrugged. "We might have to get past a couple of guards too."

He returned her smile, and they loped into the night, jumping from rooftop to rooftop, carefully making their way to the Keep.

The buildings ended several hundred feet away from the Keep, and they slid to the ground carefully.

"Now what?" Saskia asked quietly.

Kenneth shook his head. "Nora?" he asked reluctantly.

"I often go through an abandoned storage room. The guards there can't see as you climb the tower." She answered in her lilted accent.

Kenneth nodded, eyes narrowing. "Show me."

She led him around the keep for some time, until they reached one of the northern towers.

"I hope you're a good climber," she warned, scaling the wall. Kenneth followed close behind, taking careful note of where she put her hands and feet.

Eventually she paused, about a hundred feet in the air. Kenneth stayed as still as he could beneath her, fingers silently aching from the climb.

Seemingly satisfied with something he couldn't see, she took a small knife and carefully pried open the window pane and crawled through. Kenneth followed carefully, dropping the few feet to the floor as she replaced the pane.

He said nothing, afraid of being heard, and moved towards the door. Nora crept toward it as well, and after briefly shutting her eyes, opened it with confidence.

The hallway it opened to was empty. Nora turned to the right, and Kenneth followed, unsure where they were in the Keep.

They walked for a time, eventually coming to two large, ornate doors.

"I don't think—" Kenneth said, but was cut off as she threw the doors open, and Kenneth found himself staring in the eyes of Lord Iephus, Semiaza of the Fallen.

Darkness Descending

"You did well," Iephus said, eyes glinting, "very well. I will see that your body is disenchanted and returned to you. Your payment will be in your pocket. Now leave me with him." Lord Iephus was tall, dressed all in black, a uniform similar to Kenneth's. His mark stood out starkly against his pale skin, blending in with his obsidian hair.

Nora bowed and left Kenneth, who was staring in shock.

"Please, sit down," Iephus said, gesturing to the couches in the corner of the room. Seeing no other option, he sat.

"I have been told you remember nothing, or little of your past." Kenneth nodded.

"Do you remember what my savyl is?" he asked, sitting down.

At his question, memories flurried in Kenneth's head. He suppressed most of them, and focused on the answer.

"Trick question. You have multiple. Four, to be precise. I believe you can read thoughts and memories, steal memories, see, touch, taste, feel, and smell what the person smells, and can control lesser people's minds with your own," he said, ticking them off one by one on his finger.

Lord Iephus smiled. "Excellent. Now how would that be useful to you?"

Kenneth thought for several long seconds. "Can you insert memories *into* my head? Memories of myself from you?"

"You always were intelligent," Iephus said, grinning. "In answer to your question, yes. But you will have to let me. You have always had a unusually strong mind."

Kenneth hesitated. Seeing himself from Iephus's point of view would bring back almost all, if not all, of his previous memories. Even if he were to still attempt escape, the memories would be quite advantageous.

"You have my permission." As the last word left his lips, the world faded into darkness.

Patrik lay in a bloody heap, miserable and bruised, at the feet of the inspector of the week. He had not liked that Patrick could tell what he thought of them, and liked less what he had inspected. His rage had killed three people already, and he was going to be the fourth.

The man raised his sword, a smile tugging on his lips, mocking. He spun it from hand to hand, and Patrik closed his eyes, willing it to end.

There was a sickening sound, followed by a scream. Patrik wondered if it was himself.

But when he opened his eyes, the inspector lay dead on the ground, a child no older than he wiping his small blade on his shirt.

"Who are you?" he croaked, voice cracking. The kid regarded him warily.

"An orphan, like yourself." He helped him up.

Patrik felt for his mind, but found himself blocked. He wondered at it; he had never found a mind as strong as this. "What is your name?" He'd never had to ask that question before.

"Trade," Said the boy with a smile. So he wasn't stupid.

"Mine is Iephus," he said. It meant Knife of the Mind.

The kid chuckled. He knew it wasn't his birth name. It didn't matter. Patrik the kid was gone. Iephus would rule.

"You can call me Blaze," the kid replied. Iephus began to ask him why, but then he saw his eyes, like twin golden fires.

Iephus flicked his fingers, impatient. Across the room, Blaze paced, hands folded behind his back and head held high, his sword belted at his waist.

"Can it really be so easy?" Iephus asked, breaking the silence. Blaze glanced at him and nodded. He never was talkative.

"They all but know we killed him. Everything is set up so that we are the obvious successors. You were not the assassin—that much is sure, since the night he was killed you went to the library. But you rarely research something without me. So when they look up the title

of the book you checked out, they will know. And so we will be Samiaza together."

Iephus clicked his teeth together. A Pair of Kings, *the book he had checked out yesterday, lay on the table, its lacquered cover gleaming in the candlelight.*

He looked at Blaze and smiled. Apart, they had weaknesses. But together they were unstoppable.

The memories went on, swirling like a kaleidoscope of broken glass, showing memory after memory as quick as his mind could follow. After each memory was shown, Kenneth could feel countless of his own returning.

With a suddenness that surprised him, the images stopped. The room slowly returned to sight.

Iephus watched him curiously.

"How do you feel?" he asked.

Kenneth turned to face him with eyes that burned like the fires of hell.

Keys clinked as the door opened, waking Kali immediately. She gave a small hiss, and Flammeth woke from were he had fallen asleep talking to her. They had been sitting side by side in adjacent jail cells, but to their dismay, a warding had prevented them from being able to touch each other.

She rose to her feet, wary, as the guards brought in someone bound in chains.

"We brought you company for your execution," one of them joked, but at a look from the other jailer, he fell silent.

The captive was hooded, bound at the hands and hobbled at the feet. She—Kali knew it was a she by her slim figure—was thrown viciously in the cell opposite of them. The guards locked the door and left silently.

She got up with a groan, and ripped off her hood with bound hands.

"Saskia!" Kali said in surprise, forgetting to be angry with her.

"How did you get here?" Flammeth said with an undercurrent of anger. He hadn't forgotten.

Saskia sighed. "We have until morning, so I'll tell you the full story." She spoke long into the night, until none of them knew how much time had passed.

When she was done, Kali and Flammeth sat back, shocked. "Nora *possessed* you?" Flammeth finally asked with incredulity.

She nodded, looking tired. "I hardly remember that myself. It was like a dream. A very bad dream."

"So Kenneth…Lord Blaze…Who's side is he on?" Kali asked.

"I guess we'll find out," Saskia said, and Kali wondered at the loneliness that the she heard in the simple phrase.

Kenneth returned to his quarters briefly, removing his armor and weapons. He kept *Frost*, but otherwise was dressed in leathers. He glanced briefly at his discarded armor and smiled, raising his sword.

His sword hand caught fire, slowly spreading its flame until his whole body was engulfed in blue flame. *Frost* pulsed, and the flame froze, hardening into armor. He looked into the mirror that was in the corner of his room. Lord Blaze was back.

He strode outside, navigating the corridors easily now that he had his memories back. He soon entered a room full of generals. They stared at him in shock and hastily stood from where they were sitting, saluting.

"Gather your armies in the courtyard. I will addressed them in one hour," Lord Blaze commanded, and they nodded, bowing. He left as they were murmuring their obedience to him. He headed for the dungeons.

Keys clinked for the second time that night, and Kali struggled to her feet, exhausted.

The door opened, light shining into the room, reflecting off of the golden tiles, waking Flammeth and Saskia. Curious, they all looked to see who the newcomer was.

"Lord Blaze." Saskia's voice was like shattered ice.

Kali stared in amazement. Kenneth, now Lord Blaze, was dressed in his *crystintillan* armor, glinting as the torchlight reflected off of it. He looked so different from his past self that he was barely recognizable.

Frost in his hand, he walked deliberately to their cells.

"This," he said softly, "is your last and final chance to renounce the Light, and join the side that will rule."

Flammeth stared in slack-jawed disbelief. "Are you insane?" he finally asked. Kali silently agreed with him.

He turned to look at them with cold eyes. Kali shivered. He seemed to emanate power, and the air around him chilled with malice.

"You would be to not join us. We have superior numbers. We have the advantage of the full use of magic, the magic you scorn as *dark,* as *evil.* We are neither. We are vengeance. Retribution." He said this calmly, but something behind his eyes seemed to gleam.

Saskia stood. "I once told you I hated Lord Blaze and everything he stood for. My position has never, and will never change."

Lord Blaze smiled like a viper. "Perhaps you should reconsider."

Saskia shook her head, betrayal on her face.

"I seem to recall you saying that you would kill me if returned to the Fallen. How's that working out for you?" he said mockingly.

Saskia snarled silently at him, and Kali was shocked to see unshed tears in her eyes.

Lord Blaze scanned them once more and said, "As you wish. You will all die in the morning."

Turning, he walked to the door, calling to the guards, "Notify Lord Iephus that I require him in the map room in one hour. Tell him that Our Lord Lucifer said it was time."

The guards left, and Lord Blaze paused at the stairs. Turning back, he looked at Saskia and whispered, pinching the air and spreading his fingers.

Kali frowned, wondering what he was doing. Saskia gasped, her hand flying up to her mouth. Lord Blaze nodded, satisfied, and left.

"What happened? What did he do?" Kali whispered fiercely at Saskia. She pressed her hand against the warding, and Flammeth mirrored her action. It was the closest they could get to holding hands. It brought a little comfort.

But all she would do was shake her head and say, "Sleep. We will need our strength in the morning."

Lord Blaze watched as the guards brought in several recruits that had tried to kill their superior. They were pale, weak things, but they would do. He turned back to the pentagram that he had drawn. He could have had one of his warlocks make it for him, but this had to be exact.

He ordered the guards to leave and turned to the captain who stood next to him. "Captain," he said, and the man saluted. "I brought you here to observe what happens to those who attempt to kill their superiors." The man nodded jerkily, no doubt wondering how much he knew.

Lord Blaze walked to the captives. They shied away from him, afraid. He drew his sword, and the temperature in the room dropped. As always, the sword drew in heat, providing him with immense power. He placed the blade next to the first captive's throat, causing him to whimper as the blade burned him.

With a vicious slash Blaze sliced his throat. At the same instant, he removed all heat from his body, freezing him. Power surged within him. "A man is mostly water," he said conversationally to the captain, "so it is easy to freeze someone like you would water, into ice." He swung with the flat of his blade, and the head of the captive shattered.

He turned back to the captain, who was trembling. "I don't usually freeze people to kill them, but," Blaze paused, and the other captives looked in horror as frost appeared on their hands, spreading across their body, "I need the power right now."

The last captive stopped moving. The group now looked like an ice sculpture carved by an insane man. Lord Blaze breathed deeply as power inside him hummed with a growing intensity.

He turned to the pentagram, unleashing the energy with a sigh. It flashed, momentarily blinding the captain, and swirled, sparks flying from each of the points of the star carved into the rock. The runes shimmered and flared, setting the small object inside the pentagram on fire. It burned with a black flame.

Abruptly the flames vanished, all signs of magic winking out. In the center sat a crystalline black skull. Blaze walked to it and picked it up, examining it closely. He smiled, turning to the frightened captain.

"You are a good captain," Lord Blaze said, "So I will forgive you for meeting with your fellow captains and planning General Cameron's death. But I rarely forgive twice." The man bowed deeply, sweat shining on his forehead despite the chill of the room.

"You are most merciful," the man whispered hoarsely. Blaze smiled.

"My Lord Blaze," came a voice, and he turned. A servant had entered the room. It was no ordinary servant, but an Andross, a species of demon with a head like a raven, and beautiful white wings.

"Speak," Lord Blaze commanded, and it awkwardly bowed.

"Our Lord Lucifer has requested your presence."

"Take me to him." The servant nodded and spread his wings. The world *warped* and his mind spun.

When he opened his eyes, not realizing that he had closed them, he was standing in a large temple.

He swiftly walked several steps towards the dais in the center and knelt, one hand to the floor, one hand to the hilt on his sword, and bowed his head.

"Rise." The voice was rich, melodious, like the sound of wind chimes.

Lord Blaze straightened and raised his head. The sight of the Fallen Star always filled him with awe.

Lord Lucifer stood several feet taller than a normal man, shining in brilliantly white clothes. A soft golden glow emanated from him, but his face was blurred from his mind.

"You have much to explain."

Blaze nodded. There was a soft sound as he took a vial from his belt and laid it carefully on the ground. It contained a copy of his memories of what had happened. Iephus had created it for him at his request.

"I see." Lord Lucifer looked at him, and even though he could not see his face, he could tell that his eyes were leveled at his.

"It is time. Kill all who stop us."

Blaze bowed deeply. "Your will is my command." When he had straightened from his bow, he was once again in the Keep. He ignored the startled look from the captain and left to find Iephus.

He found him in his rooms. Blaze opened the door without knocking, knowing that Iephus would have felt him coming from several floors away.

Iephus looked up from his book. "Yes?" he asked mildly. Blaze bowed.

"I brought a gift, thanking you for returning my memories to me," he said, and held out the black skull.

Iephus took it, studying its shape and color. "An opseer skull. How did you manage to obtain one?" Blaze smiled.

"I empowered it not ten minutes ago. It should work perfectly," he said. Iephus smiled, placing it on his desk.

"Your gift is accepted. But that is not all. An Andross spoke to you, and then you briefly weren't here. What did He tell you?" Iephus asked, closing his book.

"It is time," Blaze said, and Iephus nodded slowly, his eye glittering darkly.

"You've given the order for the armies to meet?" he asked, and Blaze nodded, fingering his sword.

"I'm going to speak to them shortly." Blaze removed his hand from his sword, passing it over his helm. It faded in a flash of fire. Let them see his face.

Captain Blake stood at the head of his squad, waiting for Lord Blaze to address them. They stood in the enormous plaza that was in front of the Keep, surrounded by other squads. The entire plaza was filled with men, spilling out into the streets and around the inner wall.

Despite the extreme heat that was always prevalent, he felt cold. Try as he might, he couldn't keep his thoughts away from the events he had witnessed earlier. He visibly flinched as he recalled the horrible shattering noise the head had made when Lord Blaze had swung his sword.

He tore his thoughts away from the scene, determined not to think about it. He was alive. That was all that mattered. A roar sounded, and he looked up. The Lord Blaze had arrived.

Blaze walked on air, probably suspended by aeromanipulators. Nevertheless, it was impressive. His armor gleamed, the light from *Frost* throwing the beauty of the frozen armor into sharp relief. His head was uncovered, revealing his face to the army.

He held up his hands, and the army silenced. Captain Blake swallowed as his gaze swept across the army. Lord Blaze opened his mouth, and his voice boomed magically across the yard, leaving no word unheard.

"My Brothers of the Dark," he began, but was silenced as the soldiers cheered. He smiled, indulgent, and let them subside. "My brothers," he began again, "we gather on the eve of a destruction that will engulf the world." The soldiers cheered again, beating their swords against their shields.

"Darkness," Lord Blaze continued, and the cheering slowly died, "will overwhelm the light. For where there is light, there always must be darkness." There was no cheering, only stillness, as he regarded them in a cold silence.

"In this way, all things exist. Where there is joy, there is distress. Where there is hope, there must be despair. Where there is life, death hides." Lord Blaze paused again, and the army held its breath.

"But we hide no longer!" Lord Blaze shouted, and the soldiers roared their approval. He continued over their shouts, his voice booming with power. "Tomorrow we will show the worlds the strength of the darkness they scorn! Tomorrow will mark the day of a new age, an age ruled by the Fallen star! An age where we, my brothers, will rule!"

Lord Blaze stood for several minutes, waiting for the cheers to subside. Eventually, when all had quieted, he spoke. "We march at dawn." This time, the soldiers didn't stop cheering until he had re-entered the Keep. Only Captain Blake stood silent, watching him go in fear.

Lord Blaze walked slowly through the halls of the Keep, his ears still ringing slightly from the noise of the soldiers. He opened two great double doors, carved with the screaming faces of the damned, and entered the courtroom where he judged those with a high enough rank to be considered important.

The room was empty, common for this time of night. He walked slowly around its perimeter, occasionally running his hand along the wall and muttering. When he was satisfied, he returned to his quarters, sitting at his desk.

He grabbed his pen and a length of paper, thought for a second, and then wrote. When he had finished the letter he folded it carefully, dripping wax and sealing it with his sigil, a flaming sword.

He ran his finger along the edges, setting it to burn after it was read and called a servant.

"Bring me Nora." The servant bowed and left. It had been barely a minute before the door opened. He didn't turn as she entered, waiting until she closed the door before he spoke.

"I have a task for you." His voice was quiet but commanding.

Nora laughed derisively. "Do you now? And why, may I ask, Kenneth, or should I say, *Lord Blaze*, would I ever work for you again?"

Lord Blaze turned, and Nora gazed at him with hatred. He held out the letter. "I want you to deliver this." Nora sneered, flipping it over. Her face suddenly stilled as she read whom the letter was for.

"I see," she said quietly. She pocketed the letter, looking at him with shrewd eyes. "And this will get me out of here?"

"No," Kenneth said, "but this will." He handed her a small note, his signature scrawled on the bottom. She read it quickly. It stated that she had her permission to leave for a mission.

She smiled, her stance dangerous. "Consider your letter sent." She turned to go.

"It would probably be best if he didn't see you," Kenneth said as she left. She paused momentarily, glancing back.

"How stupid do you think I am?" she asked, and then she was gone.

The Fallen's Justice

Ellie ducked to the side as she dodged Pariel's blade for the third time. Stepping swiftly, she slapped his blade away twice in rapid succession and ran quickly backward.

She hadn't been allowed to return to school after she had confronted the man who'd attempted to massacre the students. Gabriel had questioned her for nearly an hour, and before confining her to the fortress underneath the cathedral. The entire town was looking for her, rumors flying about what had happened in the school.

She battered away Pariel's sword again, throwing herself to one side, rolling to stay on her feet. It was merely a survival game. She would never be able to defeat him, so she merely tried to improve on the time she stayed 'alive'.

He came at her again, feinting quickly to the left, throwing her off balance as she quickly tried to compensate. He swung quickly, and Ellie closed her eyes, bracing herself for the blow.

It never came. She opened her eyes, confused, before gasping in shock. Pariel stood, sword inches from her side, frozen. She looked around in disbelief, then backed up, her sword leveled at a small kid playing in the corner of the room.

She walked slowly to him, never lowering her sword. "How did you get in here?" She demanded. It was a small Japanese boy, making a paper hat out of newspaper.

He looked up at her and smiled. "Do you want a hat?" he asked innocently, proffering the paper creation towards her. She shook her head silently. He shrugged and put it on, his blue eyes watching her as she slowly lowered the sword.

"Why is Pariel frozen?" she asked him, and he grinned.

"Him?" he asked, pointing to where Pariel was, still in mid-swing. "I stopped time. Watch." He stood and dropped the hat. The moment he let go of the paper it froze, suspended in the air.

Ellie backed up in astonishment. She looked at her sword, and then dropped it. It did the same thing. She grabbed ahold of its hilt, and it unfroze. She turned back to the boy, who was watching her curiously.

"What do you want?" she asked quietly. The boy smiled again, his startling blue eyes gleaming.

"Follow me," he said, grabbing her hand. He took a step, and the world sighed. Grass spread from where his foot touched the ground, and the earth rippled outward from where he touched, revealing the sky filled with stars.

She stared in wonder as the grassy plains waved in the wind. The sky was clear, stars shining and giving light, but when she looked closely she realized there was no moon.

The boy released her hand, and Ellie noticed that they were by a road of paved stone. She followed him as he walked happily down it.

"Where are we?" she asked, unsure.

He smiled and didn't answer. "Do you want to hear a story?" he asked her. Not waiting for her response, he continued.

"Once, there was a town. It was well fortified against the dangers of the outside world, but one day it was attacked by a terrible monster and its warriors. The town's greatest soldier protected the town, attacking it to save the people. Despite his mighty strength and power, he could not win, for the beast's minions were many. Because of this, his friend went with him to take on the monster's warriors so he could challenge the beast alone.

"She was a mighty warrior herself, and she managed to defeat the minions while he destroyed the beast. But her power backfired, inflicting dangerous wounds. No healer could save her, because those who had the powers to heal were not skilled or powerful enough to overcome the magic that had she had used to destroy her enemies. The one who could save her was too far away, and when sent for, came to late. She died, sacrificing herself so others could live," the little boy finished sadly, looking into the distance.

Ellie didn't know what to say. She let the silence rush in, and they walked for several seconds without speaking. Eventually he turned to face her again, a mischievous smile on his face.

"This story could be true," he said, and Ellie shook her head in confusion. Could be true? But he continued before she could ask any questions. "Do you know the name of the girl who sacrificed herself?"

Ellie shook her head, caught off guard by the question. "Of course not!" she said, a little angry.

The boy shrugged, unperturbed. "I'd find out," he said calmly.

Ellie frowned, and glanced at the road. She squinted off into the distance, unsure of what she saw. "Is that a fort?" she asked, looking at a junction between mountains. But when she turned back, the boy was gone.

The sun rose without the captives' knowledge, deep in the ground as they were. But when the opened door awakened them, they knew their time had come.

Face grim, Kali turned to look at Flammeth, who's visage mirrored her own.

A guard opened her door with a clink of the key, and Kali briefly considered attempting to knock him out and try escaping.

She knew it would be a useless endeavor. Something in the cells drained her savyl's power, leaving her weak and exhausted, her movements clumsy and jerky.

She entertained the idea for another second, before allowing the guard to take her shackles and bind them to a chain with the others.

They were led out of the earth and up many flights of stairs, Kali's legs groaning in protest. Despite the pain, Kali was grateful for the change in air, eradicating the horrible smell of their cells. Eventually the stairs ended and they were left waiting outside a small side door.

Straining, she could hear speaking inside the room.

"This man, a First Captain of Regiment Six, was caught stealing from the army. This was brought here on his insistence, and allowed because of his elevated rank." She did not recognize the voice, but it's high and mighty sound made her quietly dislike the speaker.

"Explain." Despite the one word, Kali immediately recognized the voice as Kenneth.

Blaze. He is Lord Blaze now. She chided herself. She could not hear the soft explanation, but it appeared unsatisfactory to Lord Blaze.

"Enough of your driveling!" he cut in, and the man stopped. "I find you guilty of stealing and murder. This offense is punishable by death. But I find mercy in Our Lord Lucifer on this day. You will not die."

The man sobbed his thanks, but Lord Blaze cut him off.

"This blade was given to me as a gift." The sound of metal falling onto flagstones was startlingly loud. "Now it will serve the Fallen Star's justice. Count the number of coins stolen. He will be stabbed the number of times as coins that he decided would be his. He will also choose where to be stabbed, or else be beaten until he does."

Kali winced in sympathy at the cruelty, listening as the man screamed as he was dragged away.

"Bring in the prisoners," Lord Blaze said, and the door opened.

They were led inside of a large room, clearly made for holding military trials. Lord Blaze sat in the center, raised slightly on a dais. The floor, though white marble, was stained an ugly red in several places.

Lord Blaze stood, unsheathing *Frost*, its slivery radiance filling the room.

A small toadlike man off to the side coughed quietly and opened his book.

"These two," he said, and Kali realized he was the man with the annoying voice, "are charged with fighting against Our Lord Lucifer and denying his sovereign reign. They are to be executed by beheading." He moved on, and pointed to Saskia. "Saskia, Fourth Captain of the Third Regiment, you are charged with treason and the denying of Our Lord Lucifer's sovereign reign. How do you stand?"

Saskia sneered at him with disdain. "Is it not obvious?" The man colored slightly and looked at Lord Blaze.

He merely raised an eyebrow at the man, and Kali felt a small flash of satisfaction as the man wilted.

Lord Blaze walked slowly down the dais steps, and handed a small slip of paper to a nearby servant, never taking his eyes off of them.

"Deliver this to Lord Iephus immediately and without fail," he said softly.

The servant bowed and left the room. Lord Blaze looked at them in silence for another moment, before saying quietly, "Any last words?"

Kali shook her head, but Flammeth looked up angrily.

"I thought you were a better man," he said challengingly, looking him in the eye.

Lord Blaze raised an eyebrow. "That's it? Rather pitiful." He raised his sword, and the room was blasted by a concussive burst of light.

Runes sprayed against the walls, and instantly soldiers were pouring into the room, their breastplates marked with the cross of the Ranks of the Light.

"Kill the prisoners!" Lord Blaze screamed, and Kali heard the guards behind her unsheathe their swords.

She twisted, trying to disarm him, but she was too slow. He knocked her to the ground, raising his sword.

The guard froze, looking down at the crystalline sword that pierced his chest. He looked up at Lord Blaze.

"I don't..." he whispered, and then crystalized as ice spread out from the wound. Lord Blaze removed his sword, and he shattered.

Kali stared at him in disbelief as he dispatched the other guards similarly.

"Guards! Raise the alarm! The Keep is under attack! Storm the room!" he shouted, but at the same time he was throwing binding spells at the doors to lock them.

Pounding started on the doors, and Kali was lifted gently off the floor into the arms of a grizzled soldier.

"Lets get you out of here," he said, and ran towards the center of the room, where a column of light pulsed. The world spun, and she was in a large tent, medics ready. She was taken to a soft bed, and doctors examined her despite her protests that she was fine.

The column pulsed, and Kenneth stepped out, armored in his crystalline beauty, his mark of rank shimmering darkly. He scanned the room and strode to a corner.

"Gabriel!" he called, and Gabriel turned, and Kenneth grabbed him in an embrace. "Thank God you got my message."

Gabriel returned the embrace before stepping back.

"You have a great deal to explain to all of us, boy," he said, but he was smiling.

"All in due time," Kenneth responded, and turned to face Kali, as though he knew she had been watching.

To her astonishment, he winked at her.

Kenneth strode into the general's tent, uncomfortably aware of the absence of *Frost* on his hip. Gabriel had advised he leave it in his tent to not frighten the Generals.

Everyone stood as he entered, staring as he approached their table of council. General Burns looked at him with knowing eyes, and nodded as he sat. Everyone else sat as well, some looking embarrassed.

"Good. Now we are all here," he said with finality.

"Not quite," came a voice, and Gabriel stepped in, dressed in the beautiful uniform of the Exalted's personal guard. It was pure silver, engraved with the cross of the Light, spiraling outward with runes indicating his rank.

Almost everyone immediately jumped back to their feet, some looking at Gabriel in awe.

General Burns bowed. "My apologies. I did not know you were going to stay."

Gabriel waved his apology away. "You had no reason to. There is no reason to apologize. Now, Kenneth, explain everything you can."

Kenneth nodded and took a big breath.

"As many of you know, I used to be Semiaza of the Fallen. Several months ago, I was captured in an excellently executed raid designed specifically to eliminate me.

"While I was in captivity, I demanded to talk to the Exalted. After several days, they agreed. They took me to the Exalted, heavily guarded, all the halls cleared of people."

"Arrogant as I was, when I was talking with the Exalted, I demanded to talk to his superior, God himself. He rightly responded: 'I don't command my Lord.' I sneered at him, calling him coward."

"To both of our surprise, someone knocked on the doors, and then opened them. A mid-sized man walked in, bearded and brown-eyed, but with the confident stride of a leader, clothed in a brilliant white. He had scars, as you probably know, on his hands, feet, and side."

"Everyone in the room immediately sank to their knees, but I stayed standing. He walked to me, and I asked him just who he thought he was."

Kenneth shook his head as they gasped at his foolishness.

"I knew who he was, of course. But I wanted to prove what I thought of him. To my surprise, he looked at me with pity in his eyes. He asked me a question." Kenneth eyes shone with the memory.

"He said, 'Why do you demand so unceasingly to see God?' I didn't answer. The room stayed silent for many moments, until I finally spoke."

"I made a bet with God. I told him that he could wipe my memories clean from my head, and put me into the world, and when I regained them, I would choose Satan every time. He disagreed, and I challenged him to do it and find out."

"The next thing I remember is going to school in Montana. I remembered nothing, and instead had false memories that quickly faded. I was brought into the company of Gabriel and his students, and learned to love there. Everywhere I looked, I had great models of good people, and as my memories returned I was horrified at my cruelty and disgusted by my hatred."

"I returned to the Fallen Fortress with the intent of freeing my newly found friends, and was betrayed by Nora, whom I shouldn't have trusted in the first place. Given the options, I chose to fake my return, and contacted Gabriel. He and I arranged an escape, which occurred only minutes ago. That brings us to now."

Kenneth sat back, quietly amused by the officer's expressions. He saw several mouthing slowly, *He made a* bet *with Jesus?*

General Burns cleared his throat. "So how do we know you aren't actually faking that you're on our side? That would be quite the tactical mistake on our part!"

Several men agreed quietly. Kenneth frowned, unsure how to continue.

"Bring Saskia here," he told Gabriel. Gabriel nodded, and left the tent.

"What, the girl who uses fear as a weapon? What's she going to do?" said someone.

"Don't be a fool Jacob," said another, and several men snickered.

Gabriel returned with a wary Saskia by his side. Kenneth nodded his thanks, and turned to the assembled men.

"You have all heard of Saskia." It was a statement, but many people nodded. "Her power is the power of fear. She can tell the fears of others, and bring them to life." Many people glanced at her nervously, but she looked bored.

"Where are we going with this?" General Burns asked.

"Saskia can tell if one of my fears is being caught. If I do not have this fear, I am innocent. More than that, I would like her to tell of a specific incident in the dungeons of the Keep."

Saskia nodded and stepped forward. "In the dungeons, they use *auriem* to prevent you from using your savylus. Because of this, I could neither read people's fears nor bring them to life. When Kenneth came down to 'mock' us, he ordered the guards out and used a spell to transfer some of his energy to me, allowing me to briefly read his fears. At that point in time, his greatest fear was that he would be caught. From that moment on I knew he was on our side."

Gabriel nodded, satisfied. Saskia glanced at Kenneth and added, "And for good measure he has no such fear now."

"I think she's lying, and she can't tell what his fears are at all!" Jacob blustered.

Saskia rolled her eyes and stepped forward. "What is your greatest fear?" she asked the man. "I'll tell your greatest fear to General Burns, and you'll say it aloud. If they match, I can read fears. Plain and simple." Saskia opened herself, and the pattern was there. *Pain* and then *fire*, followed by *fear of being caught*.

She walked to General Burns and whispered in his ear.

Looking nervous, Jacob waited until she was finished, thought a second and said, "My greatest fear is to be skinned alive."

General Burns chuckled humorlessly. "No, your greatest fear is to be demoted by me because of your constant insolence. And you are. Leave. Now."

Jacob looked confused. "But that's not..." He stuttered and cut off. Looking around for support and finding none, he got up from the table and left.

General Burns turned to Gabriel. "Do you mind sending Saskia after him to arrest him? His greatest fear was that people would discover he was a spy."

Saskia left with a grim smile.

"Hey Ian!" Chuck called. "What do you make of this?" Ian rolled his eyes and got up. He was supposed to be off duty, but every ten minutes or so Chuck would ask him what he thought of some idea he had.

He walked further out on the wall, and found Chuck staring out into the distance. Ian squinted, trying to make out what it was.

"What is it?" he asked.

Chuck shrugged. "I don't know. Whatever it is, its huge."

Ian fumbled at his belt, producing a seeing glass. He put it up to his eye, looking carefully. He paled. "Sound the alarm," he managed, voice failing him.

Chuck snatched the glass from him. "Why?" he asked, and trailed off as he got a good look at the shrouded mass.

"Darkness and chaos," he whispered. "What is that?'

The Power of Frost

"A message for you, sir," a servant said, and Gabriel turned from where he was sitting. He accepted the letter, flipping it to reveal whom it was from. He frowned. *What do you have for me, Gimelli?* he wondered, opening the letter with a quick tear.

He quickly scanned the contents and smiled. Aelex was alive. He was severely injured, but healers would be able to take care of him. He turned to tell Kenneth the good news, but froze as a horn sounded. Its mournful keen pierced the air, and everyone in the meeting tent stopped to listen.

A second horn soon followed the first, and then a third, and soon the air was filled with the sound.

"That's not any signal, that's panic! Rally the forces!" shouted General Burns. Everyone scattered, and Kenneth found himself running side by side with Gabriel.

"Get your sword," Gabriel barked, "then run straight to the wall. We're going to need you for whatever this is." Kenneth nodded, breaking off and heading towards his temporary tent.

He ripped open its door and rushed inside, grabbing *Frost* before rushing back outside. Soldiers and common people alike gasped as he unsheathed the blade, his *crystintillan* armor clicking into place, spreading from where he held his sword.

Soon he was fully armored, pounding down the road towards the wall, his mark of rank pulsing as magical energy crackled through it. He neared the wall, and looked right and left for a stair leading up it. He saw only towers, far to the either side, and instead gathered power and speed and *leapt.*

Seconds later, his feet touched the top of the wall, and the guards stared at him in shock. He ignored them, snatching an eyeglass out of one of their hands to get a better look at the enormous shape that loomed ahead.

"Death Titan," Kenneth breathed, and one of the guards let out a cry of fear. The massive creature stood seventy feet tall, darkness swirling around its form, obscuring its body from view. Every other second or so, dark purple lightning would flash, sending a rumbling that added to the sound of each colossal step.

As it neared, the air chilled, and the guards shivered in cold as well as fear. Its eyes became visible, like two caverns of dark red flame.

"That's quite the beast," came Gabriel's voice, and Kenneth turned and greeted him and Saskia, who was standing behind Gabriel's left shoulder.

"That's not all," said Kenneth grimly, "see those shapes flitting about the bottom? Those are called daevas. They live in tribes around the Obsidian Mountains, and are extremely deadly. They look human, except with no face. No eyes, yet they see better than a hawk. No nose, but they can still track you by smell. No ears, and yet they can hear your heart beat from meters away."

"Do they fear?" Saskia asked quietly. At Kenneth's nod, she smiled, the smile of a predator on a hunt. "You take the Titan, I'll take the daevas."

Kenneth nodded looking to Gabriel. "Rally together the soldiers, and keep them inside the walls. When it gets close, weaken it with arrows and ballistae. And for God's sake, *don't let it touch you.* You'll die almost instantly."

Gabriel nodded, and left, leaving Kenneth alone with Saskia. He looked at her for a long second, and after a moment, saluted.

"If we don't come out of this alive, I must say, I've enjoyed fighting with you," he said, and she shook her head, a strange expression on her face.

Stepping forward, she embraced him, kissing him quickly on the cheek and whispering in his ear, "Good luck, Kenneth."

Letting go of him, she ran towards the tower that led out to the plains. Touched, Kenneth watched her go for several seconds, and then faced the Titan.

"This should be fun," he said, a manic grin on his face. He allowed his helmet to form before leaping off the edge of the wall.

He fell nearly three stories, landing lightly on his feet. He brought up his sword, its runes dancing on its blade. Then he ran forward, yelling at the top of his lungs.

Chuck turned to Ian. "Did you see that?" he asked, shocked. Ian nodded, looking astonished.

Ellie ran through frantic crowds of people, barely managing to keep her feet. Soldiers were running and yelling, their swords unsheathed, and townspeople were desperately fleeing to the North side of the city. She was knocked down twice, bruising her knee and cutting her cheek on a sharp stone.

Eventually the crowds vanished, and she stumbled, suddenly free. Soldiers were standing at attention in rows, swords drawn, ready. She looked around quickly, and heard a voice call out to her.

"Ellie! What are you doing here?" She turned, and Gabriel approached her swiftly.

"What's attacking the fort?" she asked desperately, "Who went out to stop it?"

Gabriel blinked. "There has been a Death Titan sighted, along with several dozen daevas. Kenneth and Saskia went to take care of it." Ellie sucked in her breath. *The champion and his friend.*

"I need to be at the gates!" she said frantically, and Gabriel grabbed her arm as she tried to turn.

"You're not going anywhere. How did you get here?" he said sternly, and Ellie shook her head.

"A little Japanese boy took me! He told me that Saskia would die if I didn't save her!" she said desperately, and Gabriel blinked again.

"Japanese boy?" he asked in shock.

"Yeah. He tried to give me a hat made of newspaper," she babbled. Gabriel's eyes narrowed.

"Newspaper? What color were his eyes?" he asked quickly.

"Blue." Ellie didn't see why it mattered.

Gabriel looked at her for a long second. "Come on," he said eventually, "You need to be at the gates."

Saskia approached the daevas, cursing their lack of fear. She usually could approach enemies shrouded in the night, but these creatures preferred the darkness and left her out in the open. That thought made her pause. If they preferred the dark, perhaps they feared the light. She half closed her eyes as she ran, isolating the waves of fear that emanated from the creatures.

They had seen her far back, and were waiting in a defensive formation, ready to counter any attack and kill her immediately. Clearly they weren't stupid.

They also didn't know who she was, either. As Saskia drew close enough, she breathed in their collective fear of the light with a sigh, and unleashed her savyl.

Light burst forth from her in a blinding radiance, piercing the shadows that surrounded and obscured the Titan. Immediately their fear doubled, and she felt one of them react in terror, guessing she was an angel.

Hmm... She thought as fear pulsed through her. *This will be interesting.*

Kenneth pounded across the plains, watching as Saskia engaged the daevas ahead of him. She seemed to be shining, and before he could confirm his thought, she exploded with white light, temporarily blinding him, and causing the creatures to scream in agony.

Realizing she needed no help, he focused on the Titan. Gripping *Frost* tightly, he drew deeply on its power, and used the water molecules in the air to freeze the Titan's legs to the ground.

Freezing things required the removal of heat, so Kenneth pulled in the heat, using it to burn great swathes of air above him, burning the Titan.

The air seemed to rip and tear as the Titan screamed in anger and pain, waving its burned arms and breaking free of the ice on its legs.

Kenneth used its distraction to dart in and slash at its left ankle, quietly blessing Saskia for her brilliance to let him see.

Frost cut deeply, severing the Titan's achilles tendon, causing the calf muscle to retract upwards.

Off balance, it tried to step backwards. Rushing forward, Kenneth leapt, his blade slicing through the Titan's knee. It fell backward with a thud that knocked Kenneth nearly fifteen feet in the air, knocking the wind out of him as he hit the ground, armor cracking and spewing fire. Rolling to his feet, he went in for the final blow.

Saskia was burning. She had used the daeva's fear of angels to temporarily transform herself into one, but the holy fire was doing terrible damage to her body.

Snarling, she dispatched the last few daevas in a burst of flame, and felt her body collapse as the power of fear left her with the angelic form that it had provided. She was still burning, she realized, and she weakly tried to roll to put out the flames.

Mid-roll she saw Kenneth sprinting towards the Titan, *Frost* blazing a bright blue in his right hand, armor shining like the sun. The Titan was on the ground, struggling to get up, and its eyes blazed in the darkness that was closing in on her fading brilliance.

Several feet from its torso, Kenneth leapt with all his strength, and Saskia felt her breath leave her body in awe.

He soared through the air like an avenging angel, flipping his blade so that when he landed it would pierce at the Titan's armor. Slashing downward, he struck the Titan's heart.

Light erupted from the wound, and Saskia saw the explosion before she heard it. The Titan was vaporized instantly as a huge ball of flame mushroomed towards the sky.

Saskia closed her eyes, curling as she felt the surging heat wash over her, followed by the concussive shock wave that threw her back several feet, sending her rolling.

The smell of singed flesh and hair filled the air. Fearing the worst, she looked up as the smoke cleared slowly, revealing a solitary figure standing at the center of an enormous crater.

Snatching *Frost* out of the ground, he walked towards her, armor cracked in several places, spitting fire.

Reaching down, he helped her up, but as she stood dizziness engulfed her, and she felt him catch her as darkness consumed her.

"Open the gates! Open the gates!" soldiers called as Kenneth returned. He jogged slowly, burdened by Saskia's weight in his arms. He had removed his armor and sheathed his sword at his side.

The gates opened, revealing astounded faces and shocked soldiers on the other side.

"Medic!" Kenneth shouted, frantic, "I need a medic!" Soldiers glanced down at the burned body in his arms, and picked up the call as Kenneth continued jogging towards the infirmary.

"Bring her here!" Kenneth heard someone shout, and he turned.

"Elena!" he said, surprised. Moving quickly, he laid Saskia gently on a white sheet and stepped back.

Ellie bent down quickly, laying her hand on Saskia's forehead and closing her eyes. She shuddered, and Saskia's wounds let off faint wisps of white smoke, wounds slowly closing, leaving black burn scars.

When she had finished, she sat back, looking tired. When she saw the scars, her eyes narrowed. "That's never happened before," she muttered.

"You've never healed wounds inflicted by holy fire either," Gabriel said, approaching from the side. He looked at Kenneth and shook his head. "I've never seen anything close to what you two did today. You've saved many lives."

He looked at Saskia, eyes sad. "She will bear those scars for the rest of her life."

Kenneth nodded, melancholy. "Lets move her to the infirmary." Less urgent now that her life was not in danger, he waited for a stretcher before following them to the infirmary, where they laid her carefully on a bed.

Kenneth turned to go, but she shifted, making him pause. Turning back, he walked toward her as she opened her eyes.

"You killed a Titan," She mumbled. Kenneth nodded. She smiled. "You looked like an avenging angel." She said, echoing her earlier thoughts.

Kenneth grinned. "Unless I'm mistaken, you *were* an angel for a while there. I couldn't even look at you."

Saskia chuckled. "I was pretty awesome, wasn't I." She looked down, grin fading, looking at the burn scars on her arms and legs.

All humor fled from Kenneth. "Ellie healed you, but it wasn't perfect. Gabriel said it was because it was holy fire." Saskia nodded, shocked.

She looked up at him, surprising him with the wavering smile on her face. "They are worth it. For those soldiers." And in saying so, she closed her eyes and slept.

Kenneth left her reluctantly and returned to the General's planning tent. Stepping inside, he found Gabriel.

"That wasn't the last of them," Kenneth said. Gabriel nodded, looking down at a map of their surroundings.

"How many are coming?" he said, looking up at Kenneth.

Kenneth exhaled slowly. "All of them. Every last regiment is marching to attack Güderam. Tonight."

Gabriel sucked in his breath. "Every regiment? What are the numbers?"

"All thirteen regiments make around twelve legions. As far as I know, we have nearly a legion here in Güderam," Kenneth answered.

Gabriel turned back to the map. "We will have to abandon Güderam." Kenneth shook his head.

"Not immediately. We need to do something first."

Gabriel looked up. "You have a plan?" Kenneth nodded. "Then we stay."

Lord Iephus paused as he crested the last hill before Güderam, watching its distant flags waving on the tops of the Towers of the fort.

Looking nearer, he frowned at the enormous crater in the middle of the plains, still smoking from the intense explosion that created it nearly two hours before.

"Set up camp ten miles out, behind the crater," he said, turning to the runner standing next to his horse. The runner immediately bowed and ran off, issuing orders to the numerous captains of the army.

Lord Iephus glanced back, eyes gleaming as he took in the sea of black clad soldiers that traveled nearly as far as the eye could see.

Urging his horse forward, he fingered a sheet of paper in his pocket, his mind elsewhere. He took out the sheet of paper and read it again; although he had committed it to memory the first time he had read it.

It read:

Lord Iephus

I have contacted the enemy and have notified them that I am on their side. Soon you will get the report that I was taken as well as the prisoners. This was to convince them that I am on their side. A few prisoners for a fortress are a good trade.

Soon I will convince the Armies of the Light that I have decided to stay with them, because 'I learned the way of love'.

They might not believe me. Therefore I ask you to send a small distraction that I can kill to convince them that I am on their side. If I am successful, when you are within sighting distance, I will go out with a white flag, seeking conference with you.

In the name of Lucifer

Lord Blaze

Iephus folded the letter carefully, putting it in his pocket. Dismounting from his horse, he commanded a soldier to take care of it.

Turning, he found a grassless area not far from the crater. Ignoring the burned smell, he ordered a makeshift pavilion to be set up there.

As the servants ran off, his advisor Adlai came up to him.

"Do you really think they will treat with us?" he asked, skeptical.

Iephus merely turned and pointed to the white flag that proceeded several soldiers as they walked out of the gates.

Minutes later, Lord Iephus stood by a chair as Lord Blaze approached with four guards as an escort.

Lord Blaze stepped forward, ignoring the chair, and Iephus reached out with his mind, feeling the guards' mental strength.

"Lord Blaze, you never cease to amaze me with you thoroughness," he said, and with a thought, all four of the guards' eyes glazed over. Such weak minds.

Lord Blaze bowed, and gestured towards the crater. "A Death Titan? You must have more faith in my capabilities than I thought."

Iephus smiled. "Not unfounded, as you can see."

Blaze nodded in acknowledgement. "Everything worked as planned. Now we must decide what to do."

Iephus nodded thoughtfully, thinking aloud. "You must have thought of something. You were always the general."

Lord Blaze smiled, confirming his prediction.

"They will notice if I start acting suspiciously. They have several men of good tactical background so I can't design something that would fail. So my plan is twofold. First, when I go back, I will tell them that you said we had one hour to surrender before you attack. I will rally my forces and keep them at watch. You will make a couple feints, continuing into the night, fatiguing their army. They do not have enough men to keep a solid rotation, so everyone will be exhausted by morning, while you will be only a regiment short."

"And then?" Iephus asked, although he knew the answer.

"Then we raze the city to the ground," Lord Blaze said, his eyes even.

Iephus smiled.

"Did he believe you?" Gabriel muttered as they led the dazed soldiers away.

Kenneth waved him away. Gabriel frowned, unsatisfied. Kenneth looked at the soldiers, noticing them being led away, and frowned.

"Halt! Bring them here," he shouted, and they returned them, some looking abashed.

Kenneth walked up to one, looking in his eyes. They were distant, as though deep in thought.

"I did not know your reach could go so far now, Iephus," he said quietly, and the soldier's mouth quirked to a grin.

"My power has grown," he said, just as quietly. Kenneth nodded.

"Do me a favor and release them when I cue you. It will impress the army of my 'power'." The soldier chuckled.

Kenneth stood back slightly, and raised his arm, willing his mark to form. "Release them!" he said commandingly.

Immediately all four soldiers collapsed, holding their heads and groaning.

Kenneth let his mark fade, turning to Gabriel, who was grinning slightly. "You heard that?" he asked, surprised.

"I have better ears than you might think. You are a good actor," Gabriel said. "That was a good idea."

Kenneth shrugged. "I didn't want him to realize that what I told him was false." Gabriel nodded.

"When will they come forward?" he inquired, watching the gates close.

"In one hour." Kenneth said, as the doors rumbled shut. "We'll be prepared."

"Advance all regiments!" Iephus commanded, his voice booming. He turned to his runner. "Bring Regiment One to the front ranks, men five deep, leaving all others in normal formation. Let those behind Regiment One rest, but keep Regiment One as though we are about to attack," he said, quietly. The runner nodded, speeding off.

Iephus smiled as they approached the walls, barely outside of bow's range. Taking out a small black crystal, he crushed it in his hand.

Immediately, the sky went dark, leaving only the army's torches and the lights in the fort to illuminate the night.

Lord Iephus smiled as he heard panic inside the walls of the fort. The darkness would keep the enemy from knowing the army rested behind a layer of alert sentries.

Iephus turned to order the first diversion when he froze, staring at the gates. They were slowly opening.

Lord Blaze, have you managed the impossible? He thought as he identified the mind behind the gates.

The glowing figure of Lord Blaze strode through the gates, *Frost* illuminating his way.

Iephus took a step forward, but stopped as Lord Blaze raised his sword parallel to the ground and slashed downward.

Four hundred pounds of magical dynamite in precise locations exploded underground, placed there by Kenneth when they had excavated various caves underneath the surface of the plain days before. The ground heaved and gave away, sending thousands of soldiers falling down into an enormous chasm to their deaths, preventing the rest from crossing into the city.

Iephus didn't move, inexplicably untouched, standing on a lone column of stone, looking in shock at Lord Blaze as he straightened, looking him in the eyes from nearly half a mile away.

Iephus felt rage rush into him like a river of molten fire as he realized he had been fooled—no, betrayed—by his only friend and companion, leading to death nearly a legion of his forces, creating a canyon that would take weeks to cross.

Lord Blaze turned away, golden eyes shining, and Iephus attacked his mind, struggling with all his strength to break him.

Lord Blaze paused, and after a moment turned back, mind like a wall of silverlight. He said four words that Iephus couldn't hear over the screams and moans of pain, but could read off of his lips.

All glory to God.

Iephus screamed in fury as Lord Blaze turned away and left, leaving the carnage behind.

Kenneth jogged up to Gabriel, mind troubled from his encounter with Lord Iephus.

"Is everyone out?" he asked. At Gabriel's nod, he breathed a sigh of relief. "Where has everyone gone?" he wondered.

"We took them to the Fortress of Light. We will be safe there, and we can consult the Exalted for further instruction."

Kenneth smiled. "Won't he be surprised to see *me*," he said lightly.

Gabriel turned to look at him. "I want to be there," he said, and they both laughed, relieved that no one had died needlessly. Kenneth started walking towards the temporal shift, but stopped as a thought struck him.

"Why is Ellie here?" he asked. "I meant to ask earlier, but," he gestured broadly with his hands, "this happened."

Gabriel hesitated, then nodded. "She came with me. I thought if we were going to have a war, it would be good to have a skilled healer on our side," he said. Kenneth agreed, and Gabriel sighed. "She's been getting more and more practice lately, ever since the demonic possessions increased."

Kenneth nodded, somber, then jerked as a war horn sounded in the distance. "Let's go," he suggested.

Soon they were both walking the halls of the Keep of the Light with Saskia, Kali, and Flammeth close behind, clean of grime and sweat. They were now dressed in simple white armor that Gabriel had explained was for court summons and other formalities. They had received a summons from the Exalted himself, and were headed to see him.

They approached the doors to the throne room, and two elaborately decorated guards opened beautifully crafted doors, revealing a long pillared room, with great chiseled statues of previous Exalteds lining the walls.

To the back stood a large throne, made of gold and silver, its high back shaped like a rising cross. It was intricately carved with thorns, and at the end of each arm was the head of lion.

Standing below the throne was a frail old man, leaning on a thick walking stick, a small wooden chair to the side.

At Flammeth and Kali's stares, Gabriel explained, "Remember, he who exalts himself will be humbled, and he who humbles himself will be exalted. The throne was ordered built for when Jesus graces us with his presence. The Exalted merely uses the small chair to sit and rest his legs."

They nodded, and knelt as they approached, resting their left hands on the floor, and their right on their weapons belted at their waist, heads bowed.

"No no no!" the old man protested. Despite his frailty, his voice was strong and steady. "Stand. There you go. Now. Tell me what has happened."

With a nod from Gabriel, Kenneth stepped forward. The Exalted eyes widened in surprise as he gazed on his face.

"I did not recognize you. You have changed, and for the better." Kenneth nodded and explained all that had happened.

Listening attentively, the Exalted slowly sank into his chair as Kenneth spoke.

When he had finished, the old man seemed troubled. "Dark days are brewing," he said quietly. He looked up. "What happened to Nora? Where did she go?" Kenneth shook his head. He had no idea.

A giggle broke into the air. "Why, look, here I am." Kenneth whirled, Nora standing off to the side, leaning on a column and examining her nails with a lackadaisical manner.

Gabriel moved so fast he blurred, unsheathing his sword and disarming Nora, pinning her to the pillar and removing weapon after weapon, throwing them to surprised guards that had moved too late.

Finally he stepped back, sword to her throat, watching her carefully. Nora seemed not to notice, instead looking at the Exalted with an eyebrow raised.

"Some welcome, brother."

Prophesying Shadows

The Exalted stood slowly, carefully using his stick for balance. "You have always had a flare for the dramatic, Nora."

Nora flipped her hair back. "Surely you know that I mean no harm, Seastán. Else Gabby here would be dead already."

Seastán smiled, his lips thin, and gestured for Gabriel to step back. Looking dangerous, he did so, violently sheathing his sword with a ringing sound that filled the quiet room.

Stepping forward, Nora folded her arms and looked at the old man. "You look older than when we last met," she stated.

Seastán chuckled. "Last time we saw each other was over two hundred years ago." Kenneth noted the number with a muted surprise. Nephilim lived a long time if they weren't killed, but living over two hundred was pretty impressive.

Nora waved the number away as if it were nothing. "What are a couple years between siblings?" she said airily.

Flammeth broke in. "You're his sister?" He sounded skeptical, and Kenneth didn't blame him. For a woman claiming to be over two hundred, Nora looked like she was nineteen or twenty.

Nora raised an eyebrow and looked at Seastán. He sighed. "Nora is my younger sister, born in the year 1479 A.D., five years after myself."

Kali gasped. "That makes you nearly five hundred years old!" Even Gabriel looked surprised.

Seastán exhaled slowly. "Why have you come here?" he asked Nora quietly. He rubbed at his temples, eyes closed.

Nora looked serious for the first time Kenneth had ever known. Pulling out a leather-bound book from seemingly nowhere, she handed it to Seastán.

"How did you get this?" he demanded.

She shrugged. "I briefly visited your room." Seastán shook his head in bewilderment.

"What is it?" Gabriel asked quietly.

"This is the only known book that has all the true prophecies of the worlds contained in one book. It was given to me nearly three hundred and fifty years ago, and has proven its value many times. All but a few prophecies are fulfilled, however," Seastán explained. It was a small book, barely over a hundred pages.

Nora took the book carefully from Seastán and opened it to the end. Taking out a sheet of yellowed paper, she laid it next the binding and whispered quietly.

After a second, the page was attached to the book as if it had always been. She gave the book back smugly, and Seastán stared at it in astonishment, reading the page in silence.

"How did you come by this page?" he breathed in astonishment. She shrugged, looking slightly guilty.

"I stole it from the person who gave it to you." She said matter of factly.

Seastán sat down in his chair, rubbing his eyes. "I am getting too old for this." Hearing this made Kenneth wonder.

"How is it that you have aged, and she has not?" he asked quietly, but Seastán shook his head.

"You must hear this. It is the last prophecy, concerning the end times," he said, and his voice rang with authority as he read.

"Listen and hear O people, for the time of the end has
come. Listen and hear the Word of the LORD.
Death shall come with he of the mind, and many
shall fall to the wicked serpent.
Four shall come to counter his will, one from the
gates of hell itself, bearing the white mark of God's
will.
The others are scattered like the wind, sown to be
reaped, thus one shall be reaped to be sown.
Heaven declares the third, righteous in all ways, he
speaks and mountains rumble, he whispers the words
of life.
The last, though the first, she bears the scars, inflicted
with years of pain. She who will invincible, but to the
most unholy.

Listen and hear, O people of the angels, for the end
times have come when the serpent with eyes of blood
turns and bites its tail."

There was silence for several seconds before Flammeth said, "Umm... Not to bash on the prophesy or anything, but that didn't rhyme."

Kali rolled her eyes at him. "It was written in a different language. It probably rhymed in that one."

Gabriel silenced both of them with a gesture. "Do you think these are being fulfilled now?"

Seastán nodded, eyes flicking towards Kenneth. Gabriel followed his vision, and his face cleared. "I see," he said quietly.

"You think Kenneth is the first spoken in the prophecy," Saskia stated softly.

At this Seastán raised his hands. "It merely makes sense. And I believe that Nora is the serpent biting her own tail."

Nora's scarlet eyes glittered. "You guess correctly. I have dealt with the Fallen long enough. The last job I did for them, they stole my body and nearly destroyed me. On this day, I pledge allegiance to the forces of God."

"I agree that the end is coming. It is more obvious every day," Gabriel spoke up, removing something from his belt. It was a roll of newspapers, their large headlines catching Kenneth's eye. They read: *Priest Reports Possessed Girl* and *Shooting at School has the Smell of Demonic Influence, Some Would Say.* There were others, but their titles were too obscured.

He dropped the papers at the foot of the Exalted's chair before turning to Nora. "You say that you are allied with us. What proof do you bring us?"

She turned to Gabriel. "To prove myself, I have something of yours. Or, more correctly, of Shalbriri's." She held out a bag of pure white cloth.

Gabriel took it immediately, staring at it in his hands. "You are destroying most of your power in giving me this," he said quietly.

She grinned. "But it convinces you, does it not?" he nodded, and left, leaving Kenneth with suspicions about what it was in the bag.

She turned to Seastán. "Now, I believe we need to search for the other three."

He nodded. "It will be difficult to locate them, but yes. We need to search, and plan for an invasion of the world. Already there are reports of demonic influence all over the world. Possessions are almost commonplace, and terrorism rampages across the nations of earth. I will need more generals," he said, looking at Kenneth.

"I will serve," he said, stepping forward. Seastán nodded, motioning for him to come. Kenneth walked to him and knelt, drawing his sword.

As it always did at the touch of magic, Kenneth's mark rose up on his skin, enveloping his body in harsh black lines. He flipped the sword, holding onto its blade, and looked at Seastán.

"Do you, Kenneth of the Flame, swear to protect and guard those of Earth?"

"I do," he answered.

"Do you stand for defense of the Human race?"

"I do."

"Do you pledge your soul willingly to Jesus, our Lord of Love and Salvation, to be your light in the darkest of places?"

"I do." Kenneth answered, and as the last word left his mouth he felt a searing pain, spreading outwards from his heart, spreading to the edges of his body.

Looking down, he saw that the black in his mark had been washed away to reveal a pure white that glowed with soft brilliance.

"He who bears the white mark of God's will," Seastán quoted, eyes shining. Speaking louder, he stated, "Stand as a First General of God."

Kenneth stood, pain vanishing, and sheathed his sword. The mark did not fade. "Where will we search first?" he asked, and Nora coughed quietly.

"I have located where one lives, but not who she is. That might be a good place to start," she said, folding her arms.

Kenneth nodded. "How did you find her?" he asked, curious.

Nora smiled a happy little smile. "She's indestructible. Her magic causes ripples wherever she goes. You only have to listen." Kenneth nodded, satisfied.

"We must go there soon," Seastán said, "but not now. First we must plan our defenses. The world's defenses."

Kenneth nodded again, face grim. "Then let's plan."

Epilogue: At the End of Days

Iephus opened his eyes and stood. "So. They have found the first, and have located the fourth. How amusing," he said, pacing the length of the room.

Turning, he pulled a length of rope and waited. Within a minute, his door opened to a bowing servant. "My lord. What can I do for you?"

Iephus smiled a humorless smile. "Get me Sam. Quickly." The servant bowed again and ran out the door. Iephus waited quietly, monitoring the minds of the guards on the outer walls as he sat.

Soon a quiet knock sounded on the door. "Enter," Iephus commanded imperiously.

The door opened, revealing a well-built man that exuded light, significantly brightening the room as he entered.

"How may the light serve you, my lord?"

Iephus smiled.

END OF BOOK 1

A special preview of

TAINTED
LIGHT

Book Two of

The Reign of Hell

Blurred Eyes

Cat rolled, skinning her elbow in her haste to dodge the ugly looking blade that narrowly missed her head. Ignoring wind and rain that whipped at her hair, she summoned a blade and rammed it into the beast's gut, causing it to issue an inhuman scream and the nauseous smell of intestine. Its red eyes burned out, and she scrambled to her feet, running down the corridor, randomly entering a room. The world was clear, but had a fuzziness that couldn't be seen, but instead was felt.

She knew she was in a dream. She always did. Lucid dreaming had always been her curse, providing her nights with vivid nightmares she rode like waves. She had learned to cope.

She walked into the room cautiously and whispered softly. The words exited her mouth, curling through the air and exploding in a flash of light that briefly illuminated the room. It was a ballroom, with high ceilings and chandeliers swaying in time with the thunderous percussion of the storm that raged outside.

Shapes lined the walls of the room, crying out as the light burned their eyes. She ignored them, running for the door across the room as they fumbled blindly after her. Cat entered the corridor and gasped. The stone floor had turned to fire. Despite the flames, no heat touched her skin. She delicately took a step forward, and then gingerly continued walking when the flames held firm underneath her.

"Most impressive," came a voice, and she whirled. He spoke in perfect Italian, her native tongue. With a thought, she summoned a gun, pointing it at the man who had spoken.

The man raised his hands amiably, indicating he had no weapon. She didn't shift her position. Men could too easily shift forms in dreams. "Who are you, and how did you enter?"

The man chuckled, his blue eyes sparkling. "Very good. But I am, as I always have been."

She raised an eyebrow. "Watcher? Prove yourself." Despite the years of speaking English, Italian flowed easily to her. It brought back memories too, memories she quickly suppressed. They were too painful.

He reached into his pocket slowly, as to not alarm her, and drew out a stone on a length of chain. The stone stayed in sharp detail, despite the fuzziness that was always attributed to a dream.

She lowered the gun, allowing it to vanish into mist. Only one person had her dreamstone, and it could not be faked. Not in her territory. She glanced around irritably, and the fire vanished, leaving stone. She walked to the railing of the corridor, looking out into the wild storm with a sigh. "What brings you into my night?" she asked quietly.

"Do you have need of my skills, or are you here for reasons known but to yourself?"

He walked slowly to the railing and leaned on the column next to it. The wind of the storm never touched him. "I am here to ask a favor." When she didn't respond he sighed. "Why do you allow yourself to be plagued with nightmares?"

The question was unrelated to his favor, she knew; he asked it every time he visited. She shook her head, unwilling to answer. She could get rid of the nightmares with a thought, but she still allowed them to come. They were what she was. Without them she wouldn't be the same.

"What do you need me to do?" she asked instead. He gazed at her for several seconds, and then held out a picture. Cat took it, before crumpling it with an angry clench of her fists when she saw the person's face.

"I knew it!" she hissed, "First, you force me to abandon her, and now you want me to do something to her, as though seeing her won't hurt me at all? You never care about people, just their precious destiny. Well, you can ask someone else." She turned her back to him, unwilling to see his impassive face.

The dream shifted as her control briefly slipped. The storm stopped, and they stood in a white landscape of snow. The air was cold, but she never noticed it. Her focus was on a sword, buried deep within the ice on which they stood. "Is this your doing?" she asked, suddenly calm.

"I cannot control the dream," he responded, and she nodded.

"You still have it? It is safe?" At his assent she turned, glaring at him. "Fine. I will help you enter her dreams. But I will not hurt her."

The man smiled. "I don't intend to do anything but warn her of danger. But we must move quickly, the night is nearly done."

"Yeah, yeah," she said, waving away his urgency with a hand. She glanced around, and the world flickered, fading to a soft blue that blanketed everything. She found her quickly. Blood always drew to blood.

Within seconds they were standing in the room of a sleeping girl. The man frowned. "This is her dream?"

"She is not yet dreaming. When she wakes in this, she will dream.

Prepare yourself," she warned. He nodded, and she shrouded herself, allowing the dream to obscure her. Taking a deep breath, she forced her to wake up.

She woke, confused, and then turned. Her thoughts would be lucid, as if she was awake, but she would know she was dreaming. Cat sighed, her mouth framing a word in the silence. *Rachel.*

"Who are you?" Rachel asked. She spoke in Spanish, and the man responded similarly.

"I am Sekai Uotchā. I am the watcher," the man said quietly. She frowned at him, and he continued. "Your life is about to change. Danger grows around you, and it will be impossible to avoid. Do not trust the light." At Sekai's nod, Cat let them fade from her dream.

They walked in the silent blue for several minutes, each deep in their own thoughts. Eventually Cat spoke. "Will she die?" Her voice trembled slightly before she mastered herself. He hesitated, and her fear grew.

"No. She will not die," he answered, and for a moment she felt relief. It faded as he continued. "It is not dying that I am worried about. That is another's fate. It is what she will choose."

Cat opened her mouth, but he forestalled her with a hand. "It must be her choice. I cannot control everything. But I can help."

"Then help." Cat said vehemently.

He nodded.

"I will try."

About the Author

Fallen Angels is Austin Golemon's first young adult novel. Austin is currently in his senior year of high school and hopes to continue writing in college. He presently lives and writes in Illinois, where he is working on the second book of The Reign of Hell—Tainted Light.